BEST SERVED

COLD

By the same author

LINCOLNSHIRE MURDER MYSTERY SERIES
Dead Spit
Seaside Snatch
Once Bitten
Dead Jealous
Or Not To Be
Twelve Days
Sacrificial Lamb
In Plain Sight
Tissue of Lies
Final Whistle
Reasons Why Not

You can contact the author by e-mail at:
carysmithwriter@yahoo.co.uk

AN INGA LARSSON NOVEL

BEST SERVED
COLD

Cary Smith

BEST SERVED COLD

Copyright © 2021 Cary Smith

ISBN: 9798709728684

PublishNation, London
www.publishnation.co.uk

1

Autumn 2020

He'd had one of those awful sleepless experiences we all suffer now and again when night just seems interminable. All that tossing and turning business, first one way then the other, feet too hot, then too cold, an inability to feel comfortable when sleep always appears a distant dream. Except frequently there never are dreams you can recall.

In his case it was the inescapable worry, the outturn from what at the time had seemed absolutely the right thing to do. Now he had his doubts and even within the cold light of day his mind remained confused by his new found circumstance.

Sat at his wooden table in the small kitchen Gordon Kenny had Retro FM turned on as he attempted to bring himself up to date with what he was responsible for. Sat there chin in hands next to a cooling Blades mug of tea with his customary dash of milk, waiting for the latest local news to come round once more.

The morning news on the radio is for so many, really critical. Unfortunately boring politics and tales of wars and atrocities in some far flung hell hole and the inevitable daily jolt of Coronavirus figures to remind us. All of which tends to get in the way of really vital news, important to the vast majority and that morning one man in particular.

The news he was waiting for?

He killed this vile woman last night.

Not an accident you understand. Not a road traffic shunt because he'd had too many bevvies. Hadn't got all drugged up and shanked her down some grubby alley like some scumbags do because she was in the wrong post code.

Gordon killed her because he had a need to. Because to be perfectly honest, he was desperate for a bit of hands-on practice.

When watching the Olympics and other major sporting contests, we all sit there glued to the action wondering how on earth they learn to do the things they do. Truth is of course, the old adage of practice makes perfect is the reason.

Those amazing gymnasts practice the same thing time after time after time, day in day out. A front flyaway or a dorsal hang for a skin-the-cat position is all part of their Monday warm-up routine when they get to work in the morning and run through just one more time, and another and again...

Bloody dedication and no mistake.

Been told those high jumpers who could easy jump over your front door, run through the routine meticulously time and again usually in some cold draughty hall.

Exactly the same reason why Gordon was in need of practice. Not something he could do time and again every day until he got it just right. There'd be no gold medal for him, not something he'd slipped under his pillow last night. No matter how good he was at it. Just the once would certainly never add much to his muscle memory.

Sat there in his jeans and sweatshirt on his wooden chair listening to the sound of the incomparable Joe Walsh, the feelings running through him that morning as he nervously waited on the news had been quite extraordinary. Which to be fair was the main purpose of the exercise, for him to experience the reactions his mind, body and emotions would be forced to endure and to suffer.

Must be loads just like him over the years who kill someone and then immediately suffer from the "Shit! What have I done?" reaction to overwhelm mind and soul. The very thought process to have kept him awake all night.

To be fair, he was only just about coping with the nerves and if he were honest he'd even struggled to eat his toast spread with Peanut Butter. When he's out and about with work, sometimes he stops off at places for a good cup of breakfast tea with a touch of milk and a couple of slices of toast.

Not exactly the sort of thing most people have running through their mind over breakfast. The person they murdered the previous evening.

2

He had never been a great breakfast man except of course when travelling. Never going to do much more than toss a few Coco-pops into a bowl or make toast when eating at home, like today. Not an eggs and bacon man at that time of day. Health warnings about fried eggs had seen him limit himself and just now and again slipped a couple on top of baked beans on toast almost as a treat for being a good boy.

Somebody had to pay the price for the way he had felt and still did despite what horrors were infiltrating his mind that morning.

The hopeless in society in effect are in the main fortunately only damaging themselves, but this bitch he had homed in on was having an effect on countless people and the higher she climbed the tree of success the more damage it appeared she was likely to cause.

Somebody had to put a stop to it. Bring an end to all her absurd costly garbage. It certainly seemed from his perspective how this female had been adamant about doing her utmost to put all her cranky schemes in place to get at Hospital patients as well as the doctors and nurses.

He was in desperate need of somebody to practice on and she was a convenient candidate as his primary target was waiting in the wings to suffer the same fate. There were others of course he'd mentally auditioned, but in the end there she had to be the one to target.

Fitting the bill perfectly. Not somebody the world is ever likely to miss, nobody crowds will rush to the petrol station to grab cheap flowers to stick where she was found, as a tacky tribute.

If asked he'd not suggest she had done anything deliberately evil. As far as he knew she'd not overdosed some poor elderly crabby old patient with insulin on the night shift, or nicked fifty quid every time she withdrew her old granny's pension.

More in her line was snorting in the loo before an important meeting, which is not the sort of thing even the low life from the land of underpass destitution would do. But you can bet your bottom dollar it's what this loathsome lump of trash does. Or did.

For the first six weeks of that damn virus earlier in the year he'd been out clapping the nurses, doctors and carers as a heartfelt way of saying a big thank you to the NHS. That was until it dawned on him how that nasty bitch might just be taking credit where it was not due. Stood there as proud as punch accepting all the plaudits.

To Gordon, this Carole-Anne Quinlan is somebody who had forced people to suffer and was doing real damage to countless others and leaving herself unscathed but with a healthy wad of cash she'd stashed some place. To his mind even her daftly composed name leaves scars.

She has links to the NHS, but you'd not find her in uniform dealing with Covid-19 or becoming concerned with waiting lists, Norwalk or Novovirus, outbreaks of diarrhoea on the wards, the scandal of agency nurses pay rates, ambulance queuing, the horrors of overcrowded A&E, junior Doctors' hours, bed blocking, old folk dying in their care or serious understaffing.

Gordon Kenny was fully aware of all the countless problems involved with a monster like the NHS, but somehow from somewhere he was convinced the country just needs to get itself a government with the nous and desire to actually stop talking and do something about it.

This Quinlan female worked in the East Midlands for some private think-tank company with a stupid name who like so many have foisted their ridiculously expensive ideas on an unsuspecting NHS.

He often wondered what role she'd actually played in the Coronavirus epidemic, if any at all. Even though she was not a nurse he could just never have imagined her all dressed up in her Personal Protective Equipment working long and utterly demanding hours.

Gordon guessed the bitch would have been at the supermarkets early claiming to be part of the NHS and would be first in line to accept gifts people offered.

Gordon's Aunt Ingrid, his mother's sister, was one of thousands to suffer. This was because the Trust in which she placed her faith and paid her dues, spent so much time and money on mad-cap ideas people like Quinlan came up with, they couldn't cope initially with the pandemic Adding to the issues overwhelming them, a slow to react government hadn't helped..

Aunt Ingrid was a lovely woman, so kind and gentle and to some extent too nice. She was his mother's sister. Was, because sadly his parents are dead.

All give and no take is how Gordon saw the lovely woman with an exceptional personality to go with it. Not just in the way of gifts of course but in her profound kindness, her love and attention to all.

With a rampant virus at the time of her death he'd not been able to be at her bedside or even attend her funeral, to represent his mother.

4

Anyway, her son Alistair years before had married this seemingly quite fairly attractive and pleasant woman and all was fine until her first born arrived. People like her are a serious pain, and there are far more of them than you imagine.

Then the trouble started.

This bitch Carole-Anne who cousin Alistair married, suffers from what some call the Mother of the Father Syndrome or Malicious Mother Syndrome others prefer. Quinlan was most certainly malicious.

Apparently almost from the moment little Matilda was born it was as if this bizarre attitude took control.

Even as the child's grandmother, his dear Aunt Ingrid was never afforded the opportunity to cradle the baby in her arms. Not once. This was a gift bestowed solely on this Carole-Anne's close family and on her mother and sister in particular. She painted negative pictures of Ingrid via deprecating comments, blame and false accusations she of course later in life shared with the child as it grew up.

Ingrid had never been allowed to develop any kind of relationship with her only grandchild. Never been invited to a birthday party, and even at the christening was never offered the opportunity even to be within touching distance of the bairn.

Apart from having no physical contact she was denied visits and when he learnt about it Gordon was amazed and angry. This loathsome Carole-Anne would actually accompany soppy Alistair to visit his parent's home but she remained sat outside in the car with the child. Refusing point blank to associate with the grandparents in any way, shape or form. Sometimes for hours.

Recent research had told him this is a grand-parents exclusion syndrome meaning there are medical signs and symptoms combining to create a medical issue. To be honest Gordon thinks she's putting it all on and Quinlan is nothing more than just a vile bitch.

This Quinlan is not the only one to suffer from this, if suffer is the right word. It has to be lovely people like his dear Aunt Ingrid who had suffered.

His Aunt Ingrid was unwell with a chest infection before she went into hospital and was listed amongst those with underlying health issues. The last time he saw her at her home he just assumed it was the illness making her look so absolutely dreadful.

5

That of course and her utter sadness of being aware of but never knowing her only granddaughter. Being punished by such a nasty bitch for something she had never done, except being Carole-Anne's mother-in-law. He's been told but is not aware how true it is, but Ingrid's birthday cards sent to Matilda each year had been torn up on arrival without being opened.

Gordon wondered of course what horrendous stories Matilda has been told about her granny, what downright obscene lies had been trotted out as part of a form of radicalization.

Of course as you can imagine Alistair visited his sick mother on his own but like all others, had been excluded by the damn virus from visiting her in hospital.

Sat at his table waiting for the news Gordon Kenny smiled to himself when the dulcet tones of Don McLean began to sing *Vincent* one of his all-time favourites he had to sing along with. In the knowledge they don't even try to make them that good anymore.

Recognizing the Retro FM jingle at the end, brought him back to the here and now. Knew it'd be the news headlines and then the local stuff he was after, before world affairs, before celebrity garbage, before the sport.

"Good morning. Mark Johns with the news. The headlines this morning. Police were called to the Cluny Priory near Gainsborough earlier to deal with a major incident. More news as it comes in and of course we'll carry full details in our next bulletin. Now our Coronavirus update for the county, it was..."

Gordon just stared at his radio. Was that it, was that the best they could bloody do?

'Shit! What d'they mean incident? The bitch is dead for crissakes!' he shouted as the news about a slight increase in virus infections, boost for tourism and police arresting some Spice druggie in Lincoln Cornhill continued. 'I should know I bloody dumped the silly cow there!'

"Now for the latest weather. The day will start off fairly bright throughout most parts of the county with outbreaks of sunshine...."

Radio off, grabbed his leather jacket, car keys and with that a fuming Gordon Kenny was off to the gym for an hour or so.

6

2

'Please go easy with her,' said this fully white robed chubby faced Sister Mary Joanna. 'She has only recently entered her novitiate,' and if he didn't know it already Detective Sergeant Jake Goodwin was now aware this was no run of the mill unexplained attempted murder they were dealing with at this Cluny Priory place. A former grand manor house set in extensive and expansive landscaped grounds.

'Excuse me,' he went to ask but was ignored.

'And whatever it is you want will just have to wait I'm afraid,' she advised. 'Under such circumstances we need to talk to our God.' She offered the merest hint of a smile. 'Our God comes first as I am sure you will appreciate.' She looked Jake up and down and a sneer would not have been out of place. 'Would you care to pray with us?'

'No thank you,' he responded without releasing the chuckle he felt inside. 'Guess I'm a bit busy right now.'

'We're never too busy to meet with our God,' he took as a snide criticism and with it this robed nun just turned and plodded away, leaving Jake just stood there. If he didn't know better, if he was not stood in a cold stark stone entrance hall of a priory he would swear the nun who had just waddled away was a drinker. Her face had the rosy complexion about it boozers usually have.

To be fair he'd known this was an odd-ball situation when the first of his team arrived to discover all seven nuns having breakfast sat on long wooden benches in complete silence. Almost as if nothing and nobody would be allowed to disturb their strict routine.

It was difficult not to be rude about these women acting as if a barely alive young woman slumped in a pew in their small whitewashed chapel was anything but normal. In fact their attitude was such he did wonder why they had bothered to phone in their discovery at all.

Perhaps Jake wondered if it was to do with the body being female slumped there in amongst others devoting themselves to a world of prayer and contemplation. He surmised how in many cases it would most probably be men they had run away from and therefore felt an affinity with a kindred spirit.

According to this tubby Mary Joanna woman who had introduced herself as the prioress, a young nun Naomi Phebe had entered the chapel first thing to prepare the venue with its huge oak door, tall thin windows and hard wooden pews for First Morning Prayers.

The first devotion of their day, every day.

The lighting of a brand new large white candle to signal the dawning of the Lord's new day was always the duty of the newest recruit, according to this nun who'd just waddled away.

There was this woman the local duty doctor was with, slumped in a pew looking for all the world as if she was just waiting to start a marathon. All she needed was her number pinning on. As somebody who had run the Lincoln 10K more than once Goodwin recognized all the gear these running people go in for and even sniggered at the sight of headphones hanging around her neck.

Absolutely never ever a good idea for a woman to be out running on her own.

Jake considered the process of sending a youngster out to light a candle had to be a strategy to put the greenhorns in their place. Bit like the armed forces odious initiation systems of making the recruits do all the menial tasks. Bullying in other words they'll never admit to.

Be up first he reckoned, washed, dressed in a robe, probably pray and then head off in her long white habit and sandals across the courtyard to this cold empty chapel to light a solitary huge candle. Still alight when he'd seen it and likely to last for hours.

Not such a bad thing this time of year on a bright morning, he mused. Bit of fresh air, touch of sunshine, but not much fun in mid-winter in the rain or with a frost on the ground or heaven forbid, a foot of snow. Do their duty without fear or favour, without an umbrella, overcoat and gumboots no doubt. Willingly suffering for their God, made the DS smile to himself.

As he stood there Jake's mind provided an image of some poor soul traipsing out through winter slush in just sandals. Reminding him of dibbos you see in town in flip-flops.

'Getting a bit fed up with all this hanging about. Still trying to interview this Sister Naomi woman who found her,' he told DS Nicky Scoley when he caught up with the butterscotch blonde outside.

'Not one's got a mask.'

'Bit of anomaly,' Jake reacted with his mask pulled down, a distance away from his colleague. 'According to her this is their home and they don't need to.'

Nicky pulled a face. 'But they're not family.'

'Not as such, no,' he mused, as Nicky flashed him a quick smile as a thank you for his phlegmatic presence she had come to depend on over the months of Larsson's absence. 'But d'you know the Coronavirus rules for nuns cloistered together?' Nicky shrugged her reply.

'Guess they'll be in a bubble.'

'Be useful if you could start to build a glossary of what this is all about.' Jake and the whole Major Incident Team had been through the Covid-19 protocols time and again. In fact he'd already called in a request for guidance on how to deal with nuns in a priory, who claimed they had no masks or any need for them. 'Start if you would with something she said - novitiate and then get a handle on the history of this lot and this place. Looks to me like it could very well have been an old school at one time.'

'Sort of place I've always known is here, but never fully aware of what it actually is.' Nicky looked all about. 'Where've they all gone now d'we know?'

'Praying apparently,' he sighed noisily. 'God comes first I've been told as if I was a naughty kid in class.' Goodwin sniggered. 'Asked me if I wanted to join them.'

'Be serious,' Scoley grinned her remark.

'Got better things to do than hang around here all day, dunces cap or not,' he glanced at his watch.

'What do we actually know so far?' she asked.

'This sister Naomi Phebe the youngster, got up at the crack of dawn apparently to trundle out to that chapel place and light a candle. When she got there she found our victim slumped in a front pew.'

'What was the word again?' Scoley asked.

'Novitiate, but don't ask me to spell it. Bit like saying she's an apprentice, is my guess.' He pouted. 'Could be wrong.'

Scoley pulled out her phone and Goodwin waited for her to Google. 'A novice's initiation period. Like being an apprentice.'

'You're fired!' he joked to lighten the mood.

'Very good,' said grinning Sandy MacLachlan the Crime Scene Manager, as he approached. The pair. 'What a bloody weird bunch and no mistake.'

'In what way?' the DS enquired.

'They were having breakfast when I first got here and according to the CSI lads, they actually had to search them oot when they turned up. There they all were sat in total silence eating what looked like sort of home-made cornflakes.' He chuckled to himself. 'Crime scene guys are not best pleased,' he told Jake. 'The chapel and the pew are absolutely pristine. There's nothing for them, and you know what they're like. One told me it was clean enough for the nuns to eat their cornflakes off the damn floor. So clean it looked as though Jesus was about to carry out a state visit.'

'You don't think...' Nicky pulled a face. 'You think they cleaned it all before we got here?'

Sandy just shrugged his reaction. 'Cannae see what else?'

'You are joking!'

'Your guess is as good as mine, but I wouldn't put it past them. There's nae black puddin' on the menu d'ya ken? CSI just told me bits of grit are from the nuns sandals which is as good as it gets. No fag ends, no chewing gum, no bits of this and that or the ubiquitous coke can.'

'Lads told me one of the nuns said the floor is washed, scrubbed and polished by them on their hands and knees on a daily basis.' Nicky looked across at the chapel. 'Thanks a bunch ladies. Been really useful. Not.'

'Don't have to ask if they've washed their hands then.'

'Lads reckon that ornate Gothic door to the chapel place opened very easily, push with one finger sorta job.'

'Easy to see how entry was achieved then.'

10

'Musta known it'd be unlocked to be fair hen,' Sandy went on. 'Alistair was telling me, only one of them has actually spoken to him since he's been here. Likely the same one you've just tried to get a bit of sense out of.'

'They worried d'you think in case these women spot a good looking bloke they might go over the wall?' Jake Goodwin glanced at his watch again. 'I'm not standing round here much longer, prayers or no bloody prayers.'

'P'raps they're living the braw life,' was Sandy's suggestion. 'No money worries, no mortgage or child care, no school run, no car needing a service, no weekly shop then the washing machine gives up the ghost.' He just looked all about. 'Even some wee woman dumped in their chapel doesn't seem to bother them by the look of it.'

'But at their age they're vulnerable.'

'Hours of contemplation and praying. How long before you run out of things to think about when you live in such a cloistered world?' Scoley naughtily mimicked a nun. 'What's the news today Sister? Edwina has cut her toenails and Freda's just picked two daisies from the lawn. Wow, really?'

'Ideal during a pandemic though. All living self-sufficient lives cloistered in here together. What was the message, stay at home, stay safe?'

'Save the NHS, save lives.'

Jake nodded, his expression unchanging. 'Our wishes are always secondary, is what she told me,' Jake offered. 'Asked her why when the poor woman was discovered around five-thirty they didn't ring in until about six forty-five, or call an ambulance, paramedic, anything.' Scoley's look told DS Goodwin she was in need of an answer. 'Our wishes are always secondary. The requirements of our God must come first nonsense.'

'Such as?' Scoley asked as she fought with a giggle.

'Morning prayers I think. All got up, washed, dressed tottered over to the chapel, said morning prayers and…'

'With that poor woman still sat there?' his colleague almost shouted.

'Must have mustn't they?'

'Jesus Christ! That's sick.'

11

'No good calling him, be tied up with that lot!' Sandy quipped. 'It's what their God would have wanted I'm guessing. As she said, their wishes are always secondary.'

'Now I know for certain we've picked the short straw. This is bloody crackers!'

Nicky Scoley had not-too-close friends who were those enthusiastic bright-eyed and bushy-tailed born again Christians, into strumming guitars and singing along joyfully and enthusiastically each and every Sunday.

'Think we need to be aware of not trampling all over this with our size nines,' was delightful Jake doing his fatherly talk bit Nicky had become used to over the years. Annoyed and frustrated he may be but it was always the calm Detective Sergeant exterior the world saw. 'PR won't thank us if this lot create a fuss with local radio and TV. Especially if we cock-up the Covid rules.'

'No news?'

'No. Think we've got all we need for now. I'll just ask this Naomi woman a few basic questions then back off. Let CSI get on with their work, then see what they and the doc comes up with.'

There was just below the surface an experienced detective's caution, treating each and every statement about this woman with a sense of mistrust he'd nurtured over the years.

'She gonna make it?'

'Apparently,' Sandy voiced what Jake was about to eject himself. 'Bloody awful smack on her head though.'

Jake Goodwin didn't need reminding how the powers that be were forever reminding all and sundry who could bother to listen, how in this day and age they were a media friendly force. Newspapers, news channels, Twitter and all the rest of it were the veins down which the news rush could link them to the public. To keep them on board and au fait with what was happening.

The senior Detective Sergeant in the Major Incident Team certainly didn't fancy getting a rap on the knuckles for being rude to a nun over social distancing.

He was also mindful of the importance of the critical first 48 hours. After, people's memories have become clogged with other nonsense, evidence can easily have been destroyed and trails just run cold as the world swiftly moves on.

Perhaps in this case the cloistered world did not move on apace like the rest of the frantic world. He guessed the Cluny Priory was not a world of flashing images and their lack of speed may well prove useful.

DS Goodwin phoned the boss. 'Nothing obvious like a good beating or stab wounds. The paramedic who discovered a jagged mark on her arm along with being dumped in a strange place made him call it in immediately. Woman's not known to us visually, but her location's a new one on me.'

'Amaze me.'

'Could be in her forties maybe, sitting,' her Detective Sergeant said slowly. 'In the front pew of a chapel. Part of the Cluny Priory nuns place out towards Gainsborough,' he added.

'You what?' Inga was pleased she'd not taken a drink of her milky coffee.

'Currently waiting for the doc and paramedics to finish up and this bunch of nuns all getting in the way of the CSI lads, to stop praying.' He paused. 'Guessed you'd want to know early doors, and in case you're wondering it's not one of the nuns.'

'Me to you or what?' Inga Larsson posed.

'Whatever suits you, boss,' he offered aware she had a baby girl to care for.

'I'll get this end set up,' she said with mug in hand. Be a shame to spoil a good coffee.

'Be careful,' he had to remind her. 'There's plenty can set the place up. If you need to keep busy could do with guidance on Covid protocols for a place like this and nuns. Talked to her outside mostly and there's no way we can organize perspex screens inside. They're not wearing masks and the Queen Bee reckons as they're family they don't need them.'

'But you are?'

'Yes, we are, social distancing the lot and CSI are covered up anyway.'

'Think they may be right. For all intense and purposes they're at home.'

Working hand in glove with Nicky Scoley when the boss was on Maternity Leave had taught them both a great deal. That had all

13

become particularly pertinent during the pandemic lockdown, which had started just after Larsson's daughter was born.

As they bonded well as a matter of needing to, it had never been a situation where they could call on the Inspector for a chat and a cuppa. They'd used Zoom but they'd kept all that to a minimum with all the post natal she had to put up with stuck at home. Fortunately with her husband Adam being a physiotherapist he had been with her for weeks and weeks before his business could re-open.

3

Apart from the manner in which she had treated his favourite aunt over the years, Gordon Kenny had realized what sort of person that Carole-Anne Quinlan bitch was.

She's one of those who use their attendance at events such as health related charity get-togethers to enhance their own credentials without making the slightest contribution. Take all the plaudits without offering help, advice or a measly pound from their pockets. Using people's lifelong struggles to boost their own self-esteem epitomizes the very reason he was sure this Quinlan woman was just what he had been looking for.

He had never been able to fathom the reason for these blogs people write. Beauty bloggers appear quite sane compared with some strikingly odd efforts. Discovering people who constantly write about weird worms, about edible flowers and eating insects had Gordon intrigued enough to delve more deeply into this very odd world.

It was then he came across Quinlan's effort.

Allow me to take you on a word journey. As the IIA Lead Co-ord I live and breathe with my dynamic IIA Navigator who provides me with so many opportunities to network with other like-minded effectiveness parties, to make the whole experience effortless. Just remember to always include all the touchpoints as we tinker with the strategy for all our futures. This is our journey going forward and even though there are headwinds desperate to halt our ambitions we must do all we can to stop others tampering with the shoots of growth... blah blah...

It took Gordon quite a while to discover exactly what half of that nonsense meant and the IIA business turned out to be, he eventually discovered, Impartiality In Action piffle.

As far as he had been able to gather, her area role is a spurious link between the NHS and Social Services. Apparently there are what they call think tanks who publish their theories on the future of the NHS. She runs a team who make decisions about future care for patients once they leave hospital. Not practically of course, but based purely on theory for the future.

Serious time Gordon had spent researching on-line provided him with in insight into how most of these organisations were created to facilitate debate, impartial or otherwise in order to build through careful analysis the problems facing the NHS.

In short all this hogwash he'd read about sat at his PC meant she was nothing to do with the NHS, most certainly not a nurse qualified or otherwise. Not now and never had been.

The tripe he'd come across continued with silliness such as, *I am striving for a united vision across my portfolio linked headlong with diversity...* just the sort of garbage you'd expect from these weird techy-geeks we all come across these days.

What staggered Gordon more than anything was the fact she had written some of her nonsense weeks into the Coronavirus lockdown. The world was struggling to get to grips with the awful pandemic. Nurses and care workers were dying, some had even been forced to stay in hotel rooms to avoid contact with their own family. Grandparents were isolating themselves as directed, unable to have visitors or see their grandchildren. People were being furloughed if not sacked by unscrupulous bosses and new temporary hospitals were being set up in no time as death and tragedy surrounded the whole nation.

Forget all that. That nasty bitch was more concerned with spouting about headwinds desperate to spoil her ambitions garbage.

He had wondered over the months if hospitals had not been distracted by the insistence of the likes of Quinlan with all their ridiculous and frequently absurd schemes, would they have been better prepared initially to deal with the vicious virus.

Gordon was fully aware how through taxes we are all paying for hogwash like her crass nonsense. Some of the people forced to fork out hard earned cash for this utter clap-trap, struggle to feed their family and pay for a roof over their heads, let alone deal with the horrors of a pandemic.

He discovered how the only time in three pages the word 'health' was mentioned was the second word in NHS. It was all her spouting self-important sinister jargon about the delivery options and pathways. Gordon did wonder if she at any time had ever for one moment stopped to think to herself how ridiculous she must appear. Copying the self-righteous with her own brand of utter bunkum. All set amidst the tragedies unfolding around her.

Not once did she mention the hard work and dedication of consultants, nurses, practitioners, doctors, paramedics or even the hard working cleaners and porters. It was very obvious she was using our National Health Service, the envy of the world for her own good, not developing the service for the benefit of the nation as a whole.

All this in the very same place where they never ever have enough wheelchairs.

One of Gordon's personal hobby horses is hospital car parking. He has never been able to understand why people complain about paying for car parking at hospitals. After all, it's their fault.

He will remind anybody willing to listen how now when car parking is free, the public who had absolutely no need to go anywhere near hospitals fill the car parks and just head off to work or into town for a shop. Sod folk with appointments or people limited to just an hour when visiting sick relatives. Yet these same dimwits now complain about something they themselves caused.

4

'*Nungate*' it had already been christened by one bright spark once the team got word of where, what and when.

In the Major Incident Team's main office in Lincoln Central, the team had been spread out as far as was possible. DCs Ruth Buchan and Michelle Cooper had even been moved into a small annexe nearby they normally used for research interviews. Work stations had been moved to create space between officers. Downstairs in the interview rooms, perspex screens had been erected to protect the interviewee, his or her lawyer and the officers involved. One had even been set-up to enable remote interviewing if necessary.

'You're first up Nicky, if you please,' the DI commanded.

'Think severe penitence,' said DS Nicky Scoley. 'This is not your normal order of nuns. To be fair, I understand the Catholic Church is trying to show what goes on in such places. Have organized sort of tours, open days if you like, where the public can see how they live and what they do for the community.' She hesitated. 'Not this lot.'

'You saying this is not some normal holy order?' boss Inga Larsson asked for all her team.

'Far from it. From what I can gather, women in this day and age join an order of nuns for three main reasons. The world has become far too materialistic and if you're low paid on zero hours or unemployed, life can be a real bitch. An Xbox some regard as a must-have at close to four hundred quid, is always going to be out of your league unless you nick it of course and we know where that leads. Too sexual and far too dependent on technology. When I say technology not the good things it brings, but the nasty tweets, the sad trolls and paedophiles and all the bad elements of modern life. All the virtual world stuff.'

'I always considered they were running away from responsibility,' said DC Jamie Hedley. 'Running away from men, from real life and quite often have financial problems, frequently brought about because they don't fit the norm in society. Always a bit cranky and weird. All a bit like your prim and proper soppy maiden aunt Nellie on a bad day!'

'I know this is not easy to get your head round,' Nicky continued. 'But the majority of women joining these days, have no such hang-ups but just know deep inside they have been chosen by their God to devote their lives to him. That's what motivates them. Apparently,' she added with a smile.'

'Like I said, weird.'

'Like all these eco warrior hippies.'

'This lot are not like that,' Nicky went on. 'These women it would appear, and I'm still looking into it, want to be punished and are desperate to pay the price for the world's sins. Sort of, I'm sorry they crucified Jesus and somebody must be punished. Please punish me, somebody has to pay the price for what they did to him. Please, please I want it to be me.'

'Some weirdos live in constant pain with things strapped to their legs, all part of the same masochism principle is my guess.'

'Sort of thing some people pay good money for!' was quipped in.

'You're right there.'

'Can I just say,' said Jake Goodwin. 'Yesterday morning they waited over an hour to phone it in, and when Sandy got there just before us, they were all just sat eating their breakfast, in silence as if nothing was cracking off.'

'After early morning prayers lasting over an hour, then this silent breakfast was followed by what they call private contemplation in their rooms.'

'Washing?' Detective Inspector Larsson tossed in. 'Toilet?'

'They have to troop off to a sort of communal latrine area to wash and use the toilets…'

'My guess,' Nicky interrupted Jake. 'They have to do it in the dark at night. No en suite there let me tell you. And,' she emphasized. 'No mirrors. Anywhere.'

'Why?' a frowning Inga asked for them all. 'Washing your hands is good at any time, but doing that won't change the world. Might keep the virus at bay but it won't return us to a world where it was possible to sleep at night without locking your front door.'

'What sort of god are they worshipping who thinks this is all an extremely good idea?'

'Only seven of them, so it's not exactly popular.'

'So you see, that lot out there are not the norm,' said Nicky. 'These are not nuns as we know them, involved in a serious proper religion, who go out into the community, often working in schools and to some extent do a certain amount of good. Not this lot. They only eat what they can grow so they reckon and...'

'Yeah right.'

'And,' Nicky went on. 'Spend the rest of the time hurting themselves because they think some idol somewhere will be really impressed.'

'More research please, Nicky,' Inga just slipped in. 'You've done really well already.' Inga knew from experience how Nicky Scoley was to all intense and purposes her truffle hog. Capable of hunting down anything and everything they might need given time. 'Just get as much as you can for us.'

'What is it they grow for breakfast then?' was Raza Latif sat against the far wall.

'Some sort of wheat by the look of it, and they make all their own bread they appear to eat dry. According to the CSI lads there was toast on the table when they walked in, but no butter or marmalade, nothing apparently so they reckon. Guess that was eaten dry too.'

'Penitence,' said Nicky to remind them. 'Bags of conscience, guilt, pain.'

'The nun I spoke to yesterday,' Jake then offered. 'In fact the only one who would speak to us, except the one who discovered the body we had to insist we interview, gave me some hogwash about by chance she'd had a chat with a priest once upon a time. There and then realized just talking to him she had to devote her life to paying the price for others sins.' He smirked. 'Said something about the pain she suffers is a pain her God doesn't have to endure.'

'If her God is still in pain after two thousand years he needs to see his GP.'

'Not getting an appointment for weeks, could be her problem.'

'Some people pay good money to get punished!'

'And the one who found the body?' Inga asked and her look said enough now of the sarcasm and wit.

'Waste of time with that Sister Mary woman stood over her. African descent is my guess and looked scared stiff to be honest, as if she dare not say what went on. If somebody told me she'd been forced into joining I'd not be surprised, she looked frightened to death.'

'So you didn't get much out of her I take it?'

'Only the basics you know about. Went off to light the candle, discovered the body, went to find this Sister Mary woman and it was her who phoned us.'

'Eventually.'

'Another worrying aspect was with this Sister Naomi, the young one who found the victim. As we say she was suffering badly from her nerves all to do with the shock of it all. Said it was the first time she'd ever seen a dead body and I suggested perhaps she should see a doctor, but they weren't having any of it. I was told in no uncertain terms how they will not be beholden to anyone; said that was the way of their God.'

'What do they do for money?' big DC Sandy MacLachlan popped into the mix.

'Little job for you?' Inga slid back to him. 'Get me a complete financial breakdown of their operation. Need any help I'm sure Jake will point you in the right direction.' She peered down at her notes. 'Initial assessment from both the doctor at the scene and from Jack Black and his CSI team, whoever our victim turns out to be had not been attacked there. Suggestion at this point is she was clobbered the previous evening. Get more when they take her out of the induced coma and we can ask her.'

'Evening Prayers would finish before seven,' said Jake. 'And according to this Sister Mary nobody would go into the chapel until this Naomi walked in there to light the candle at around five thirty.'

'Around?'

'They don't have watches or clocks,' he had to stop to snigger. 'Get this. They tell the time by God's light,' produced a whole range of grimaces amongst the team.

'Do we by chance have any surnames at all?' Sandy queried.

'No,' Jake responded. 'I've asked for a list of all the nuns including last known normal address, name, date of birth all the usual gubbins. All I've got so far from this Sister Mary Joanna is they only use their real name linked to a name God has given them.'

'Naomi, the kid who discovered the woman, is her real name apparently then it is followed by Phebe, a name God had given her,' said Nicky. 'Truth is as far as I can discover, the second name is nothing more than one out of the Bible. What they must mean by God's name.'

'Is it all God this, God that?' Sandy MacLachlan asked. 'What about Lord or Jesus or Christ or maybe Mohammed?'

'Only God. Seems idolatry,' Nicky responded.

'Sounds like a God botherer bunch to me. Sort who knock on my front door spouting all their mumbo jumbo.'

'Can we go back to the wee hen who found the body?' Sandy asked.

'Naomi.'

'Whatever,' Sandy continued. 'How many keys are there to the chapel, and…' he stopped when he realized both Jake and Nicky's heads were shaking.

'They never lock the doors,' Jake advised.

'Never?'

'No,' Jake smirked and looked across at Nicky.

'To allow their God free access…'

'For god's sake! Whoops!'

'This is not the nunnery norm,' said Nicky. 'This is not about Christian women living behind cloistered walls who in this day and age apparently go out into the world a great deal more to preach and teach. From what I've been able to ascertain so far, modern nuns are on line, even on things like Facebook.' She stopped to shake her head and sigh. 'Read about one crowd who produce their own wine and sell it. This lot literally have nothing along those lines, as far as we know.'

'And you don't see many out and about these days.'

'Can I make a suggestion boss?' Jake asked an attentive Inga. 'I think we should bring this Naomi in, move her from their world into ours. Sit her down and allow her to go through the sequence of events in her own words away from the rest of them.'

'Or, we go to her,' said Inga. 'We,' she said looking at Nicky. 'It very well could be they're not happy dealing with men, if abusive relationships is one of the things they're all trying to escape from.' She moved to look at her second in command. 'Could be why you got nowhere Jake.'

'CSI had Siobahn with them but they still didn't respond.'

'I want to know why somebody would dump a young woman on this bunch of weirdos? Did you ask why they phoned us?' Inga posed to Jake.

'No,' he responded with a frown. 'Seems they consider it to be the norm. Natural thing to do.'

'But they're not natural, they live a far from natural life, so why suddenly decide they want to conform?'

'They waited long enough to call us,' he emphasized.

'Everything they do is so far removed from the way normal people live including waiting to phone. Then suddenly up pops this Jo Bloggs and after prayers, probably seeking divine guidance in the meantime, they follow the rules they want nothing to do with the rest of the time.'

'Hang on!' said DC Ruth Buchan sharply stood at the door. 'It means this lot were in the chapel praying and didn't give a toss about a seriously ill woman in the front pew.'

'Sick!'

'Thought it was just men they didn't like.'

'Alert from Mispers,' said Nicky loudly. 'Could be her,' she added as she frowned at her screen and let her breath just wander out. 'Got a Carole-Anne Quinlan missing for more than twenty four hours. Below average height, brunette short hair. A...' She hesitated. 'IIA Lead Co-ordinator,' Nicky said slowly and carefully. 'IIA means...er...Impartiality in Action...something to do with being linked somehow to the NHS. Lives in Gainsborough, divorced,' she read and looked up.

'We've come across one of these before,' said Jake. 'People who somehow are linked to the NHS for some obscure reason.'

'Now you know where your money gets wasted.'

'Be fair,' the DS responded. 'She was probably on the front line during the virus, could be people owe their lives to her. Be somebody we clapped, remember?'

'Jamie,' Inga aimed at the DC. 'A word when we finish, if you please.' She had important questions to which as yet she had no

23

answers. Had the body been placed there deliberately? If so, why? Was it just somewhere conveniently close by? Did the killer know how quickly it would be found, that a candle is lit that early? Why a nun's place, why not an empty disused building, an old warehouse or dump it in the River Trent? Why had she not just been chucked in the hedgerow, a ditch, down a grotty back alley?

'Welcome to MIT again,' Inga said in her poky office to DC Jamie Hedley after the briefing but refrained from shaking hands. 'I'm particularly interested because the resume about you reminded me you once lived in Gainsborough.'

'Mum still does.'

'D'you still know people over there?' He nodded. 'I take it you can still find your way around, can't have changed very much.'

'Over there quite a bit actually keeping an eye on her. Still support the Blues. Still have a friend or two over there.'

'The Blues?'

'Sorry. Gainsborough Trinity.'

'Good. Need you to be our eyes and ears on the ground over there probably just for starters, and to keep us up to date with what's going on. Use Gainsborough cop shop as a base when you're over there. I'll tell them you're coming. Easier for you than travelling back and forth every day when you might have inside knowledge.' She could see the look on his face. 'Rest assured this is not me farming you out of sight out of mind, but it would be remiss of me if I didn't use your local knowledge. Word on the streets is so frequently important.'

'Of course, ma'am.'

Jamie Hedley had a clean-cut look and a muscular physique to go with it. Working out had been his way of attempting to move himself away from the world of bullying he had suffered for so long at school. Outgoing, brash thugs picked on boys including Jamie from a one-parent family. Now tormentors would certainly think twice.

He'd worked with MIT before on Operation Themis and until the call went out for extra hands he had been gaining a month's valuable experience with the fraud team.

'Please make sure you ask if you miss out on what's going on with the case. Start over there first thing in the morning and we'll text you to arrange coming come back here from time to time. In the

24

meantime check with Detective Sergeants Goodwin and Scoley about what they discovered yesterday at this Cluny place.'

'Cluny Loony.'

'What?'

'What the locals call it.'

'See? I'm not such a silly old fool after all.'

As part of the Prisoner Handling unit downstairs Jamie had a daily grind involving in the main the very dregs of society. The waste of spacers, the druggies, the shoplifters nicking stuff to earn cash for their fix, the shoplifters helping themselves stuff to earn cash for food. Plus the alcoholics of course and the ones he could never fathom often with hideous tattoos on their faces or straggly hair down to their shoulders. Last but not least were the domestics he'd had to attend which were on the increase. Cowardly so-called men bashing their women about.

Moving back to the town of his birth had good and bad elements. He would be living with his mother temporarily which he knew she would be really pleased about, to provide company in the troubled times. He'd be nearby to get to the Blues home matches.

Downside was he'd back on his ex-partner's territory and his most recent experience had left a bad taste. During the early stages of the pandemic he'd organized food deliveries for his mother in addition to checking up on her during the week when the rules allowed.

Now with the worst subsiding, six weeks previous he'd gone to Tesco for his mother to get a few bits of pieces and a treat for her tea when he spied his ex in the store on her own. He was no closer than double the 2 metre barrier when she spotted him.

'Don't you dare touch me!' she shouted to attract others' attention pointing at him.

He'd had no intention of touching her, just aimed to enquire after her health and well-being and that of his daughter he'd still never seen. Loath to get involved in some shouting match in public, Jamie put his hands up, spun round, dumped his basket, left the store and sat in his car with a boiling of emotions under his skin.

He still couldn't fathom how anybody could just turn off their feelings for somebody without due cause. Had he been a nasty shit, the sort of sadistic bully who bash their women about, the type he'd had to deal with many a time. Had he been a control freak leaving her short of cash, deciding who she could talk to and where she could go, he could understand the attitude.

Except that sort of imbecile wouldn't have the brain to understand what he'd done.

In all his time with her he'd never laid a hand on Kerrie or any other female come to that. She'd never had bruises she'd have to hide, no black eyes, no burns or broken bones there was a need to lie about in A&E.

He wanted no more of it.

5

Since landing on Quinlan as his target practice Gordon Kenny had taken an even keener than normal interest in the working of the National Health Service.

He personally knew exhausted nurses who are disillusioned by the utter shambles they work with at times

He knew it was all about the likes of Quinlan getting their priorities right round their neck and wasting the one thing the NHS is desperate for: quality care and our money. Completely pointless 'Our Vision' and 'Future Together' priority diatribe posters littered the hospital walls with messaging patients a distinct afterthought it seemed to him whenever he visited. Why no posters warning of the harm caused annually by the foolish public not taking up the offer of free flu vaccines?

As a simple aside, he had read somewhere a while back how having a 'Family Doctor' is now considered bad for your health. His gran he knew always made her appointments with one specific GP, a Dr James, but he did no such thing.

Before the pandemic with all the waiting lists as they were, how on earth would anybody know they are going to feel unwell in a fortnight? These days it's a case of phoning up and putting your health in the hands of as receptionist to arrange a virtual consultation. At times he understands you may have to wait a bit, but at least in the end you do get to talk to somebody.

The suggestion of seeing the same GP each time means in effect you only receive the opinion of one solitary person, right or wrong made real sense to him. Since the pandemic it really was pot luck.

Gordon discovered at a very early stage how this Quinlan now lives in Gainsborough and with all due respect to the place it is hardly the epi-centre of the universe and not at all what he imagined the bism had in mind for herself.

27

The modern shift of people behaving like cloned sheep had in this case played right into his hands. This Carole-Anne was a case in point in the way she ran her life to a tight schedule, never veering from the path she had set for herself in her career and behaving like the woolly jumper growers.

Every evening he had also discovered the stupid woman went jogging. We've all seen the sort of thing. All the branded lycra clothing edged with pink, the bum bag, the earphones blasting out what some bozo has told her is music, the heart-rate monitor, one of those daft expensive watches and a water bottle full of some over-priced H_2O all dragged around the same course.

Be the sort as soon as Boris Johnson said people could exercise she'd go on line to get the latest pair of snazzy trainers.

Every time he spotted her, Gordon was absolutely delighted at how too pre-occupied and most certainly vulnerable she had allowed herself to become.

First time he followed her at a safe distance – on his mountain bike, he was surprised by her route. Not as he had had imagined a well-used, well-favoured course of well-lit streets used by others in order for people to see her. Folk like her doing this are usually puddings on legs or skinny ma-links we've all spotted out a few weeks before London Marathon and Lincoln 10K.

Gordon considered this to have been a serious dent in Carole-Anne's armour. For once in her life every day she appeared not to want the world to see her in action. Possible, despite the great love she had for herself she in truth recognized how she lacked a figure to capture attention. Her ungainly slow plod-plod left a great deal to be desired as he watched her from afar going through the overhang of trees.

Silly girl. By choosing her route Carole-Anne had in effect signed her own death warrant, not the decision about whether she would die or not, but how it would happen.

Razor wire and a staple gun were amongst the early items Gordon had investigated and cast aside, but then Puffer Fish meat was on the database on his untraceable laptop for a few days.

That fell by the wayside when he could simply not fathom a way of feeding it to her, no matter how big a gob she had.

Had she lived Gordon Kenny's mother would have been coming up to her seventy-fifth birthday soon. He is seriously not the type to leave messages on Instagram for dead friends and relatives as if they're sitting up in heaven with a cuppa, a packet of Hobnobs and an iPad

Be another year where there's no requirement for him to scour M&S for a nice blouse or top to suit her in the green she loved.

6

When this Sister Mary Joanna advised the two policewomen how their timing was very inconvenient when she met them at the front door of the Cluny Priory, DI Inga Larsson sensed almost immediately how she and Detective Sergeant Scoley both wearing visors would not really be welcome at any time.

'Stock excuse for everything,' said Nicky sat opposite her Inspector on a hard wooden bench in the small entrance hall. 'Pray before breakfast is why Naomi had to light the candle, pray before lunch I imagine has to be a bit more than saying grace like my gran used to, and certainly during the afternoon and in the evening think she told Jake they have a community prayer session.'

'Surely you must run out of things to pray for.'

'Some people do tend to dip out of main stream society to an extent, keep themselves to themselves but this is madness. Be interesting to see what Sandy comes up with about their finances.'

'I've asked Ruth to do a police and open source search on every one of them, see what it throws up. Getting them off the electoral roll for starters.' She shrugged. 'Have to say Jamie seems switched on.'

'He was good when we used him before on Themis,' said the DS. 'And I'm told he's just done a month or more with the fraud guys,'

'If Ruth discovers they're on there under the names their God has given them, we could well be up a gumtree.'

'Would the council accept that d'ya reckon?'

'Got the sense I hope to try the census, if Council Tax throws up next to nothing.'

'HMRC is probably blank with no income. I bet this lot hand over their worldly goods when they first arrive.'

'I know people who willingly give ten percent of their salary to their church.'

'More fool them.' Inga looked all around. 'How cold must a place like this be in winter?'

'They'll not take any notice, after all they're suffering for their God so he doesn't have to. Good trick that, get someone else to feel cold for you.'

The house was Georgian, very large and in its heyday considered very grand no doubt. Sort of place some folk these days pay a pretty penny to wander around with an air of envy and strange reverence to the owners, or previous owners if the National Trust have added it to their burgeoning list. Sort of place Nicky's mother Paula had enjoyed visiting at one time.

Inga Larsson just blew out a breath of frustration. 'What's keeping them?'

'Now know what my bedtime reading will be tonight,' whispered Nicky. 'I'm gonna be looking at a few nuns websites, try to get a real feel for how others operate.' She looked all about. 'Can't all be like this surely?'

'Bedtime stories are becoming a bit tedious.'

'How is she?'

'Starting to sleep much better. Certainly difficult to start with the little madam. Slept for all she was worth during the day, but night…' Inga shook her head as she remembered vividly the nightly trials she and Adam had shared with Terése in the early days.

Months of chewing over a variety of names and in the end Inga and Adam came down on the side of an early choice. Not for them any of the child name silliness which tends to abound in some quarters. A movement towards gender-neutral names such as Aman, River and Sawyer in order for them unfortunately to be either sex. Even a girl named James was one Inga had sadly heard about. She just wished such people would put an end to stereotyping their children as the offspring of idiots or planning things in order for transition to be made a great deal easier. 'This is worse than Strangeways.'

'Worse than any prison I've been in.'

'Prison reform folk would have a field day here.'

'Wonder if we'll be offered a cup of tea.'

'Don't hold your breath,' Inga scoffed. 'Be some vegan nonsense if we get anything at all.'

'Is this really necessary?' this Sister Mary asked the moment her sandaled feet shuffled back through the door. 'I'm sorry, but you look ridiculous.'

'We are wearing these to protect you and your ladies as well as ourselves as we have a protocol to follow.'

'We have no need and anyway I've heard they don't work.'

'Your choice, but can I suggest you try wearing a mask and blowing out a candle.'

'Our afternoons,' the nun went on after a snigger of contempt. 'Are spent working outside in the fresh air. You telling me that's wrong too?'

'Not at all.'

'We have a great deal to do today, our foodstuffs don't just grow on their own. You seem to have forgotten we have half a dozen hungry mouths to feed.' She just plonked herself down and folded her arms.

'I'm sure you'll cope one short for a while,' said Inga Larsson as she sprung to her feet. Nicky Scoley looked up at her boss and wondered about their meals and what they were harvesting at that time of year she'd check with her dad. Would these women tuck into steak and chips tonight, perhaps tagliatelli or lasagne like she was having? No chance. 'Can we get on please, I'd like to interview the nun who discovered the young woman.'

'You're under a misapprehension,' said the prioress sat there arms folded. 'I'll need to be with Sister Naomi Phebe, or have you forgotten already how very young she is?'

'Nineteen I understand,' said Larsson. 'Old enough to drink, to vote, to get married, have sex, fight wars, join Gay Pride and a lot more besides. In fact old enough for pretty much anything. We'll see her on her own if you don't mind, and if we feel she is in need of legal representation, then she'll accompany us down to Lincoln or the local police station across in Gainsborough where we'll arrange professional legal support for her and a responsible adult if deemed necessary.'

'I don't think so.'

'And why is that?' Larsson asked hands firmly planted on her hips.

32

'Dereliction of duty, and I owe it to my God to do all I can to protect his children.'

'All very well Sister, but we have to operate in the real world. Sister Naomi Phebe on her own if you please, and bear in mind social distancing.'

'And if I refuse?'

'I'll arrest you.'

The nun pushed back the sleeves of her habit and put out her hands as she did so. 'Please do.'

Did Larsson need the hassle involved in arresting a nun, not to mention the ensuing publicity such a fuss would bring on the force? She ignored the reaction for fear of the twitterati hiding under her skirt.

'Depending on the outcome of this interview it may well become an operational requirement to interview Naomi on her own, and if that proves necessary I will be quite willing to arrest you and throw you in a cell while the interview takes place. Do you understand about perverting the course of justice?'

'I understand you are providing me with a perfect example why we live here as we do. Why we want nothing whatsoever to do with the petty silliness you appear to deem necessary in your sorry little lives.' With that this Mary turned and clip clopped ahead of them down a passage and then turned to usher the pair of them into a small room. 'This is where,' she said abruptly and walked off.

The two women sat in silence this time side by side on wooden chairs at a scrubbed well-worn wooden table. The room apart from two more odd high-backed chairs was empty, save for a wooden cross hanging crookedly on a nail on the whitewashed wall opposite.

Larsson was reeling against a tide of frustration she had no cure for.

The door opened quietly and a rather painfully thin fresh faced young woman with skin like polished ebony tentatively entered.

'Hello,' said the Detective Inspector as gently as she could. 'Come in, have a seat, dear.' She waited until the young woman and the one they both guessed was in charge had sat down. 'Just a few simple questions, nothing to bother your little head about,' she offered and smiled but received a slightly opened mouthed blank look in return. 'If you'd be so kind,' said Inga to the Mary woman.

'A list of all occupants please,' and slid a sheet of paper across the table and then rolled a black biro in her direction.

'Tell us about this morning,' said Scoley in her best sympathetic voice. 'From when you first got up.' This Naomi made no secret of the fact she was looking at Sister Mary for some sort of permission or confidence boost.

She cleared her throat. 'Have to be up at five, then got myself ready and that and went...'

'What does get yourself ready mean exactly?' Inga asked and the youngster looked slightly confused. Possibly because it was now the taller older blonde DI asking.

'Washed and dressed.'

'And then?'

'Walked over to the chapel.'

'Did you see anyone?' blonde Larsson asked and put up her hand. 'Just a moment,' she told the youngster. The DI stabbed the sheet of paper in front of this Sister Mary with her index finger. 'List please,' she told her. Back to Naomi. 'Carry on, sorry about that, dear.'

'Went into the...'

'Did you see anybody?' Inga Larsson had to remind her and got a shake of her head.

'No,' she mumbled and shook her head slightly. 'Just went up to the altar, took a new candle out of the box, put it in the holder and lit it.'

'What with?'

Naomi scrunched up her face as if the answer was obvious. 'Match.'

'Then?'

'Prayed,' was said with a flick of her eyes to her right, and Inga guessed in reality the prayer just might have been skipped. As if preparing herself, Naomi sucked in a breath and allowed it to slither across her bottom lip. 'Turned round and there she was. That...'

'Woman?' Naomi nodded. 'Then what?'

Naomi shrugged her shoulders. 'Told Sister Mary Joanna.'

'And what time would this be do you think?' Scoley asked gently.

'Dunno,' she pouted. 'Could be half past five.'

'Yet nobody phoned for an ambulance until around six forty five.' There was the slight shrug again. 'Sister?' was aimed at Sister Mary scribbling down a list of names.

'Sorry?' she pretended.

'Naomi here found the woman at five thirty or thereabouts, but you didn't dial 999 until six fifty one I think to be absolutely precise.'

'And?'

'Please explain why.'

'First Morning Prayers.'

'How do you mean?'

'We have prayers first thing in the morning.'

'And you couldn't wait a few minutes while you phoned? Is that what you're saying?'

'What time are these Morning Prayer?' Nicky Scoley the note taker asked.

'Six.'

'So you had time between Naomi here telling you what she'd found and the start of prayers, to phone us?'

'Had to wait for the Sister to be ready,' this Naomi piped up in a way which said they should know the system.

'So,' said Larsson with her eyes closed. 'Are you saying, when you found the body in the chapel you didn't run hell for leather back into here and bang on Sister Mary's door.'

'Not allowed,' was all wide-eyed at the suggestion.

'What's not allowed?'

'Banging on doors.'

'It was an emergency.' The shrug was back to annoy and Larsson spun her head to Sister Mary. 'Why couldn't prayers wait until you'd dealt with it?'

'Really,' she woman sniggered. 'You seriously think our God had nothing else to do. Other than sit around waiting for us to stop messing about with things of little or no concern to us let alone him?'

Inga Larsson pointed at her. 'Don't take me for a fool, please. I've never met the guy but I guarantee he's not there waiting at exactly six o'clock every morning having had his Weetabix and a cuppa waiting just for you to call him up. It's not Zoom!'

'You really should meet him, dear,' annoyed Inga because the condescending bitch had not reacted. 'I can assure you my dear, time spent with our God can only change your life which will I guarantee, never be the same. You will be fulfilled, at one with him and at peace, as we all are.' The smile was sickly sweet.

'Do you really think waiting over an hour to report a woman unconscious in your chapel is acceptable because you were otherwise engaged?'

'In most circumstances of course not, harvesting in the field for instance, but interrupting our special time with God is something we'd not even consider I'm afraid.'

'Please stop it,' said an angry Swede. 'You're not harvesting in the field, you're growing a few runner beans and a lettuce or two.'

'We harvest our God's provisions.'

'How's the list coming on?' Larsson questioned to put an end to the rot being spewed out. She pulled the sheet of paper towards her. 'Real names,' she said stabbing a finger on the sheet. 'Not this.'

'They are their names,' Sister Mary insisted and pushed it back at Inga. 'We have a right to our own secrets, a touch of privacy that's all ours.'

'The names they were born with, the ones on their passports, the names the tax man knows them by, those we probably know them by too I should imagine.'

'We have no need of passports,' prioress Mary slowly slid the sheet back. 'We have no earnings, we do not crave the objects people like you hold dear, so pay no tax, we do not become involved with the police and all the rest of your paraphenalia. End of.'

Inga took the sheet, glanced at it and passed it to butterscotch blonde Scoley beside her. What a very peculiar remark from a nun.

'Any chance you might have touched the woman, checked for a pulse maybe?' Larsson asked Naomi, who shook her head. 'You?' she asked Sister Mary.

'No.'

'How did you know she wasn't dead?'

'She didn't look dead, and anyway she was trespassing.'

Inga did have to wonder if her intolerance of the likes of this Mary Joanna or whatever her real name was, could be quite simply down to the company she now kept away from the force or just her maturity would not allow her to suffer such antagonistic fools.

'Nicky,' she said to her colleague sat beside her instead of aiming her vitriol at the woman who was no doubt expecting it. 'Would you please go with Naomi and let her walk you through her whole process this morning. From when she first woke up, step by step please through to the first of our team turning up which was most probably Sandy MacLachlan.' This Mary Joanna went to get to her feet. 'Not you!'

'I will not…'

'You madam will do as you're told for once,' was firm and up a notch from her normal tone. 'You will sit here and shut up and you will speak only when you are spoken to.' She glanced at both this Naomi and at Nicky. 'Off you go, take your time.'

Larsson noticed how scrawny Naomi looked at her mentor, almost as if she was desperate for her approval. In return she received a glare which spoke volumes for the Inspector, who watched the pair of them leave the room.

'This is quite intolerable, you…'

'I said shut up!' Larsson pulled the sheet of paper back in front of her. 'Anna Hushim, Esther…,' she shook her head as her eyes scanned down the list. 'I don't think so. Let's start again shall we? How about you start with yourself Mary?'

'And if I say no.'

'There'll be two dozen big hairy coppers rampaging through this place for the rest of the week, I'll get you on every radio and television station in the land, you mark my words. When I do, some numbskull looking for her moment of fame on social media will twitter how she knows you, where she knows you from and what you've been up to in the past.' Inga stabbed the paper again with her finger. 'Just cut the crap lady!'

'Can we start exactly where your day began,' Nicky Scoley suggested gently as she walked alongside with Naomi Phebe down a corridor of highly polished wood. 'Please call me Nicky, relax and just tell me everything you can remember.' As she walked, Scoley picked up the musty smell of mildew here and there. The whiff she associated with old stately homes her parents had enjoyed visiting at one time.

'This way,' was no more than a whisper but even so Nicky had no difficulty in hearing her as the whole place was eerily quiet. They turned right at the corner.

'Where is everybody?'

'All be out gardening, preparing our crops.'

'Do you grow all your own produce?'

'The majority.'

'Must take a lot of doing.'

'Keeps us busy,' and at that juncture Naomi extended her arm to guide Nicky Scoley through an open wooden door into a small room, which was more like a cell.

Cells in every women's prison Nicky had ever been in were absolute luxury compared to the stark empty cavern she had walked into. The wood everywhere did tend to make corridors dark, dull and dour, but having the wood painted white did brighten the room as a positive. However, it was all too stark. Not one thing out of place, no personal knick-knacks but then having noticed, Scoley realized there probably was nothing to be out of place.

The detective did what she often did in such situations. She checked the ambience impression. Just something she'd picked up in a novel she'd once read on holiday years previous. This detective, she'd read about always gave smell a priority. Her attention had already been drawn to what was missing and even in what in effect was this young woman's private bedroom there was something not right. All these women together and there had not so far been as much as a whiff of scent or perfume. Not at all the place to wake up and smell the coffee or even the smell of cabbage.

Polish out in the corridor and what she sensed was air freshener, wafted about, but in the cell where the youngster spent her time, nothing at all.

'You're in bed I take it. Then what?'

'Got up, did my blessing, went out to the washroom.' Scoley gestured to her, and Naomi clip clopped out and joined her for a walk down another corridor past similar bright white cell rooms all with the doors open and what she could see they were regimentally all exactly the same. Scarily alike.

In the washroom Scoley saw wash hand basins, communal showers of the sort which once upon a time were provided in school changing rooms decades ago and toilets. Red quarry tiles on the floor and the white ceramic tiled walls inevitably.

No trails of perfume any of them had left in their wake. No sense of shower gel or a soapy freshness she'd normally associate with such cloistered women.

The slightness of the young thing with her was a major cross in the box if she was to consider this Naomi as a potential killer. The Detective Sergeant doubted whether she'd have had the strength to carry or even drag their Jo Bloggs into the chapel. It would most certainly have been a serious case of huffing and puffing if she'd even tried.

'Then after I went back to my room.'

'Hang on.' Naomi stopped in the doorway. 'You had a shower?' was answered with a nod. 'How did you dry yourself then?'

'With my towel.'

'You brought with you?'

'Yes.'

'Where do you dress?'

'Back in my room.'

'And to get from here to there?' Naomi just looked at her. 'You put your habit on in here?' There was a silence lasting just long enough to become awkward. 'Did you?' Scoley said at last before it became embarrassing.

'No,' the young woman said sheepishly and gave an apologetic smile as a way of saying sorry for the long pause. Her bright white teeth as perfect as she had ever witnessed.

'The nightie you wore to get here then?' was answered with another shrug to annoy Scoley further. 'You put it back on and...' A shake of the head pulled her up sharp.

'I just walked back to my room.'

'Naked?'

'Yes,' was hardly audible, and there was the start of a look of real embarrassment which explained everything.

'You have to do that every day?' Scoley had to ask as the idea of plodding back naked in such a stark cold environment made her actually shiver. The girl nodded weakly and bit here bottom lip as she did so.

From the ablutions they returned to her room where she said she had dressed, then set off for the long walk out to the chapel but the DS could not rid her mind of the image of walking naked in the freezing cold at times, all the way back to her bleak unwelcoming cell.

'Could you go through exactly what you did?' Scoley asked as they entered and she watched the young thing open a wooden cabinet, produce a huge white candle she lifted out with two hands and then a box of matches. She watched fascinated as Naomi pretended to place the candle on a spike next to one already lit and mimed the action of lighting it. Naomi then returned the matches to the draw, stood in front of the candle and prayed for at least a minute, then she spun right round towards where Nicky was watching from.

Had she really prayed she wondered or was this more mime, more pretence?

'Then I saw her,' she said and stuck out a chubby finger. 'Sat there.' Her finger pointed to the far right hand side of the front wooden pew.

'And you did what exactly?'

'I erm…went back in and told the Sister, Mary Joanna.'

'Straight away?'

'Had to wait for her to rise,' Scoley's look asked for more. 'Get up.'

'You didn't knock on her door and tell her there's a problem straight away?' While she was still speaking Naomi had started to shake her head. 'Why?'

'Against the rules to wake a senior Sister.'

'But it was an emergency. To be honest it was a matter of life and death.'

'Erm…,' she sucked in a breath. 'Rules,' she offered as she shrugged and grimaced as if she had said completely the wrong thing.

'Then what?' Scoley asked as she struggled with the gobbledygook.

'Think we 'erm... all gathered for First Morning Prayers.' For the umpteenth time Naomi seemed unsure of herself. 'Yeh, yeh that's right,' she said as if she hoped she was still following the party line. To Scoley, at times she looked all mixed up and guilty.

She so felt for this young woman and prayed she was there of her own free will and had not been force fed into all this business by uncaring ultra-religious parents. Thoughts of her trundling naked along the corridor to her cell still rankled. This Naomi was quite obviously not at all the sort who are forever yearning for approval. Could possibly benefit a great deal if she were offered an element of kindness, but Scoley was not at all sure Sister Mary would be the one willing to or capable of providing it.

Nicky ushered young Naomi out of a door and into fresh air.

'Just so I have this clear in my mind,' she said as she pulled out her notebook. 'Would you please run through who it was were gathered for Morning Prayers.'

Back to the hesitancy and the nerves, back to looking almost frightened about the consequences of what she might reveal and Naomi glancing around as if desperate for somebody to come to her aid.

'Me of course,' was almost whispered as if she dare not do what the policewoman wanted. 'Susanna, Angela, Esther, Anna, Sarah, and Mary you've met.'

'Sister Mary Joanna you mean?' Nicky Scoley queried as she wrote them down. 'Real names?' was enough for her stood there looking at the poor mite with her eyes closed, hoping to god this would soon stop. 'Don't worry about it, thank you Naomi you've been most helpful.'

From there they walked together back to the small room where Inga had managed at last to obtain a list of the seven names.

'I don't care what you say, that poor kid's never a Naomi,' was almost the first thing Nicky had to say the moment they had removed the visors and were alone in the boss's car.

'And neither is it Jasmin.'

'What she told you?'

'Sure did and all the rest could well be hogwash too,' Inga glanced at her young DC. 'So, what's this all about?'

'Nuns giving false names, have you ever heard the like? Job for the team, find out exactly who it is we're dealing with.'

'And there's me thinking this woman has got nothing to do with a bunch of nuns.'

'Did you see the look on the woman's face when you said hell for leather?' Inga visibly questioned her. 'Was as if you'd come out with a stream of four letter words. She was visibly shocked.'

'Hell has got four letters,' Inga offered with a grin.

'Unreal.'

'Tell me this,' was a very serious Inga Larsson. 'Why was that Mary Joanna so obstreperous? Surely nuns, are some of the easiest people in the world to get on with. Yes, possibly a bit naïve about life as we know it and out of touch, but not like she was. And another thing, have you ever heard of a nun being done for attempted murder?'

7

'First things first,' said Inga Larsson to her team. 'DS Scoley has more for us after researching on nuns and priories.'

Nicky Scoley cleared her throat. 'Priories first appeared as subsidiaries of the Abbey of Cluny in France,' she read from her monitor. 'They were all subservient to Cluny and were named priories and were all based on Benedictine ideals.'

'So, this bunch are Benedictines then?'

'Doubt that very much,' Inga interjected. 'Nicky.'

'The Cluny Priory we're interested in was closed as a practical nunnery just after the war and bought by a series of property developers the last of whom planned to turn it into luxury flats. Never happened because he went broke soon after. Since then it's been bought and sold a number of times and been home to a whole host of different people over the years until it is now once again infested by nuns in inverted commas.'

'Why d'ya say that?' Raza queried.

'I'm sorry. Because they're really not quite right,' Inga told him.

'Now of course the locals call it Cluny Loony,' a snippet of information picked up from Jamie Hedley, the guy she'd borrowed again.

'Think you need to explain to the boss,' a grinning Jake told Nicky, both unaware she had already heard the name from Jamie.

'Apparently Cluny has become known as loony locally, and the word loony comes from loony bin,' said Nicky talking direct to her Swedish boss. 'Loony is slang for a mental hospital or asylum.'

'Was that what it was?'

'Was what?' Nicky asked.

'An asylum.'

'No., not at all. Just what the yokels call it probably because it rhymes with Cluny and the women are a bit odd.'

'How long have they been there do we know?'

'Couple of dozen years or more according to Jamie.'

'And Cluny Priory is back to being a nun's home from home again.'

'We shall see,' said Inga. 'Seven names,' she said to her team as she tapped the white board.

'Ma'am,' from Scoley stopped her. 'Looked up the names business. Some change their names simply because the apostles had their names changed by Jesus. Supposed to depict the change in their status, like taking your husband's name on marriage.'

'Good, useful. I want to know everything there is to know about all of them.' As her team went to react she cut them dead. 'Wait on,' was firm. 'That's not all. Something's not quite right, not right at all. This chief nun or whatever she is has grey teeth and body odour, not how I see nuns. All scrubbed faces and glasses and no room for halitosis!' She looked down at DS Nicky Scoley.

'Not sure I'd have a good wash in the morning if I lived there, and what's the betting the showers are freezing?'

'She could still clean her teeth.'

'I'm still concerned,' said Nicky to voice in public what she had already told her boss. 'How a group of women in a religious order all by sheer chance have names from the Bible. Naomi, Susanna, Esther, Angela, Sarah, Joanna and Mary.'

'Sorry Ruth,' Inga said to her Detective Constable. 'Need a fresh start to your Open Source Search to tell us whether she's even close to telling us the truth. Get onto everybody PMC and DVLA for a start then HMRC, Councils, NHS, Banks, the works. At least the names she gave me are a better bet than things like Naomi Phebe. The lump in charge claims the girl who found our woman is Jasmin Palmer. Sorry no. She's African is my guess, or at least her parents were, doesn't sit right.'

'First check we've done on the Cluny Priory,' said Jake Goodwin, 'Has drawn a blank. There is nobody on the Electoral Roll for the Cluny Priory but it's not mandatory, and the Council Tax is in the name of,' and he looked carefully at his screen. 'Traa-dy-Liooar based in Jurby near Ramsey in the Isle of Man. And just out of interest gas and electric are in the name of ...'

'Hold on there,' said Inga before anybody else could stop him. 'Say that again.'

44

A grinning Sandy responded. 'It's a Manx saying. Traa-dy-Liooar, and I know what it means because the gas and electrics are in the name of an associate company at the same address called Timenough.com.' He knew he had to explain even without the looks his colleagues were giving him. 'Traa-dy-Liooar is Manx for...time enough,' he sat back with a self-satisfied grin on his face.

'Tax Haven.'

'Exactly. So what's that all about, why would a bunch of nuns with no income need to be based in a tax haven?'

'Church of England is the largest land owner in Britain,' DC Sandy MacLachlan offered. 'What's the betting they've got a few quid in the Cayman Islands or somewhere?'

'Or unscrupulous bankers are using them to hide their ill-gotten gains.'

'And you think this lot are stinking rich too?'

'It doesn't look like it,' said a chuckling Nicky Scoley. 'Not by what I've seen. The place is really basic, in fact it's horrible. Talk about no expense spared, looks like they've had no expense.'

'But surely Nick, it's what they sign up to. Isn't it all part and parcel of the deal, isn't that why they go through this slow progression?'

'This is what I discovered,' said Nicky. 'The young nun who found the body has to get up at five, has to wash in cold water in a general washroom place, walk back to her cell stark naked, get dressed and traipse across a courtyard to the chapel in her habit thing and sandals in all weathers, just to light one bloody big candle.'

'And this is where our Jo Bloggs was?'

'Hang on,' Inga said to stop anymore interruptions. 'Naomi has been with them at least a year, been given her habit and the Naomi Phebe name to show she has an aptitude for their way of life.'

'How far are they from reality?' Sandy asked. 'They must have some creature comforts.'

'No television, no magazines, books or newspapers I saw, in fact everywhere is so bland and bare. No mirrors or pictures, just a cross here and there and whitewashed wooden walls in the bedrooms if you can call them that. Wooden benches in the chapel, nothing in there to steal like there are in every other church I've been in. No gold or silver on the altar which to be honest looks just like a huge wooden crate with a wrought iron cross on it.'

'She's right,' commented a nodding Jake in case any were doubtful.

'And all the doors are unlocked during the day, and as I say, the chapel remains open 24/7.' Nicky looked at DI Larsson. 'Got to say boss, I felt sorry for Naomi. At one point when we were on our own in the chapel place and she'd explained about lighting the one candle and turning round and seeing the body. She looked like a frightened kid. Sort of got the feeling she didn't want to be there.' Nicky sucked in a breath. 'Tried to get chatting to her, talked about everyday things and sensed she wished she was out here, but and it's a big but.' Nicky pulled in her breath. 'Then became so self-critical, mentioned her weight more than once and how she'd come across trolls on the web who'd bullied her, called her awful vile names due to her looking like skin and bones. Thing is how do they know with that habit on? And...to be honest she's not the prettiest girl I've ever seen. Just felt so sorry for her. Almost as if bloody trolls had done that to her.'

'Not win a beauty pageant to be honest, and being coloured would set some trolls going,' was Inga. 'What on earth's she doing on line? We never saw anything.' Larsson put her hands ion her head. 'What on earth is going on?'

'That a mistake you reckon? She given the game away?'

'This not a form of slavery is it ma'am?'

Inga shook her head. 'Think we've got enough on without heading down that road, but we'll bear it in mind.'

'Took me to her room to start with,' Nicky continued. 'She's not on line, there's nothing in there. All so stark and horrid and I'm in there looking all around at next to nothing and been reflecting on all those soppies who spend their nights in scary pink bedrooms looking like a pigsty and wondered if perhaps she'd actually got the best deal.' Nicky put her hand up. 'Sorry, just me being a bit sarcastic.'

'No life for a young woman.'

'No certainly not, but then nor is a pink bedroom with fairy lights.'

'Could have a phone,' was another issue to face.

Inga knew if the revised list of names she had dragged out of Mary 'Joanna' Johns was to be believed, Susanna Chapman it seemed, had quite possibly not changed her name when entering the Cluny Priory. In this day and age Inga accepted almost anything is possible with names. Women taking or not taking their husband's name on entering marriage as they see fit, kids using one or the other of their parents or at worst both to emphasize their illegitimacy when looking for a career was never a good move so she understood from friends in staff recruiting about the stark realities of life.

'We always root out all those who can't spell for starters', a friend had told her. *'Chuck away those they've downloaded from the net. Then we throw all the illegitimates in the bin and you're quickly down to a manageable amount'*. But worse was to come. *'Slanting lettering usually means they're left handed so they go too, and if a department has a no gays policy we deal with by ditching them at interview.'*

She'd heard about some men taking their partner's surname on marriage and in some cases doing so without bothering to get wed. Such nonsense was going to make researching your family tree in the future an absolute nightmare.

'Another thing I need to mention,' said Nicky. 'The poor kid admitted they each have a chamber pot they take with them to the ablutions place when they go to get washed.'

'What in hell's name for?' Sandy demanded.

'Once you're in your room, the door is shut and you must not leave for any reason.' Nicky put her hand up. 'But once you walk out in the morning with your potty in your hand from then on the door must never be closed.'

'It's like a concentration camp.'

'What that lot are running away from has to be pretty horrific if that place is a better alternative.'

'What's the worst it can be?' Sandy asked. 'Abusive relationship, homosexuality, ordination of women some are dead set against, and sex-abuse scandals probably.'

'None of which need actually affect them. What about poverty in this day and age and being prudish maybe.'

'Has to be more,' said Inga. 'You seem to be forgetting we'd not be looking at this weird bunch at all if it were not for our Jo Bloggs slumped in a pew. People drive past the end of the road all day long and don't bat an eye lid. Back here at four with all the answers you've got.'

'And the poor kid who found the woman is African we think,' said Nicky. 'Chance she might be Muslim, so somebody needs to explain to me what is going on.'

'You're not the only one,' added Inga. 'Could be they're planning to convert her.'

'We suggesting this is radical Islamic indoctrination in reverse?' Raza asked. 'Instead of forcing her to profess the Muslim statement of faith this lot are teaching the poor kid the Lord's Prayer and all that loaves and fishes business.'

'All we need!'

'Part of the problem is who they claim to be. You all know what witnesses are like. Those who can remember regularly get it totally wrong. Those who can't just make it all up for a minute of fame or repeat something off You Tube. Nuns would by their very nature be different. How much tele do they watch? Never saw a set when I was there.' Nicky was nodding in agreement. 'Apart from *Songs of Praise* on Catch Up what do these people watch of a night? *Countryfile* maybe or even the *Proms* when it's on would be as much as they could cope with I should imagine. Be all fussy about people swearing and everything else about real life.'

Just something DC Jamie Hedley had once done for a large part of his adult life. Pop into the Spread Eagle of a Tuesday night for a few jars, having arranged to meet up with those who once were school pals and folk he'd known a good while. Nothing too heavy, no daft crap songs, no getting wasted, no heaving in the lavvy, no weed, no immature mooning or buying stuff off the back of a lorry, just none of that. Despite being British there was little or no bragging about it all.

Supping a quiet pint or two of IPA or real ale, game of darts maybe now and again but a good chin wag putting the world to rights along with The Blues.

Rather than traipse back and forth from Lincoln with being seriously involved with this case his decision to stop with his mum for a few days was proving right. He could just walk back home after, rather than drink lime and lemonade all night or some alcohol free nonsense.

As Scott bowled in he made a drinking motion with his hand and Jamie was pleased to accept. When the tall bloke in navy sweatshirt and good jeans asked the barman for 'same again' for his friend pointing at Jamie, the landlord had been so bored he could remember exactly.

Sat at opposite ends of a long wooden table, Jamie deliberately took his time sipping his pint for he knew Scott was bursting with curiosity, and once he'd supped, wiped his mouth and sat back - he was ready for the questions or as ready as he'd ever be, but also very wary.

'Why here?' Scott Casey asked sat at the far end of the table. 'Not been here in ages.'

'No idea where all my mates meet now.'

'Not here for sure,' was sarcastic. 'World's moved on matey, since that virus crap. This is on its last legs, and to be honest I'm surprised it survived.' He looked all around to spot next to nobody. 'Think they pretended to be on lockdown,' he almost whispered. 'Story is, few dozen folk were in here on the quiet. Or so I'm told and he did take-aways.'

'How was I to know?' At least it told Jamie why nobody else had responded to his text.

'Bit bloody strange this nun business,' was not the inevitable direct question but even so Jamie knew he wanted, needed almost, demanded an answer. Scott had gone for a bottle of Heineken much to his chagrin when he discovered they didn't sell Doom Bar any longer.

This was now a real problem. The Cluny story was all over social media but he understood the press had not been informed officially. He had no media guide lines to follow.

He and Scott had met some time back through Gainsborough Trinity or to be precise an event at their Blues Club. Jamie had been to some fund raising night at the club and they'd got chatting over a pint. Had then met up on the away coach a time or two. Not inseparable good friends by any stretch of the imagination now he was based in the city, just someone he knew with the same local footie interest.

These days with the virus the club prefer tickets to be bought on line, but with his job Jamie tended to turn up on the day when he could, sign in for Track and Trace and look for Scott.

Jamie had just never broached the subject of his Kerrie relationship collapsing to this Scott. Not one of those man to man relationship to be fair, and anyway he was quite sure he didn't need bothering with all his troubles or craved a hug the virus had put a stop to.

'Boss says when the hooter goes you never know what's coming up. This time it was out at the Priory.'

'She one of the nuns this girl?'

Jamie always knew he had to be so careful. According to the County Hospital she was more than a girl. 'Can't imagine so,' was what he said although he knew she had now been identified and a couple of Family Liaison policewomen up in East Yorkshire on the coast had been lumbered with the unenviable task of telling her parents the news before details were released.

'D'you know it was a nunnery place?' Scott asked.

'Knew it was called the Cluny Priory these days, musta been past it a hundred times over the years when I was a kid, but can't remember ever seeing any nuns about the place can you?'

'P'raps they wear civvies,' Scott chuckled and supped. 'How many are there do we know?'

Jamie knew exactly how many there were and knew Ruth Buchan had been tasked with identifying them all. The way Scott used 'we' amused him.

'No idea,' he offered for starters. 'All got sort of religious names, things like Hepzibah and Esther all out of the Bible,' he'd made up and hoped they weren't real ones off the list on the board back in the MIT Incident Room at Lincoln Central. 'I deal with low level crime remember,' was normally true.

'What happened then, do we know? This a rape d'we think?' Scott pushed for.

'I'll tell you this fella. If I catch my mum reading a murder mystery on her Kindle next year by some Scott Casey about a bunch of nuns I'll know where it all came from. You could get me into serious trouble.'

'All trending on social media, so don't worry yourself mate. Got too much on anyway.'

'But not the nitty-gritty about what actually happened. Just guesswork with the trolls on the web. Taking a punt like they do.'

Tall Scott sniggered at him. 'Get the nationals onto it they'll have their bra sizes before you can turn round. They'll all have it come Sunday, right up their street that sort of thing, a nun and a tart in a nunnery, chuck in somebody off *Coronation Street* and they'll revel in it.'

'Who said she was a tart?' Jamie shot at his friend.

'What I have to do if you don't fill me in with procedure. Pretend she's on the game, maybe gay and having a romp with a nun.' Scott took a sip. 'There's a thought. Wonder how many nuns are gay?'

'Don't be ridiculous!' stocky Jamie chuckled as his brain told him to tread very carefully. He knew being loaned to MIT for this case was another opportunity to impress which would not come round very often.

'We've had gay priests coming out, so anything's possible these days. I just mix fiction and real life and it's the latter with most surprises. Might just store that idea away.'

'You really think lesbian nuns is the norm?' he offered.

'Don't be so bloody naïve mate,' Scott scoffed. 'Battered wives, religious freaks, love torn lesbians I could run riot with such stuff. What's the betting it's what those places are full of?' Scott took a sip. 'Anyway what's happening now, what's the latest?'

'Waiting for all the tests to come back then we have to wait even longer for toxicology. Could easy be the middle of next week before we get results. If it's complicated all the forensics'll go down to Leicester to East Midlands Forensics.'

'CSI Leicester I take it,' Scott jumped in.

'You watch too much crap television where it's all done and dusted in an hour. Find a body, post mortem, forensics, car chases and culprit found before *News At Ten*. Murder solved, all sorted with adverts in between,' he chuckled.

'Just curious that's all,' said Scott before he took a good drink. 'Sort of stuff I can store away,' he looked at Jamie. 'You're always picking me up on things in my books you say I've got wrong; all the procedure bits. If you won't tell me, how the hell will I ever get it all right?' He turned his head to look seriously at Jamie. 'Some writers have half their police force feeding them info, and I struggle with the one solitary copper I just happen to know.'

'It's all right for you, but I've got a career to think of.' Jamie grinned. 'Be easier if you let me read the next one before it comes out then I could point out the blatant errors.' How it would delight his mum, being able to read a book before all her friends. She'd talk about it at the WI for weeks. 'Or why not go down official channels, try the PR team at force headquarters?'

'This writing business is hard enough as it is without coming up against a brick wall,' Scott saw the hint of a grimace from his drinking partner. 'I have to do this on my own. I don't have a team of highly trained professionals like you do helping and advising and no doubt joining you in combined efforts.' He stopped to drink. 'I have to create people almost on a daily basis and their complex lives, then come up with a twist or two when I'm all locked away in my own little world of solitary confinement.'

'Sorry mate.' Jamie shrugged. 'The offer's there.'

'Spend most of my life in lockdown remember, not just a few months like you.'

Jamie spent the best part of a good ninety minutes with Scott Casey and fortunately the quizzing gradually subsided. They got onto football and Scott's great gripes surfaced.

His novelist friend has this pet hate about football commentators shouting and screaming unnecessarily on television and teams wearing their away strip even when colours don't clash. He thinks turning out in yellow when the fans are all dressed in blue is completely disrespectful.

8

As he trudged back home Jamie's mind wandered fleetingly back across the years, back to those early days of how one or two of them had first become pals at what was then Yarborough School and then as he strolled along hands in pockets with utter inevitability once school came into his brain a recent event came back to mind.

Tamara Diagne had been a year ahead of him at school, and she'd been, he was not ashamed to admit, the first real life female he had ever lusted after. In addition to having, according to the eyes of a fourteen year old, a fabulous figure and the looks of a superstar, she also had money. At least her old man did.

Lived out near Hemswell Cliff at one time in a big house, but sadly she was never a love he had lost. Sort of place some sad people get very envious of. Big long drive between tall trees up to the house when most folk just have a garden path next to the lawn from the garden gate.

Jamie Hedley had never got close to her, and doubted whether in their schooldays she even knew he existed. His problem then apart from the zits to occupy almost every waking moment were his hormones. Looking back now this Tamara was as pretty as a picture. Not exactly what his hormones had in mind for her, being in a picture.

Next time their paths had crossed Jamie was doing a six month night stint as a PC patrolling the streets of Lincoln. On the late shift one night he'd come across Tamara by sheer chance during a break when she was being booked in by the Custody Sergeant. By this time Jamie was already aware who her nasty piece of work father was. Terry 'Tez' Diagne was at that time doing a term inside for drug trafficking and a few other bits and pieces and his only daughter was in a right mess. Thin, gaunt, bedraggled and a mouthy shambles was a real shock to behold.

At the time he'd cursed to himself for being a stupid bastard and not making more of an effort with her at school. Then he reminded himself how fanciful such a notion was in reality, and the moment he had realized who she was he'd made himself scarce and busied himself to keep well out of her way.

He was thoroughly gobsmacked at what he had seen and wanted nothing more to add to the horrors he was already trying to deal with, and no way was he going to be the poor sod ordered by the sergeant to deliver her breakfast in the cell.

Once upon a time his hormones had wanted to deliver her breakfast in bed, but it most certainly had never been like that in his mind!

Once he had got over the loss of looks and luscious body he became aware of the piercings. Multiple cheap rings in both ears, a silver one dangling from her nose to further spoil what hint of great looks still remained.

Time and tide wait for no man or woman and Jamie, now DC Hedley with PHU (Prisoner Handling Unit) and his new temporary move to MIT in Lincoln had by sheer chance bumped into Tamara Diagne just a few days previously.

As he walked across Marshall's Yard he was staggered she'd recognized him but when she went through the annoying habit some insist upon about exchanging mobile numbers, he should have waited a while, snuck round the corner and then just deleted it.

He didn't, because deep down inside he was so proud of the recognition from a much better turned out Tamara than the last time. She was showing considerable improvement on the skeletal emaciated nose-ringed horror he had seen previously – yet still a good way from her heyday.

Was his tide of life on the turn he wondered? Move to MIT again had come out of the blue and a chance meeting with Tamara. Been a long time since life had been doubly good to him for once.

The horrors of the demise of his relationship with his Kerrie still lingered in the back of his mind along with brooding for his child, his daughter he never saw. Had never seen.

Next day he'd got a Text GETTIN 2 NO U TAMARA.

Took him a minute or two to delete the message, when he really should have deleted her number too. It was not a good idea at all to associate with her because of her misdemeanors and because who her father was, and he knew it.

The potential bane of his life Jake Goodwin, his MIT Detective Sergeant he knew by reputation and previous encounters, would read him the riot act if he were ever to find out. Goodwin he had known for some time was an absolute stickler for doing things by the book. All about keeping his nose clean, be careful who you associate with, about public concept and service image.

Goodwin worked, lived and breathed by the book, and it would be a very brave man to cross swords with him. Jamie saw him as being out of touch to some extent with his ultra-disciplined ways, but he still had to give him credit for being a really first rate copper.

Don't you dare fiddle with and certainly don't you dare answer your mobile when Jake's talking to you. Be equally rude whilst being served in a shop, and in particular doing it in places like the Doctors then woe betide you when he's about. Dropping litter was another of his Sergeant's pet hates, along with wearing headphones he saw as being akin to spitting or eating in the street. Deemed as being totally anti-social and fortunately by chance Jamie did neither of those objectionable things. He was currently exasperated and angered by idiots just dumping face masks all over the place.

Jamie had wondered back those three years or so when he'd first caught sight of this waif of a thing at the cop shop whether her old man was into more than just a bit of drug dealing alongside serious fraud and tax evasion. There are drug turf wars he knew everywhere. Not as big, brutal and vicious as you'd find in some big cities, but they existed all the same. Across in Lincoln they had a drug issue apparently with a high number of crack cocaine users and the availability of Spice the synthetic cannabis particularly in Lincoln Prison, but he'd only ever seen the city as a tourist place. Now he knew it was indeed the tourists who were the magnet for county line gangs.

Had Tamara become a victim of her own father's impropriety, was her fall from grace inevitable with her background?

One of the reason Jamie had considered the idea of joining the army when he left school was the instant income. He and his mum had not exactly lived hand to mouth and gone down the easy benefits road. Life had been hard for the pair of them and he just wanted to make a contribution. The only way he knew to say thank you.

He knew his mum would have been as proud as they come and just loved him to be a student, to go to uni. In truth it was never on financially, as it will never be for so many.

Jamie was not scared of dying for himself, he was scared of dying for his mum's sake. What on earth would something like that do to her? Getting the knock on the door, his empty beret, a worthless medal and being tainted as a vet at his age. What use would they all have been to her?

The reason in the end why he chose the police. Always aware he could die at the hands of a scrote with a chib, he knew there was a greater chance of living long enough to take his time to thank his mum, to do what he could for her in return for all her sacrifices and to make a social contribution.

By the time he reached the semi he was currently sharing with Rebecca Hedley he had gone through the whole chain of events in his mind. He walked into the kitchen, checked the kettle had water in, flicked down the red switch, lifted his mug off the draining board, spooned in coffee and two sugars, lifted the milk from the fridge and stood there with his back resting against the sink, waiting.

'That you pet?' he heard.

'Tea?'

'You've not been long.'

His phone rumbled as he wandered through to see her.

FIX A MEET? It said and Jamie Hedley smiled to himself as lurid images about Tamara and DS Jake Goodwin came to mind back waiting for the kettle. For once he'd seriously take on board the behavior discipline the great man instilled in his team and slipped his phone back into his pocket.

'Lads weren't there, but I've been talking to big Scott.'

'The one who writes those books you mean?'

'The very one,' he confirmed. 'Tea?'

'Didn't give you a free book I s'pose.'

'Not this time. Be a while before the next one's out I should imagine. Tea?' he asked again.

'Yes please pet. You think he gets the books free?'

'Guess it's probably author's perks, can't see him dipping his hand in his pocket for it.' Best not to mention he might get advanced sight of his next best seller. If Scott changed his mind she'd be real disappointed, so best to keep it to himself for now.

Waiting patiently for the kettle, his mind went back to the call. Nowhere near as vivid as it had been all that time ago, and he had no way of recreating the feeling which somehow remains in some form. Just two texts, and yet despite what he knew whenever he mused about Tamara his stomach turned and Jamie felt himself almost being drugged into a feeling of longing for her. What an amazingly beautiful, cute and funny girl she had been back at school.

Been there, done it with his Kerrie. All the big romance thing, hugs and kisses, love of his life and then moving out and setting up home had all been such a fabulous and exciting time.

Now where was he? Back home it seemed almost in the twinkling of an eye on his own in his old bedroom, a few clothes and possessions in his backpack.

Just as the kettle boiled, Detective Sergeant Jake Goodwin came to mind and what he would say if he heard one of his team was dreaming of and lusting after a young woman with a record of naughtiness as long as his arm and her daddy doing another lengthy stretch.

Was this pure frustration? Following on the loss of his Kerrie to another and now the unavailability of a past dream if he stuck to the rules.

It has crossed his mind more than once how Tamara just might know something about what had gone on at Cluny. So far everybody he had asked seemed to know less than he did. Trouble is these days, folk don't read local papers and something like the Cluny attack would never be on a BBC website folk just might take a peep at on their phones and tablets. These influencer woman'd not be in the slightest bit interested in such events.

How was he ever going to impress the foreign DI and disciplined DS Goodwin? Then a sudden thought of how Tamara might very well still be on regular doses of Methadone brought him up short.

Time to take mum her cuppa and sit with her for a while.

9

No matter how many times he'd checked on his phone social media was still just a load of scurrilous twaddle about nuns, but to be honest Gordon Kenny never expected much more.

He was starting to feel slightly uneasy because he had a feeling the coppers were playing mind games. They had to be. It all started off with the news of what was described as a major incident out at the Priory place, but since then it'd not moved on. Except for bits and pieces about serious crime officers being at the scene together with experts in forensic investigations.

Did they really need all those people for what was in effect a simple matter, he wondered? Like television programmes he got annoyed about, who at the end list the fifty people or more it had taken to create a silly simple quiz.

He'd been onto various websites but there was nothing much more he could see. Once upon a time he guessed a murder would have stuck out like a sore thumb. These days it'd be treated as just another in a long line. He'd not been on trend and stabbed anyone and because of that his attack was probably seen as less interesting. When that virus was at full pelt the lack of other normal news really annoyed him, but the media did that anyway.

There'd been no mention of a body, an unexplained death or talk of them launching a murder enquiry and some specialist team moving in. Apart from going on about nuns, they were still on the incident business, a word he knew they use for all sorts.

He'd found stories on the local news sites about "Woman accused of attempted murder in Sutton-on-Sea…teenager dead after stabbing…and the very latest virus figures update."

By now he was spending his time in a state of nervous exhaustion and the tension was certainly getting to him. What he'd done was for the benefit of others and they would be relying on him to be self-disciplined in everything he did, if they knew what he'd been up to.

Gordon had no wish to bore anybody with a whole screed of this Carole-Anne's philosophy, even if he dare open his mouth about her; but her blog was there on line to constantly remind him what she was involved in and what he had got all het up about.

We need to concentrate our efforts in future on the Millennials as important specifics within any generational cohorts are always a key sign. I fully appreciate how this generation's confidence may tend to dribble over into the realms of entitlement and narcissism but I know you will agree this is the time to ignore these so-called baby boomers. Even so I do have to say I am slowly coming around to the suggestion we offer them a patient portal.

The Millennials cohort garbage was bad enough, but Gordon really did wonder why seriously intelligent and supposedly highly educated people fall for such weird and wonderful off-the-wall hocus-pocus ideas. Always presented to them by some daffy female with a degree in gender studies, geometric topology or palmistry. Where on earth does she get such nonsense he wonders, or did she really just make it all up after a few gins?

He'd then remind himself there was no distinct connection between education and common sense.

Morning after with his mind still in an utterly confused state, he'd been reluctant to go the gym first thing, in case he missed the news on *Breakfast Cavalcade*. Be just his luck for them to report her death and then some major event takes over and it's not mentioned again, or it's on air when he's pounding the treadmill.

Always the way with governments. Wait for a major catastrophe to unfold and they leak out the bad news under cover almost.

Gordon did go for his workout in the end, as in the days to come he knew he would need his attendance there on a regular basis as a major part of an elaborate alibi when he gets down to the proper job he had planned.

10

'Quieten down, please,' was tall, blonde and elegant Inga Larsson emerging in her Royal blue suit from her office.

'Haud yer wheesht!' was the stronger Scots version from Sandy MacLachlan.

The DI just stood there smiling hands on hips, cream blouse showing, waiting for her specifically reduced team to settle.

In some cases for individuals to quickly find a seat and for others to stuff a bit of something in their mouths to chew on or suck. One of the things she was used to. When she spoke, people listened.

'Looks as though we're talking ecstasy with our Miss Quinlan, with the possibility of a little extra.' Inga looked down at the notes she had made. 'Ecstasy pills in case you're not a fully qualified chemist, contain one active ingredient MDMA.' She hesitated.

'Be serious!' Jake exclaimed. 'How many athletes take that crap before they go training?'

'Please listen Jake,' was a serious rebuke. 'Don't ask me to repeat what it means or spell it. Save to say in addition from time to time, the drugs lads upstairs tell me they come across dodgy ones containing the drug PMA. This has a sleeper dose-response curve.' She stopped when the door opened and Detective Superintendent Craig Darke annoyingly walked in and then dropped down onto the first chair he came across, left empty for social distancing.

'Carry on,' he told an annoyed Inga who was going to anyway.

'This PMA. The amount needed to send your heart-rate, temperature and blood pressure into overdrive is far less.' She nodded at her boss at the back she could see was itching to speak. Sometimes he really annoyed her. Why couldn't he wait until after morning briefing or just sit there politely until she was finished?

'Excuse me, but who we talking about Inspector?'

'The nunnery congregation. This Quinlan woman.' She waited in case there was an annoying follow up. 'Too much MDMA usually won't kill you so I'm told, but add PMA and you'll find it doesn't seem to have had an effect.' She smiled.

'Pardon me,' was Darke again. 'Are you seriously telling me this woman took ecstasy and went off running?'

'Please sir, please allow me to finish. PMA,' she went back to. 'That's the big catch; that's the dose-response curve coming into play. Lunatics on a Friday night think it's not working, think they've been sold a pup and so, desperate for what only idiots think is a good time, they take another one. After all they're only a tenner,' she smiled broadly. 'Problem is, they then never see Saturday.'

'This from the hospital?' the Darke boss annoyingly asked.

'Yes,' was her annoyed response. 'Plus input from the drug experts upstairs. We've not had full toxicology yet of course and her bloods will tell us more but this has already come to light. The cut to her forehead needed stiches, they checked for a skull fractured it was that severe along with bad bruising and lump to her forehead suggests she took a hell of a wack on the head, but it wasn't all. According to our pathologist wiz…by the way sir, Bronagh asked to be remembered to you. She had at some time recently taken ecstasy. Not just before she went jogging, but they found signs in her system, that's what I'm saying. Tells us the sort we're dealing with here.'

'Why do we need a Pathologist when she's still alive?' Darke asked as if it was going to cost an arm and a leg.

'Phoned Bronagh O'Connell to ask her advice. Had our woman been dead, we'd have got chapter and verse on what they'd found. As she was only close to death we had no inside information, to coin a phrase,' she chuckled at. 'Just bits and pieces but your friend and mine was in and around the County, so being a good friend she popped to have a look for us.' Inga hesitated. 'If you're an Olympic athlete beware, Ecstasy can stay in your urine for a good four or five days, which is how it was discovered. Toxicology will tell us more in time.'

'This her clubbing?' Darke posed. Inga was tempted to assume her boss was still talking about Dr O'Connell but thought better of it.

'She was out jogging,' Inga retorted. Had the boss not read her reports? 'Or at least she was dressed for it with the headphones still round her neck and girly trainers. Who in god's name would go jogging after taking such garbage?'

'Then somehow she was delivered to the Cluny place.'

'Did I read you right? They've got no masks?' Darke questioned.

'Claim they're from the same household,' Jake answered.

'What about when they go shopping?'

'You ever seen a nun in Waitrose?'

'One theory from the doctor,' Inga carried on. 'Looking at the damage to her forehead it could well have been a metal pipe or even a baseball bat.' Her hand went up. 'Is possible the pills were part and parcel of her normal weekend social life.'

'Pretty much answers my questions,' said Darke as he got back to his feet. 'Just passing, thought I'd pop my head in see what the news is.'

'Not at all sure how we link any of this business with a group of very strange nuns.'

'Good question,' he said at the door. 'Been reading all your reports; certainly does appear you've got yourself a very strange crew indeed. Thank you Inspector.'

DI Inga Larsson watched him head off down the corridor. 'Just passing eh?' she whispered. 'Wonder how much of the Cluny report he actually understands?'

'Save you all looking it up,' said Jake Goodwin sat nearby. 'PMA is Para-Methoxy Amphetamine. Looks like another one to steer clear of.'

'Some sort of party trick amongst footballers at one time.'

'Are we surprised?' a chuckling Sandy asked.

'Why I want to know did somebody go to all the trouble of dumping her in the chapel?' Inga asked the team. 'Was it to guarantee she'd be found soon enough, does this all have some connection with the Cluny Priory and is anybody there involved in some way?'

'Answers on a postcard please,' was not helpful.

'My feeling is the place has to be involved in some way, because surely you don't bother with taking a body to a place like that on the off chance the chapel just might be open.'

'Somebody knew it would be open.'

'Exactly, and opening hours are not published on the net like Waitrose or Lidl. Could possibly be a former nun, sorry…sister.'

'What about if this is a nun getting her own back, this revenge for something untoward? Been kicked out for some reason.'

'Redundant nuns? Be serious!'

'Jake,' said Inga. 'When you were there, how many other people did you see apart from the nuns, sisters call them what you like. Any deliveries, callers, postman, maintenance or odd-job men?'

'No,' was simple with a slight shake of his head.

'Nor did we,' she said looking at Nicky for confirmation. 'Until we get the full toxicology results we have only got seven of the most unlikely suspects. Doesn't fit with how they operate. They are shut in their rooms at night, so are we saying one of them opened her door and crept out to do what...give this female her ecstasy tablet she'd laced with PMA or walked to the end of the drive in her nightie to collect a body she then carted in a wheelbarrow back to the chapel?' Inga scanned the room. 'Well what?' she insisted. 'Any ideas? Somebody, anybody.'

'Or waited for a car to deliver her to them.'

'Really?'

'And whoever drove the car you think helped her hump the woman in.'

'How do they communicate?' Nicky Scoley asked them all, but then posed her next question at the boss. 'Did you hear a phone ring when we were there?'

'Now we're starting to think out of the box,' Inga nodded.

'In this day and age, no phone ringing. How very odd in a world of stupid ring tones.'

'They're never going to have smart phones though ma'am.'

'My parents only have a landline and that only rings once in a blue moon.'

'If you ask the youth of today why they're never off their phones,' said Jake. 'They tell you it's because they live in the real world. Trouble is of course in truth they don't, but these nuns do. Might not be the world as we know it, but its real not some fantasy fake news nonsense.'

'Or porn.'

Inga Larsson looked at her team as she sighed her frustration. 'We've already said during the time some of us spent at Cluny yesterday, there were no deliveries, no Amazon or Yodel no calls.

Now we're talking about there being a special one off order. They can't just spend their time in there with no contact with the outside world, nothing going out, nothing coming in and nobody calling. Only the vulnerable lived like that during the pandemic.'

'What if our victim was lured to the chapel, smacked round the head, had stuff pushed down her throat and then just propped up in the pew?'

'No, no, no,' from Inga came with her head shaking. 'I'm coming to that. Quinlan already says she can remember running down through the trees. Then nothing.'

'I don't understand how a woman with some very peculiar job linked to the NHS gets involved with these nuns,' was Jake. 'If she was a nurse say, then I could maybe find a link, all part of their care in the community business. Nuns visiting people in hospital or a hospice maybe, somehow got to know her. Bet she doesn't know the difference between an epidural and a bed pan.'

'Candles,' said Nicky. 'Somebody delivers them, and they're big. You'd need two hands to pick one up.'

'Exactly,' was Inga. 'Where do they get the candles the poor kid had to light? Who goes off to buy them, in fact where would you buy big white candles – where do churches buy stuff, or are they delivered? And if they are delivered by Parcelforce say, what else is? Have we,' she glanced at Nicky. 'Just by sheer chance happened to have been there when nothing was going on? No deliveries, no callers, no phone calls.'

'No postman.'

'Or they'd arranged things.'

'Raza,' made him blink. 'Down in Grantham they've got an ANPR vehicle made to look like an old scruffy white van. Nip along to the chief and ask him if he can get hold of it for a day or two for us. I want to park it just along the road from the Priory turn off. What goes in, what goes out, you follow me?'

'You think anything does, boss?' Sandy asked his boss.

'Candles,' said Nicky. 'Forget the food and stuff some of which they could grow at a push, what about those blinking big candles? Where do they come from?' Nicky knew what the look from Inga meant. 'I'll see what I can find out, but it took two hands for the girl to carry one, they're big.'

'Be a church shop somewhere.'

'Ma'am. What about Tesco?'

'What about them?'

'Home deliveries. Tesco, Sainsbury's, Waitrose. What about them delivering what these women can't grow?'

'All yours,' she tossed back. 'Thanks everybody,' meant time to move on, before there were click and collect suggestions. 'We'll know more when the full toxicology screen comes back and see if we have anything in the realms of DNA from her clothing.' Inga waved the report she had in her hand. 'I'll issue a resume of what this contains.'

11

Donald Mackenzie was of course a rank or two up from the normal copper. Had considered himself a big cheese at one time back up in Yorkshire, when Gordon Kenny first came across the bloody bully.

Getting on for more than two years he'd kept my eye on him in case he decided to drop out and do a runner. Be just his luck to decide to retire to some place they're keen on as a holiday retreat. He didn't want former Detective Inspector Donald Mackenzie to do that and head off to start throwing his weight around in Brixham or Swanage or a hundred and one other delightful holiday places.

Sort of thing he'd heard people do, then once there regret it for the rest of their decreasing lives. Holidaying some sunny place is not the same as living amongst meagre facilities, away from the norm and all your friends and relations.

Mackenzie as he discovered, had been born and brought up in a small place near Huddersfield and his only link with Scotland is his name, so there was little chance of him just skittling off up to the Highlands. Thoughts of him trying to claim he was part of the clan and throwing his weight about north of the border would not have painted a pretty picture.

Gordon guessed he'd probably sold his place in West Yorkshire when he moved to the county and struck lucky with cheaper housing and was grateful he could transfer to the agricultural landscape in the east. The ex-copper probably saw it as a bit of a backwater where he could be a big fish and see out his last few years. Gordon Kenny had certainly had his work cut out tracking him down back then.

Researching his career on a PC in the local library had been a whole different ball game. Once he realized Mackenzie was not prominently highlighted he turned to well know major serious crimes. One he found interesting had been the case of the Nude in the Nettles, about a naked body of a woman dumped next to country road which remained unsolved.

A Donna Keogh and Vicky Glass had extensive coverage both murdered but also unsolved.

It proved difficult to find a major case of any notoriety with the Mackenzie name attached.

Dealing with the likes of him he knew would be an altogether different experience from the way he had decided in the end to handle the Quinlan trash. Strength of course is in the detail and if his voyage into the world of murder was not to end up on the rocks he had need to check and re-check. Even things like her height had been on his list. Not a real list you understand, not scribbled notes about why he needed to know how tall she was, just a mental list of do's and don'ts.

Gordon had a pretty good idea how tall she was but confirming it was fairly simple. He just sidled up to her at a bar one night when she was in full flow spouting to all and sundry and noted where her head came to on his arm. Five foot four or thereabouts it turned out when he marked the spot on the wall at home and got his laser rule out.

The jogging route she took he was able to quickly establish, which turned out conveniently to be well worn in places. During his research he had noticed there was not much in the way of litter. No cans, hardly a fag butt these days, no condoms he could see, but there was he'd spied an old McDonald's box almost hidden by stinging nettles. Just a partly worn path but it was still engaging a degree of grass alongside the fence and through the trees just before that rickety old gate leading to the nuns' place he had decided just had to be absolutely ideal.

Silly bitch had done his planning for him.

12

Preliminary forensic report, witness statements allocated into four groups - relatives who just happened to all live miles away. Friends were few and far between, colleagues who Inga understood were quite scathing and then the bunch of nuns.

To add to the pile of papers there was a file all about what little they had on Carole-Anne Quinlan or Carol Ann Quinlan they discovered from her passport application.

Her apartment according to DS Nicky Scoley was a shameless shambles in total contrast to the occupant's public image. Control on the one hand they gathered from her underlings' revelations, clutter on the home front and a domestic goddess she definitely was not. Just stuff everywhere in an untidy mess. According to young Nicky, not dirty filthy you understand, just a mish mash of 'stuff'. Old magazines and knickers just lying about, bits and pieces, odds and sods just left where they had fallen. Food remnants, a smelly full kitchen bin, washing up bowl well stocked with old dirty crockery.

'Then the bedside cabinet in the bedroom, and lo and behold bits of cannabis,' she sighed. 'Talking personal use at most, unfortunately.'

'Seems like don't do as I do, do as I say.'

'No suggestion of supplying and no suggestion of anything else untoward.'

'Party's got to be a good bet then for that.'

'One person told me,' the blonde looked down at her tablet. 'She's an 8-bit enthusiast,' she grinned and looked up.

'Go on.'

'Looked it up. 8-bit is all to do with size capability of computer information from the era back when computers could only store a process up to 8 bits of data.'

'And?' a confused Inga had to ask with a partial grimace.

'She collects them,' was smiled. 'But don't ask how or what, I've no… idea.'

'If we need to know I guess your eTeam friends will have the answer.'

She also told Larsson how this Quinlan may well have been a control freak but one thing was for sure. By the state of the place she was certainly not one of those with a tidiness obsession to go with it.

The food was so weird according to Nicky she'd actually stopped to make a note of it from labels and a shop receipt just screwed up on the work surface. Silliness like Tofu, Gogi berry, Quinoa and Asparagus tips plus a load of dry washing just hanging on a concertina clothes drier plonked in the spare room could easily have been there a week.

As it turned out it wasn't long in coming, and the lab report turned out to be none too helpful.

Simple combination Inga had seen before many times when she worked with women in trouble. Close to death the report said caused by the toxic combination of the evil thrill pills and a whole heap of booze.

Not your average run-of-the-mill ever-present gin and tonic or a scotch or two. Booze as it turned out, so high proof the scientists had decided it must be neat alcohol.

Very nasty lump and a black and blue bruise on her forehead. More good news for the woman but not for the team, no recent sexual activity so nothing left behind they could work on.

Inga knew all these people had a job to do, but was such an invasion of privacy really always necessary?

But then the other side of the coin was, she might well have been struck down and been unconscious when some evil bastard decided it was an ideal opportunity to leave a calling card.

Apart from the good news and in addition to the mess just above her eyebrows that'll take time to heal, there was just slight scuffing and bruising consistent with being hauled into the chapel. Just bumps and bruises.

'Now she's come round, they've established from the Quinlan woman it must have been some time just before seven. Ten to or thereabouts she thinks, give or take,' Inga informed her hand-picked team in the CID room.

'Down where, do we know?' was from Jake a question, the answer to which he was already privy to.

'According to her she was running slightly downhill through the trees. Then it flattens out to…? The DI hesitated. 'Down the side of Cluny.'

'Of course,' said more than one voice.

'Route she uses and suddenly there's this blinding flash and pain seared across her head and bang lights out.'

'We all leave traces of ourselves wherever we go. Robbie Tudor is now with CSI and a uniform team going over every inch of the path down where she says it happened. Be easy from there to unceremoniously dump her in the Cluny place,' said Inga as she hurriedly scanned her way through all the medical bumph, some of which reminded her about ambient temperatures. 'Chapel would have been quite cold overnight.'

'Clubbing and ecstasy go hand in hand but not early evening, they'll not have even pre-loaded by then.'

This was all adding up to a barrel of nothing much. Only CCTV was a good mile or more away at a garage more interested in folk bilking fuel. Anything else passing by and the odd bods who think they're detectives because they watched two episodes of *Vera* and a repeat of a *CSI* phone in with daft suggestions had been absent from the overnights.

'Ruth,' said DI Larsson as if she was in a hurry. 'Let's start with you. What've you come up with about these nuns?'

'No vehicles according to DVLA so a nationwide ANPR search was a waste of time,' said the Detective Constable. 'You asked me to look at these individuals, these nuns,' she glanced across to Nicky waiting her turn. 'Who I understand may not be actual nuns at all.'

'Can we stick to the remit initially, please?'

'None of them are paying Council Tax, well not in West Lindsey anyway in their own name, although the DS has his Isle of Man connection. Found three on PNC for driving offences, but the last one of those was more than a six years ago in Wakefield. HMRC need more than just names, if we can give their National Insurance Numbers they can cut it down for us. Only thing we do have is Social Services locally who have gone through their database and come up with Tracey Monaghan aka Sarah Judith who according to

70

them was subjected to violent physical abuse a good while back. The reason Social Services got involved was because concerns were raised by neighbours about the two kids living in such an environment. They reckon she just suddenly fell off their radar, not heard about her for getting on for a good eighteen months max.'

'And the children?' Inga popped in.

'Can I just add the name Quinlan ma'am? She's got an overarching link between her NHS role and Social Services staff allocation of care.'

'What does that mean?'

'She's some big cheese who decides if the care being allocated is correct. Has overall medical input.'

'Interesting,' Inga nodded and made a quick note. 'The children. You were saying?'

'Taken into care just about the time she did a runner,' saw Inga make another scribbled note on her pad to investigate further. 'Next is Miriam Levine they call Angela Lydia who is a similar case, except her daughter is much older. There was talk of sexual abuse by this Miriam's partner towards her daughter and physical against the mother, but once again they've disappeared. Imagine that was her escaping down to Cluny. And neither of them were willing to testify in court.' More notes for Inga.

'Until she popped up at the Cluny Priory.'

'Third one I'm trying to get my head round.'

'This the one you've been looking at Jake?' Inga Larsson queried as she caught Jake's eye.

'For my sins,' he remarked as he pushed his chair back and crossed his legs as he concentrated on his monitor. 'Jean Sloan is the real name of Esther Leah married to a soldier, and together they had a daughter Kachelle. Unfortunately he was killed in Afghanistan in 2010. Two years later she married Anthony Rufus Smallbone but he wasn't exactly new on the scene. Truth is they were having an affair while her husband was away fighting the Taliban.' Jake stopped to shake his head and sigh. 'Then the fun begins,' he grinned.

Inga blew out a breath. 'The lives some people lead,' she mumbled to herself.

'Kachelle then falls pregnant and one guess for who the father is?'

'Go on,' Inga sighed and sagged.

'Tony Smallbone.'

'Like I said, the lives people lead. God I must be bloody boring,' she chuckled with.

'But not the end,' said Jake. 'The daughter and her new husband kicked Jean Sloan out of her own home and one day she went back round there apparently to collect a few clothes and when doing so confronted daughter Kachelle.' He hesitated as the chatter began. 'I know all this because it all came out in court when she was done for ABH.'

'And now she's in Cluny.'

'Told you they were loony!'

'Got twelve months, did just over six and my guess is she then joined Rita Appleyard at Cluny having picked up a contact inside.'

'Not a battered wife then? More the batterer.'

'Do you blame her?'

DS Nicky Scoley was up next after the chatter subsided, aware she'd need to let the team recover. 'This could take all night if I go through it all, but here's the general gist, and I promise this is not as mad as Jake had to offer. Nuns for those of you who are not aware are not just Catholics, some are Hindus, Anglicans, Buddhists and of many more religions. All of them live a cloistered life of meditation.'

'Drop outs in other words.'

'Best I can come up with is, this lot claim to be the Livonian Order linked to Textonic Order,' she said slowly to get it right. 'Only one problem,' she grinned. 'This Livonian Order disbanded some time back in the 16th century.'

'Our lot are nae that old!'

Nicky ignored Sandy. 'I've read enough about all this to turn my brain into mush, but I reckon the crowd we're dealing with are actually religious sisters not nuns. It's all to do, as far as I can make out, with the level of solemn vow they make. Having said that though, the nuns of old orders make no such solemn vow, so the issue is confused. The sisters which I think our lot are, also confuse me because normally nuns live in, and sisters live out in the community and this lot don't.'

'On the one hand you're talking about them making the solemn vow business and on the other we have to consider they are involved in some way, shape or form with an attempted murder.'

'Not nuns,' said Nicky firmly. 'Nuns don't murder.'

'And what makes you say that pray?' brought a few sniggers.

'Best I can come up with is a woman who murdered her own new born child and did it purely to hide her sexual activity in order to become a nun. Not found anything at all about a nun committing murder anywhere.'

'Always a first time,' Jake tossed in. 'Ours was pretty close according to the medics.'

'And in case you're wondering,' said Nicky. 'The collective is a superfluity of nuns.'

'Get you!'

'Means surplus or abundance.'

Inga Larsson was just thumbing through the pages of the case file in front of her. 'Something's not right boss,' was Nicky Scoley's opening line next morning in MIT before the briefing, with scribble weary flip charts and smeared white boards somebody had forgotten to update.

'I could have told you that,' came across the desk from behind her bosses steepled hands. 'Sister Mary Joanna our prioress aka Rita Appleyard has a criminal record of some interest. Starting with Section 4 of the Public Order Act 1986, a threat to destroy property belonging to a third party, namely her next door neighbour. Public Order offence for abusive language plus shoplifting twice. But as far as I can see, she's not committed any offence in this case or been nabbed for a year or two'

'That we know of,' Scoley commented with a smile. 'But this Quinlan woman got herself dumped there somehow.' She hesitated. 'Why?'

'Search me,' Larsson just shook her head. 'What on earth is any of this about?'

'I was going to tell you about the girl we saw remember,' she said overlapping. 'My hunch is she's African and never called Jasmin Palmer in a million years, all plumby sounding south-east girls school type and scared to death probably for good reason. She or at

73

least her parents or grandparents are from South Africa or somewhere like Uganda. Called Palmer after a missionary a generation or three back is a possibility. It's my guess, anyway.'

'What's with these odd-ball names anyway? Naomi, Esther and especially the Appleyard woman.'

'I'll accept they want religious names, but when I asked for real names one sticks out like a sore thumb. And if these are not highly religious totally dedicated to their god sort of people why the hell do they live the way they do? This some sort of punishment they undertake for their god, like some force upon themselves?'

'Like the Opus Dei sect you mean?' Jake butted in.

'A cilice, a form of penance,' Nicky advised.

'Maybe not be quite as crackers as them.'

'I'm pretty sure had we gone to a real pucker nunnery we'd not feel at all like this. The nuns would not be like the Sister Mary woman. She's just not right. Forget her bad teeth and the look of her, there just something amiss. I think if somebody told me it was a fancy dress party with a Monks and Nuns theme it'd be what I'd expect to find.'

'Apart from the lads who just have to dress up as Mother Superior in fishnet stockings.'

'You know what we forgot when we were there?' Inga asked and quickly answered. 'We didn't ask what order of nuns they belong to. Considered about looking it up last night, but then realized we didn't know which one they are?'

'Not sure they're anything in particular, from what I can tell. This Jasmin Palmer is my priority,' said Nicky as she clasped her hands together around her knee. 'I know we should just tell social services about her, but we don't have any actual proof there's anything amiss. All she's done so far is find a body. And to be honest do we need a third party trampling all over our murder scene? Thought I'd take Jamie with me, or d'you think it'd better be female?'

'Take Michelle,' Inga rested her head slightly on one side. 'Not being sexist, just the poor lass has spent too much of her time recently being lumbered with family liaison issues, must get on her nerves a bit. Fresh set of eyes, just brief her thoroughly first though.'

DI Inga Larsson looked back at the boards. 'Who was supposed to have updated the boards,' she demanded and before Nicky could react with a name: 'Whoever it was, tell them from me, snap to it, get it done.'

'By the way you can buy candles on line. Girls have discovered a website selling anything and everything. Hymn Book trolleys and vicar's shirts,' she read from notes. 'Communion cups, a silver plated chalice, chairs and for just £500 different colour Chasubles.'

'Say that again.'

'Chasubles. Frocks with wings.' Nicky was up and gone across to go out to talk to Michelle next door leaving DI Larsson just sat there.

Inga waited a few minutes before she too got to her feet, having watched the scurrying about from her office. *'Time to brief them all about nothing much I suppose,'* she mumbled to herself with what little enthusiasm she could muster.

Something in the back of Inga's mind told her to investigate two of the women. Miriam Levine and Tracey Monaghan, so she took herself off down to the Public Protection Unit where she had served as a Sexual Offence Officer prior to being moved to head up MIT.

She was right. Both had been assaulted by men in the past, but there were no recent records of Levine having need of the team since one incident when Inga worked there.

Tracey Monaghan was different. Since The Detective Inspector had moved to deal with major crime this woman had been on the PPU radar on two further occasions. The most recent being when she was seriously assaulted during violent sexual role play with her then partner.

The defence in court had suggested Monaghan had invited her then partner Brian Wasyliw to join her for sexual role play during which it was alleged he inflicted serious violence as they re-enacted a rape scene they actually filmed on his phone.

Wasyliw admitted slapping and punching but denied his violent attacks including kicking her knee with shoes on and knocking out two teeth were anything more than she had begged for.

He'd been sent down.

Why had Monaghan like other women she had come across gone from one violent man to another? A puzzle Inga Larsson had never been able to fathom and women admitting they preferred what they called 'real men' as they had done at times was always an utterly ludicrous suggestion with frequently tragic consequences.

Maybe she'd seen sense at last and was now simply biding her time by hiding away at Cluny from the monsters she had become involved in.

For Nicky Scoley it was a return to the hard wooden bench of the penance type they still have in many churches in the cold uninviting entrance hall of the Cluny Priory. Back to waiting, back to chatting amongst themselves.

'This what it was like before?' DC Michelle Cooper with her warm shade of chestnut hair and clean scrubbed face, queried in a low whisper through her mask. Towards plump if she wasn't careful but pretty with a gathering of freckles. Great hands which Nicky was envious of not to mention her delightful nails without layers of varnish or anything garish.

'Excuse me for being sceptical, but it's as if they plonk us in here while they get everything ship-shape. Left the boss and I in here a good twenty minutes last time we were here. You can guarantee when we get released they'll all be bustling about, working away out in the garden or praying. You won't see one having a cappuccino with sprinkles and Kit-Kat break, reading *Hello* magazine or having a fag round the back.'

'Is it me or is this place cold?'

'Imagine what it's like in January and...' Nicky Scoley stopped when they heard creepy footsteps.

'This way,' was very abrupt from Rita Appleyard aka Sister Mary Joanna the moment she pushed the wooden door open. And the pair traipsed after the woman down the wood encased dark corridor and into a room Nicky had been in before. There sat this thin dusky Jasmin Palmer or whoever.

'If you wouldn't mind,' said Nicky Scoley as this lump of Appleyard went to sit down. 'We need to talk to Jasmin on her own.'

'I don't think so,' and Appleyard wriggled her fat bum down to make herself comfortable. 'I know the law.'

'Would you please join me?' DS Scoley said to the youngster and held out a gloved hand of friendship. 'It's a nice day, how about you and I go for a walk in the garden?' The youngster looked at her chief nun call her what you will, then peered up at Nicky. 'C'mon,' Scoley said to encourage her, as thickset Michelle Cooper moved round to block Appleyard in.

'She's too young to be interviewed by police,'

'This is not a formal interview, we're just having a social chat and anyway I think she's quite old enough, thank you.'

The scrotes Larsson and Scoley normally had to interview rarely disguised their emotions, and, when they managed to, they very often were too young or too unsophisticated to hide their real feelings. Time and again her gut feeling came to the fore.

'You can't,' Appleyard suggested. 'Don't talk to them,' she instructed the young woman. 'D'you hear what I'm telling you young lady?'

'Carry on and I'll charge you,' said Scoley sharply. 'Let's go,' she said down to Jasmin and offered her hand again. She looked at the blue rubber gloves but then didn't take hold of the fingers, just stood up slowly and wandered out into the corridor. The policewomen simply turned her and walked back out the way they had come in, wandered around the building and found a wooden bench under a big oak tree. The three sat themselves down equally spaced and Nicky in particular sat watching two women gardening for a moment or two.

'First things first,' she said gently. 'You are not in any trouble. We need to talk to you because you found the body, nothing more.'

'What's your name?' DC Cooper asked. 'Your real name.' Jasmin bit her bottom lip and wrung her hands together. 'Tell you what,' said Scoley when an answer was not forthcoming. 'You tell us about your home life, about your mum and…' Tears brought what she was going to say to an end, as the young woman just sat there shaking and sobbing.

'Whatever's the matter?' Michelle Cooper asked. 'Talk to us. Please.'

'You'll…send me back,' she managed. The word illegal just sprung to mind.

'Is that a problem?' was the wrong thing obviously as more tears arrived and the poor wretch looked very distressed. 'Look after her,' said DS Scoley as she got to her feet. 'Excuse me,' she shouted to the two nuns appearing to weed the vegetable patch. 'Any chance we could have three teas?' The two nuns just looked at the policewoman. 'Teas...three, please. Cups of ...tea,' she all but swore. The DS pulled out her warrant card as she moved closer. 'We're police. And if I have to pay for them I will, now snap to it!' With that Scoley was striding off back to the main Cluny Priory building. Once inside she went in search of Rita Appleyard remembering to ask a nun she came across for Sister Mary Joanna. She found her eventually pretending to be reading a Bible in a small room. 'What's the score with Jasmin?'

'I don't know what you mean.'

DS Nicky Scoley pulled handcuffs from her jacket pocket and waved them at the woman. 'Think we'll carry on with this at the police station in Gainsborough.'

'You wouldn't dare!'

'Try me.'

'What's the matter with you people? She had hell on with social services, now you walking in here with your size tens. Just leave the poor kid alone will you.'

'Why should we? Have you forgotten she found what she assumed was a dead body, but she's scared witless when we ask for her real name. What is going on?' Nicky demanded slowly and loudly. 'She looks frightened to death most of the time. Don't give me all this Palmer rubbish, you and I know it's not her name. Where's she from and why, and while you're at it what's her real name, and what's she doing in a place like this?'

This Appleyard took in a deep breath and closed her eyes. 'Forced marriage,' was almost gasped.

'What?' was more breath than voice.

'Parents lined her up to marry some forty year old fat git in Malawi or somewhere, she'd never even met.' Nicky knew she'd been right. This woman was never a nun. Somebody from a religious order would never say things like "some forty year old fat git" in a month of Sundays.

'How'd she get here?' she asked.

'Ran away, sleeping rough then social services picked her up and guess what?' Nicky Scoley didn't bother, as it was never really a question. 'Took her back to her bloody parents.' Having answered her own query Rita shook her head. 'How damn naïve are they? Make me so angry!'

Something clicked again inside Nicky's brain. She had the confirmation she was after, twice over. The way the woman spoke was never a nun. Unless she was very much mistaken and with her experience of nuns being non-existent she still could not imagine "damn naïve" being the normal nuns turn of phrase. Wasn't it close to swearing in a nun's world? She knew some daffy women who would think it was. The sort the BBC warn about on television when "blinking heck" is about to be said.

Catch her on the hop, introduce a subject close to her heart and she's back to normal, and underneath the starched habit was the real Rita Appleyard.

What she'd said about Jasmin and the forced marriage was not new. Nicky was well aware how quite often the victims such as this young woman were being failed by social services, the police she was willing to admit and even their schools. They miss the signs of forced marriage and then put the victim in greater danger through their ignorance or lack of understanding of the issues involved.

'And you think it we take her in, hand her over…'

'Please,' said this Appleyard calmly. 'Just let her be, she's safe with us. Ask your questions, but please I implore you don't put her in danger again. Not fair at all, really it's not.'

As it turned out, even with a cup of weak tea, and a distinct change of emphasis from Appleyard, Jasmin could add nothing very much to what she had already told them about finding the body in the chapel.

With a promise to leave her where she was at least for the time being, DS Nicky Scoley was able to obtain a sprinkling of information from her about her home life.

In the end with gentle persuasion she was able to discover how English speaking Whyte Mulilima was originally from the city of Blantyre in Malawi in south east Africa bordered by Zambia and Tanzania. Her grandparents had moved to the UK for a better life and now her parents had apparently told this vulnerable and isolated young woman quite openly of their plans for her. They were very enthusiastic about how they would take her 'home' to Malawi for a holiday which would in effect be her honeymoon as a marriage had already been arranged. They planned to dump her back in the very environment their own parents had managed to escape from.

Social Services then amazingly went to her parents and did their level best to get her to go back home.

She had somehow managed to escape and through help from friends and bed hopping to keep ahead of her father and brothers had in the end come to the attention of Appleyard.

Scoley was not aware of any religion advocating forced marriage, this was all some cultural issue, and quite probably involved money all wrapped up in the form of a dowry.

13

People talk about sheep, but as Gordon Kenny knew we're all creatures of habit, particularly when we are of employment age. Wake up at the same time, get out of bed on the same side, shower, shave, dress, eat breakfast (the sensible ones), drive, bike, walk or train to work. Same route day in, day out. Same arrival time, same procedure.

People who have unfortunately had to have lengthy periods off work through ill health recall how difficult it is to get back into a routine again. Just the everyday task of simply going to work is under those circumstances real hard going they say. Something you really cannot imagine until it happens to you.

Gordon was sat in his kitchen wondering to himself about how many people commute to work. Really commute that is, not just get on your new fancy Boardman bike and career down the cycle path to work or jump in your car for a journey you could walk if you were not such a lazy sod and got out of your bed at a decent hour.

Not live in some pokey place in North Hykeham and work in Lincoln and try to claim you're a commuter. No such silliness.

Just tootling up Lincoln by-pass as far as Gordon is concerned doesn't count. Commuting to him includes a brisk walk, good bike ride or drive to the station if you must, jump on a crowded train, and then be forced to stand all the way to Victoria or Waterloo, scamper across to the Underground and hang on for dear life all the way to Bank or Blackfriars all the while fearful of some horrid little eastern European shite picking your pocket.

He'd seen all that when in London. Off the tube and then a fast walk jostling through the crowds the fitness guru's never mention when they talk about people sat there at their desks not being healthy. Walk quickly to the station, stand on a train for an hour, brisk walk in a hurly burly crowd to the Circle Line, another fifteen minutes hanging on for dear life, walk against the tide then trot up the stairs and jog along to the office.

Some folk have ridiculously long commutes. One guy he'd heard about travels from the Isle of Wight to Milton Keynes. Why?

How does that journey compare with some of the so-called super fit in their sweaty vests in the gym or nearby park he wondered, who then drive to work polluting the atmosphere?

Start of day it's called, and then as if all those habits are not enough to cope with how many millions of us have logins and passwords to remember these days for one thing or another? The front door, office door, the PC, till, photocopier and even the bloody coffee machine.

He wondered how many people go through life on a 'qwerty' login or AbCd999 or in an attempt to be really cute, the opposite way round? Gordon knew of one berk a while back who used 'password' as his password. The devilishly daft use their date of birth or the name of their mistress. 123456 is exactly what the hackers absolutely love.

Knew of idiots who when they get home use the same combination for their laptop in the spare room where they keep all the nasty stuff hidden from their partners and the sexual offence officers.

"By gad it were a lot easier tha knows lad, when all one had to do was wake up, get yersen up, sup up and brisk walk out int'fields".

Don Mackenzie his target of course had retired. Knew how that would make his start of day a darn sight easier than those aiming to catch the 07.36 from *"Newark Norfgate....Newark Norfgate...."*

And of course made the job of tracking him so much easier for Gordon, as far as start of day time was concerned. Then once he'd worked out old copper's daily patterns it was so easy peasy to track him, follow and choose the perfect spot to cut him down to size so he'd fit snuggly in one of those body bags the coppers will want to use.

Gordon's meandering deliberations sat at home with a fresh black coffee were interrupted.

"Lincoln County Police have not as yet released the identity of the young woman discovered in the chapel of the Cluny Priory just outside Gainsborough. Their enquiries as to the circumstances surrounding the discovery are ongoing, according to Detective Inspector Larsson. 'We are hopeful of having a formal identification of the victim in the very near future. We would appeal to anyone who was in the vicinity of the Priory between 7pm on Thursday 22nd and 5am on Friday 23rd or saw anything suspicious, including parked vehicles to please come forward

and phone Lincoln County Police or Lincs Crimestoppers. More news in our next bulletin. Sport. Lincoln City have today…"

Gordon was shocked and dismayed. 'What the fuck's going on?' he shouted at the radio as somebody gabbled on about stolen sheep. He couldn't fathom how they'd not know who she was. This couldn't be right surely. Hadn't somebody missed her? What about family and friends, bloody workmates? Told himself they gotta know who she is and decided this is just some con he was supposed to react to.

He sipped his strong tea and closed his eyes. This was not part of the plan. He'd never imagined they'd take all this time to start scouring the county for him or at least suggest they were looking for somebody.

'And another thing,' he chuntered to himself. 'How in God's name does anybody steal a fucking herd of sheep?'

He pushed out a breath of frustration slumped in his chair but was somewhat pleased murder had still not been given a mention. Maybe that was for the best. Takes away some of the worry he'd been struggling to cope with, and now hopefully he could concentrate on Mackenzie. Now he *would* be dead there'd be no getting away from that.

Sat there, Gordon in a strange fashion almost felt sorry for the ex-copper. Knew the poor wretch had no idea what pillocks he'll have trying to solve his murder. Almost feel like warning him: "Hey Don old fella, these cops are a bunch of wasters. Don't get yourself killed me old son coz this lot'll not be any damn use to you!"

He knew all about Mackenzie having a part-time job. Working for a couple of estate agents handling property viewings, doing one or two a week, now there was a bit of a boom on with folk wanting to leave the nasty big polluted cities. Used to be more of course, but all that Brexit shemozzle and the damn virus kicked the property market where it hurts before it started to recover.

That and young folk demanding a massive tele and even more take-aways than saving for a deposit. One perk Gordon had noticed was Mackenzie getting use of a car with the estate agent blurb emblazoned down the side. Probably think they're in safe hands, handing over the keys for property to a former policeman.

14

The average man in the street never gives the idea of being followed a second thought, and so it was for dear old Don Mackenzie. No rhyme nor reason why anybody would be interested in him had to be his mind set. Probably knew deep down, although of course he would never admit it, he was not popular. Sort of sloth you really want to steer clear of in life. The great know-all, all mouth and trousers, and just out of interest he was still wearing baggy ones. Just the one person you don't ever want to be stuck on a train with. Go on a cruise and find the likes of Mackenzie is sat on your table. *Stop the boat I want to get off!*

Gordon Kenny has not got anything against these tight trousers youths are wearing these days – they'll be something different next year forcing you to buy new. At Mackenzie's age he'd have looked a bit of a prick had he tried to keep up with trends. Folk wearing jeans these days are often the ones who made them popular, and any silliness about them going out of fashion has long been ditched. Just the in vogue silly stuff would look utterly daft on an old geezer like Mackenzie. Utter stupidity like the nonsense of paying for jeans with holes ripped in the knees. To his mind they look equally ridiculous on some of the youngsters especially when some dope-heads still insist on the decade old idea of showing their shreddies and the cracks of their dirty arses.

One of the things Gordon had done at the library was to look up old newspaper reports on cases where Detective Inspector Donald Mackenzie played what he considered to be an important part. Important to him of course, but not in the grand scale of things. These provided a real insight into the man, confirmed what he already knew and thought.

He could have done such research back home but it was better to be safe than sorry. The library IT system would no doubt record he'd been on newspaper sites, but so what? What does that tell anybody?

As he'd never attempted to download the articles he was interested in or tried to print them off, the only pathway was to look at media sites. What would that ever prove?

Folk at the library were helpful too. Just told them he wanted to use a PC and they'd lead him over to five or six huddled together, ask if he wanted to use any one of them in particular and when he said it didn't matter they just started one up for him. Random selection done by others would he knew hide trace of him even more.

Kenny had no real need to go over the one case to have set him off on this crusade in the first place, but he did. In a strange sort of way reading it all again confirmed in black and white how the passage of time had not altered his concept of what had actually gone on. Being true to himself he knew exactly what had happened, most certainly more than anybody else.

Next thing he had to do was get close to this Mackenzie. Not prop up a bar with him or become his pal, although he did consider suggesting to an estate agent the git worked for, about wanting to view a property. Then after second thoughts decided against it.

Realized when he assessed the situation how he'd then have to go through all the false name rigmarole, using the number for the old phone he'd bought from a charity shop. Too much hassle he decided in the end. He'd always known he'd need to check Mackenzie's routine, comprehend his habits and those of his little wife who Gordon knew he was about to rescue from her lifelong torment.

He just wished to god somebody could have done that for his dear old mum. Saved her from the years of endless misery dished out by his bastard father. Had that been achieved, and had Mackenzie gone about his job properly and honestly the chances are his dear mum would still be alive today and he'd have a decent retirement to look forward to.

Not many a day goes by without him thinking about her, as he has done over the years. How absolutely dreadful and frightening it all must have been for a good honest god fearing woman who never saw ill in a soul, having to waste years languishing in jail.

He'd think of her at night and what she must be going through in the slammer, the tears she must have shed, sharing with women she could not stand the sight of knowing there was no escape from the daily and nightly torment. In the dark there'd be no sight of the four walls incarcerating her, but come the morn she'd discover they were still there when she'd prayed all night it just might be all a bad dream. In truth an absolute nightmare.

He knew she must have heard the stifled cries and screaming from others on her wing. Gordon guessed how she must have yearned all those years for a full night's sleep and he'd often wonder if she secretly and silently cried out for help, the help she knew deep inside could not and would never arrive.

All around her the low-life bedraggled women would swear and fight over next to nothing, as they self-harmed to gain attention and threatened. His dear dear mum Lynda had wanted none of it and her boredom threshold would he knew have surely been bad enough without adding to her woes. She'd be the only one on her wing probably not having drugs and phones smuggled in.

Nowadays it'd be Spice landing tied to a drone some clever dick is working from outside. He'd read how if crims offer at least five hundred to the screws they'll bring a phone in for you. His dear old mum didn't have a mobile on the outside let alone in her bloody cell.

To be an innocent in circumstances like she endured year after year, he just dare not think about too intensely. Abused day after day and then cast aside without fear or favour and told repeatedly awaiting trial it would be to her credit if she confessed. Say you did it even though you're totally innocent and they'll cut a month or six weeks off, then find any excuse inside to add that back on, with some ridiculous trumped up charge.

What good in the end had pleading guilty done her, was a question he had tortured himself with over the years. What credit was there for telling them what they wanted to hear, because they were unwilling to accept the god's honest truth?

How the incessant catcalls from some of the less intelligent inmates aimed at the screws must have driven her to distraction. Sometimes Gordon can just manage a simple smile when he thinks back to the sight of his mum in there at visiting times. The things she would say, the characters she would talk about, in particular the munchkins as she called the dimwits with their absolute desperate need for drugs. The way mum used slang words she'd picked up at first came as a shock, but if nothing else he had also learned a few new words. The majority he simply did not understand, such as joy juice he had to look up when he got home, beamer he assumed initially was a German car, and kinda understood when she said a munchkin in the next cell was a meth freak. Seemed so very strange at the time with such stuff coming from his own dear gentle innocent mother who'd not normally say boo to a goose.

Like so many folk Gordon is full of regret. All those things big and small we all choose to ignore, decide to put to one side for now that make us angry so we react in an involuntary way.

One regret he has to this day amongst the pile of many others to litter his life, is not keeping safe and sound any of the letters his mum wrote to him from prison. Why?

Truth is he was just too damn angry every time one arrived. This poor, kind, hardworking woman was writing to her son only about her soul destroying desperation when clearly there should never have been a need for her to do so.

Gordon will tell anybody who cares to listen. His bloody mother was never guilty. Never ever.

Read and rip became a sort of ritual for him back then. Took in every spidery word in her own neat handwriting, and then just ripped them to shreds in his anger. He's not scared to admit many is the time he blubbed like a baby as he read her letters, sat at his kitchen table at the old flat he had in those bad days, tears just dripping down to soak the cheap paper.

He knew there was no going back. No copies laid somewhere for him to retrieve at a later date and they're not amongst his trash or spam. Her writings from the heart were on cheap as chips lined paper with the name of the prison at the top. As if he and her didn't know where she was.

There was never anything of real significance in her letters. How could there be from someone cast aside by society living a hum-drum boring life of four walls, if you can call what she endured a life. What an absolute and complete waste.

Now this Covid-19 business had closed the natural order of things and it is entirely possible he's not been able to grieve for his aunt Ingrid, without the normal funeral closure.

15

Jamie Hedley was not at all sure he was not being dragged to a garden centre by his over enthusiastic and underused groin.

He'd forgotten how many times he'd brought up FIX A MEET? on his phone and looked at it and how many times he had ignored it, been rude and not even said thanks but no thanks. Not something he worried about too much, as the social etiquette his mother insisted upon has all gone for a ball of chalk these days.

Send a Christmas present to some young nephew, and do you get a hand-written 'thank you' letter? The answer these days inevitably is a two letter word.

Jamie wished he knew somebody within Tamara's close circle of friends, but then had to laugh at the prospect of exactly who such hideous characters might be. Only ones he was likely to come across popped up regularly on the Police National Computer (PNC) or at one time had made guest appearances on *Crimewatch*.

On the one hand he had the memories of the absolute delights he used to dream of alone just laid on his bed in the back room.

Times were hard back in those days, just him and his hard working mum and though he tried to big it up with older lads and tell them he was into all sorts such as Arctic Monkeys and Snow Patrol, truth was there was no spare money for music and Jamie knew he could not expect his mother to even consider a PC at home. Instead for entertainment he could still remember avidly watching *Dr Who* and *Outnumbered* but it was his mother who kept him away from the likes of *Big Brother* and *X-Factor*. Life wasn't all bad and Jamie could always recall seeing jeans for around £15 and the arrival of Primark.

From his point of view *Match of the Day* was worth watching back then with Man United winning title after title and the double with some of today's moneybags clubs in lower divisions. Those were the days.

Thinking about it life back then for Jamie Hedley really was not bad at all.

Was it an accident the pair of them almost crashing into each other walking across Marshall's Yard on his way to Costa to get a coffee a few days back? Had it been deliberate, was it all part of a plan by her, by her father even to suck him into their world? Was she simply playing a game with him, reeling him in on behalf of her old man, slowly slowly catchee monkey sort of thing. Copper on the take on his payroll would suit Tez Diagne's business plan down to the ground. Coat Jamie Hedley in a layer of corruption he'd never rid himself of.

Not sure he'd ever been to a garden centre with Kerrie. Not really her scene, gardening. She had been more into having coffee with her mates and getting her hair and nails done than deciding whether ericaceous compost might be best for the begonias.

Of course these days they're a whole world away from what they once were. Now plants seem to have become of secondary consideration. All chasing awards it seemed to Jamie for the best garden centre café these days rather than hoping for a petunia of the year rosette.

He could only surmise what it would be like to be with Tamara. Caressed by her sensuous lips would be an absolute thrill in itself and he guessed a woman like her would very likely be demanding. Nowhere near the take it or leave it if you must attitude Kerrie had turned passion into. An attitude to this day he'd never been able to fathom.

Was all this subterfuge really necessary Jamie asked himself more than once? For his part, tales of who he'd been meeting up with getting back to MIT would not bode well if DS Goodwin or the boss got wind of who he had been seen with.

For his part the location was in some respects too open to the public, but on the other hand was unlikely to be the regular haunt of the sort of ne'er-do wells Tamara was used to mixing with they needed to keep well away from. Tuesday morning was also a plus sign compared with two in the morning in a dark and dingy bar or club somewhere full of the world's worst and rife with the virus creating another surge.

Tamara had certainly made an effort, and from Jamie's point of view although she was a good sight for his eyes, it made him more wary. Was she looking for some sort of liaison, of the very sort he had to steer well clear of? Please, not a stupid school reunion.

He'd not been with a woman since Kerrie and looks wise his ex was still a better bet than Tamara even though she'd certainly improved.

Once they'd chosen a table freshly cleaned and masks had been discarded, Tamara chose to start with a black coffee. Tucked away in full sight of any comings and goings, the centre was as it turned out, a good choice.

Tamara showed how she had most certainly moved on from the desperate spindly wretch Jamie had seen back in Custody late one night. At her suggestion they ordered oatcakes with plenty of real butter, red onion chutney and a good selection of local cheeses, all brought to their table. A degree of sophistication he would never have imagined from her not too long ago.

'You've changed from the skinny kid at school,' Jamie took as a compliment. He of course was surreptitiously scanning her attributes, but Tamara was blatantly looking at his muscular build. Working out to him was a major part of who he now was, forced upon him by his peers.

Once all the usual intro stuff was over and done with she put her cards firmly on the table verbally. No going round the houses, no alleged, no hints, no innuendos, Tamara just came out with it.

'You anything to do with that woman what's been attacked?' was not at all what Jamie was expecting. First up he'd had Scott picking his brain for snippets he could use in his books, now this Tamara. He could understand why his pal was asking, but why on earth would she want to know?

'Why d'you want to know?'

'Just.'

'Just what?' How he hated such conversations.

'Just that I might be able to help in return.' Now he was stuck between a rock and a hard place. In return for what? He was being offered information from the outset, from the one person in the world he really wanted nothing to do with. Jamie was really only in need of a simple social chat, a case of bringing each other up to date with their lives. Talking over old school times possible, but not an attempted murder. Not from her!

He'd been back in Gainsborough just a few days and so far he'd heard of little to please the boss.

'I doubt it,' he offered as his response.

'Try me,' and they were back to this nonsense.

'Go on then.'

'Can I trust you?'

'I'm a policeman,' Jamie offered in a whisper with a grin.

'Exactly. That's my problem,' Tamara admitted and returned to her latte to annoy him. 'If I'm to cleanse my life of all the shit that's gone before, I can't be involved. Can't be seen to be the grass who brought her own father down. Be the one who kicked his nasty evil world into touch.' She looked right at Jamie. 'D'you follow me?' Jamie went to speak, but she beat him to it. 'There's a whole different world out here I've never been part of. Doing simple things like this is some peoples every day, not for me it's not been. Folk I know'd think I'd lost my marbles if they got wind of me sat here like this eating oatcakes. Different bloody world let me tell you from doing a line, booty juice or a day's shoplifting trip to Meadowhall to feed a crave or planning the next scam.'

She really didn't need to tell him. Jamie knew all too much about the sort of world she had inhabited, and maybe still did if the truth were known.

'To be honest if my chief knew I was talking to you right now he'd probably slap me round the head and give me all the boring jobs for a month. I can't be seen to be associating...' he flipped his hands up in an act of surrender. 'With the likes of somebody like you without good reason, if you'll accept what I'm saying. Not you personally, but...you know what I'm on about.'

Jamie knew Jake Goodwin would never permit members of his team to allow a crook or known low life to buy them a drink or god forbid hand out a bit of dosh in used tenners for insider information.

He knew to Jake Goodwin the world was simply governed by right or wrong, black or white with no gradation. This stance people had told Jamie had served the DS well and nobody sensed there'd be any change anytime soon, if ever.

Jamie had made sure he bought her black coffee and oatcakes and himself an Americano with an extra shot at the outset and paid with his card so he had a record of it all. He kept the till receipt he would normally not bother with.

'But we could work together?'

'Why me?' he wanted to know.

'Because I don't know any other coppers, silly,' she insisted. Then added, 'I might be able to trust,' as an afterthought. 'Heard you was one now on the grapevine, saw you the other day remember. All got me thinking. Maybe a lifeline, possibly just what I need, a line to acceptability, to the establishment I've never been part of.'

Jamie was surprised Tamara had not dressed down for the occasion if she wished to be out of sight and out of mind.

A dark grey vest, with what looked to him like a velour top label version of a tracksuit top, clingy jeans and bright red trainers. Those alone probably cost an arm and a leg, and he didn't want to think about where the money had come from for such a get up.

'I'm on a two year plan to change my life completely,' she went on. 'On a personal health level I'm getting there and I've bin free for a couple of years. Now I'm getting closer to who I want to be, I need to rid me life of all the things what dragged me down once upon a time and still tend to.' Tamara took another good drink from her coffee cup, then hands tightly clasped she rested her forearms onto the round table. 'Don't want to be laid there on me death bed thinking, well that was all shit,' she smirked then glanced to people two tables away in case her language had carried. 'That nuns' place is just a front.'

A breathy grimaced 'What?' was all Jamie could manage to muster.

'Can't do right for doing wrong seems to me. Yeh give 'em credit for what they're doing but all the time they're doing what they're doing I got no chance of pulling the rug from under me old man's feet.'

'Are you saying the nuns are up to something?'

Tamara laughed and shook her head. 'They're never nuns, you silly sod,' she responded in a whisper, and Jamie felt so foolish as she leant right into him he then took a drink of Americano as an excuse to increase the space between them. 'Don't know all the ins and outs but me old man tied the sodding rich prat who owned the place in knots over some heroin shipping deal involving the guy's stupid half-baked son. Had him over a barrel, looking at a long stretch the lad was if me old man had told what he knew. All to do with publicity ruining his social standing and affect share prices or something or other. In the end to get his lad off the hook he had to give in and signed over that place. From what I heard he could easy afford it.'

'And the nuns?' Jamie asked having been staggered by what she had said but was desperate not to show it.

'Top dog there is some nasty old bitch me old man's known for ages, running a sort of safe house place for battered wives and all that business.'

'And who's in there now?' Was he hearing her right?

'Clever me old daddy in some ways. Just a pity he never went legit, could have made a real fortune - a proper pucker one. Too clever by half he be. Set that old woman up in the place, and uses her as a hidey hole. Somebody else he's got over a barrel,' she shrugged. 'Way he works o'course.'

DC Jamie Hedley had checked what he could about Tez Diagne. He knew if the notorious bastard continues to behave well he could be up for parole in about twenty three months some of which was more than likely to be spent in a casual open prison somewhere.

'Drugs you mean?' he queried very quietly across the table.

'And the rest.' Tamara sighed. 'Feel sorry for the women who've been through a bad patch corse I do, but all the time the Cluny place is still going, his empire still thrives.'

'And without it?'

'Look,' said Tamara as she fiddled with her glass. 'Old man's had a minor stroke, left him with his left side not working hundred per cent. Be limited when he gets out. If there's no nuns to run his cash and carry it'll be a major part of bringing his world falling around his ears.'

'But those women apparently live very austere lives and...' Tamara chuckling stopped Jamie.

'That's a bloody front,' she said and continued to chortle at his naïve remark. 'God, they saw you lot coming! Bloody hell! You need to open your eyes. Why you lot always dicking about shit all?

Wake up Jamie, there's a big nasty world out there, and I should know.'

'I've not been over there,' he admitted. 'All being done from Lincoln. How d'you mean it's a front?'

'They seem to the outside world to be carrying on like proper nuns, I'll give you that,' she stopped to snigger at him again. 'Appear to be praying and growing stuff but that's all a charade. Surprised it's not obvious to clever clogs like you lot.'

'Apparently not.'

'Look,' she sighed. 'What nobody sees including you lot, is the cellars are all fitted out with normal home comforts. Nothing too lavish mind, but the moment there's any hint of visitors they go through with their routines as if they really are pucker nuns.'

'Have you been there?' said Jamie as he tried to take in what he'd been told. Tamara answered with a shake of her wonderful head of hair, as Jamie struggled. 'If it's all make believe then why do they make one of the younger ones get up at the crack of dawn to light a candle?'

'All part of the charade I guess, and if I know that bitch chances are it's a form of punishment.'

'You been there?' he asked.

'Don't be silly! Mum's bin, mum knows all about that Appleyard skank out there. You met her?' Jamie shook his head having not been near the place. 'Not bosom buddies or anything, just knows her. More by reputation than anything else I reckon. Sort of shit we've had our fill of.'

'And this is for battered wives you say.'

'Battered and beaten up mostly, running away from the bastards they married or lived with. Stay there a week or two, couple of years some of them getting themselves straight. Others use it as a sorta staging post, couple of nights to doss down to pull themselves together and off they go, hiding from you lot I bet, some of 'em,' she chuckled then sipped and ate an oat cake. 'Clever really, like they've disappeared off the face of the earth.'

'And in return for handling your old man's ill-gotten gains he allows the place to be used as a safe haven and provide a staging post for these women.'

'Good cover the nun business. Not like it's an old house and folk wonder what's going on.'

'This all women?' he asked.

'Course, but not all battered ones. Be plenty of low life amongst them don't forget, an' he's got his scum bags to do all the work.'

As he sat there looking at her he knew she could well have been the most beautiful woman he'd ever seen. Before she had almost been destroyed through her own stupidity and a generous helping of illegals from those who claimed to care for her.

Jamie guessed she was the apple of her obnoxious father's eye, the one he doted on from his dank prison cell.

'This woman they found, you know anything about her?'

'Haven't got a clue, just heard it on the radio. Wonder what's cracking off with that? '

'Just a woman,' he shrugged slightly. 'We're waiting on her family. Some issue about them not wanting her details released for family reasons. Not from round here I don't think. Trouble is being stuck over here I'm not up to the minute with all the latest info,' Jamie took a good drink of his cooling coffee. 'Thought you'd know what it was all about.'

'Just coincidence. Been thinking about talking to you when I saw you that day, then this dead woman popped up outta nowhere on the news. Gi'me the shock of me life I can tell you. There I was just having a coffee, reading me Kindle and there it was all over the radio. Up it pops out of the blue, I was bloody gobsmacked I can tell you.' Jamie sniggered. 'What so funny?'

'Just how things have changed, sipping coffee, oatcakes and reading your Kindle. All sorta real middle class proper.'

'S'pose it is.'

'And your interest is what?'

'What I wondered was, with what's going on there'd be a good excuse for you to close the place down. Cut off me old man's supply chain, close down where he stashes stuff, place where folk can hide away for a day or two out of sight, out of mind of the law. And while you're at it you can close down his three head shops.'

'What?' a grimacing Jamie managed before she went on.

'Head shops, legal highs,' she said in a manner to make him feel naïve. 'Somebody said you need a reason for doing things these days, looks like a good enough reason to me.'

'Head shops? They're illegal been for years now.' Tamara just sat there with a self-satisfied grin on her face and shook her head. 'What d'you mean no?'

'All over the place. Not actually shops, silly boy,' she chuckled to make him feel stupid. 'Now it's all illegal, but he makes a tidy penny from them let me tell you.'

'Where then?'

'Moves them about, people's houses. One good one's a caravan somewhere they can tow about. Do really good business at the coast in summer. Takes a fair bit, good two or three grand a week at least. Bank holidays make a real killing.'

'So even without this dead woman you were going to suggest we take a look at the Cluny Priory place anyway?'

'And the head shops, yes. She's just an app if you like,' she considered amusing.

'What a pity.'

'Please don't say you're not interested,' she almost pleaded.

'We'll be interested,' Jamie admitted. 'Just have to find a way of telling the boss of the murder team, without saying I've been cozying up to Tez Diagne's daughter,' made Tamara smile and run her bottom lip through her teeth.

'D'your people think this woman's got something to do with me old man?'

'Not a connection they've passed by me.'

'Wouldn't put it past him like. Always had a bit on the side.'

'To be honest at the moment…' he sucked in his breath. 'Keep this to yourself…we don't have a clue. Can't see the connection, but anyway your old man's still inside. Clever trick if he killed her. Not out on day release I guess?'

Tamara shook her head slightly. 'But he's still got people out here, still has some influence,' she said pointing out of the window with a thin digit. 'Running errands for him, at his beck and call.' Just for a moment Tamara stopped to check all around her, sipped her drink and was soon back to it. 'There's half a dozen cannabis farms on farms,' she smiled. 'Sell more ganga than milk I bet in old barns in all sortsa places.' She looked at Jamie. 'That's if you're interested of course.'

He was interested if it was all true, but had to be more contemplative in his response. 'And if you destroy his supply line so to speak, what'll happen when he gets out, surely he'll be after you.'

'I can't go on like this, nor can me mum. We've had a gut full of it. Enough now and she's not getting any younger. We just want a normal life without looking over our shoulders all the time, coming up short every time you hear police sirens. Get him all closed down and we can forget him, and his henchmen'll be gone as soon as. He'll not come chasing us in the state he is now that's for sure. Need a fresh start, a new life, don't want him with me as a hang back.' She stopped to chuckle and look all around. 'Sorry but I'm not becoming a bloody carer for dregs like him.'

'The nuns. They all clean d'you know?' Jamie knew they weren't, but had to check to see what Tamara knew. 'Or just battered and bruised? Domestic violence.'

'No idea don't know who's who. Certainly not that Rita Appleyard. Me old man'll not use someone he hasn't got something on. Could always ask me mum I s'pose.'

'No!' was Jamie's turn to be sharp. 'We need to keep this to ourselves, could be our people will want to keep tabs on the place to see if there is anything going on, rather than just bash the door down. Must be a reason why that woman was found there. Remember it will remain their priority. Gotta be attempted murder.'

'What about me?' Tamara threw at him a touch too loudly. 'Brilliant,' she sighed. 'I've told you what's going on so now you'll just go your own sweet way and I'll never get me own back on him. Never get me life sorted properly.' She suddenly looked unhappy. 'All about you and your lot ticking bloody boxes I bet.'

'No not at all. But I'm sure we won't go in there all guns blazing and kick the Appleyard woman out, just on your say so. I don't know for sure obviously, but my guess is we'll keep an eye on the place, because our priority has to be the woman who was beaten half to death.'

'Get more points for her do you?'

'No,' he insisted. 'We rattle the Cluny cage and could be we'll never know who did it and why. Doesn't mean we won't raid it for

97

drugs and all the rest of it, catch who we can and close it down in the end, just need to bide our time is my guess, but I could be wrong. Need to have a word with the boss.'

'How long?'

'I don't know, I'm not in charge. But if your old man's still got a couple of years to do it won't be too long. Week or two possibly, couple of months maybe at the outside.'

'She attacked there do you know?'

Jamie shook his head before he'd had time to consider his response. 'Apparently not.' The coffee shop had begun to get busier as it approached mid-morning and more people arrived to spend an hour or two looking through all the things they have in garden centres these days. More potpourri than pot plants; more dresses than dahlias. Jamie was sensitive about their subject matter. 'Think we need to be careful,' he suggested and looked all about, then drank the remainder in two visits to his cup.

'What happens now?'

'Now I've got to find a way of telling my immediate boss, and as I'm the new boy on the block I need to be very careful. Might go above his head, talk to the DI see what she's got to say and…'

'She?'

'Yes,' he reacted. 'We do have women you know. In this case she's Swedish.'

'Why bring a Swedish copper over here?' Tamara asked firmly. 'Aren't ours good enough? Like nurses is it? Train ours up for a couple of years then say there's no jobs and go off to recruit a load from the Phillipines who struggle with English.'

'She's not come over,' he advised. 'Born in Sweden and moved here with her parents when she was in her teens I think. Went to school and university here so I heard, got her degree in law, been in our force ever since. I'm sort of on detachment for a while.'

'S'pose that's what comes of being out of Europe,' Tamara quipped. 'I was told that's what Brexit'd get rid of, all these damn foreigners.'

'Anything else I should know?' was better than reacting.

'I could tell you all about me personal troubles,' she let out a sighed breath. 'Save that for another time eh?'

Jamie shrugged. 'Up to you.' And for a moment she appeared to be going to tell him something.

'Huh, best to stick to things like that cheap skunk couple of year back in the summer what done the rounds based on some Rumanian strain. All my old man's work, 'specially over at the uni,' she obviously considered amusing, then blew out a big breath.

Not the time or place to hear about her dependency on drugs, about the dealers she became totally reliant upon, about her nights in a cell, her court appearances and detox. Jamie was not at all sure there would ever be a good time to hear it. He wanted to praise her for losing the stupid thing through her nose and all the cheap tat in her ears, save for small delicate earrings she now wore. Time and a place for everything.

'You a gardener?' he asked to move her off subject.

'I know all about grass and weed.'

Just as Jamie was thinking perhaps he'd better renew the coffees, Tamara indicated it was full time, but when he stood up and waited for her to join him she remained seating.

'I thought...'

Tamara grinned. 'Being picked up. Off you go,' she said as if he was a little puppy dog.

'Want me to get you another coffee before I go?'

'No, no you're fine,' she said, looked at her phone, then towards the door. 'You'd better be off, you don't want your boss moaning about you wasting Police time,' she sniggered at.

What had happened, what had he said, who had she spotted? All questions to ponder as he slipped on his black mask and made his way out.

16

White crime boards and marker pens were the order of the day back in the Incident Room at Lincoln Central, with each of the team aware they would be asked to make a contribution as DI Inga Larsson began to build the background from all their actions and more importantly their interviews.

'Who exactly is this Carole-Anne Quinlan?' she asked them all. 'Over to you,' then just sat down and crossed her legs.

DC Ruth Buchan was first up. 'Born plain Carol Ann Quinlan in Tewksbury. No e's and no hyphen, has a first class honours degree in business management, there's talk of her going for her PhD and is a high flyer with one of these business profile companies people like the NHS feel they need to employ...'

'Can I just say,' Inga interrupted. 'I see no sense in what people like her do, it's almost as if the universities have churned out all these people and something needs to be done with them. They can't all work for Starbucks or McDonalds. No need for everybody's opinion on what she does and whys and wherefores. Just the facts. How come somebody tried to kill her and how come she finished up dumped in the nunnery of all places?'

'Been there just about eighteen months,' Ruth went on. 'Divorced with one child, well teenager now.'

'What's happened to him?'

'Husband's Alistair Quinlan. Shacked up with a female down south. According to the boys in Kent when they checked him out he attended a seminar in Tunbridge Wells with witnesses the evening before she was attacked and at breakfast and spent most of the next day there.'

'And the daughter?'

'Not yet confirmed but looks as though she might be down south with him or at least nearby.'

'Quinlan sounds popular. Ex doesn't want to know her, daughter feels the same and somebody tried to kill her.' Inga smiled and nodded. 'Interesting.'

'Try as I may around and about,' said Jamie. 'I've not found people who are her best pals. Think it's why Ruth's been struggling. No girlfriends you'd find her out with on a Friday night or if you'll excuse the expression ladies, doing girly things with. All the talk from those I spoke to was about her utter dedication, how she has a one track mind. Career orientated. Her working in Lincoln doesn't help with getting info from Gainsborough. Almost as if she's an unknown.' He hesitated. 'But a really nasty piece of work by all accounts.'

'We saying a nasty piece of work in the caring profession?'

'Social services link they say is the issue.'

'Tell me more.'

'Part of her remit, we understand,' said Jake carefully. 'Is to align the home care former hospital patients are said to need, with the actual facilities allocated by social services.'

'Go on,' the DI urged.

'Extra services or the removal of care are on her say so,' he put his hand up. 'On her say so, based upon her strategy. She is never hands on. Chances are she's never met a patient.'

'So if you mum's carer is removed you'd describe her as heartless.'

'Her policy. And all the names under the sun.'

'Men in her life currently?' Inga popped in, and Ruth, Nicky and Jamie all glanced at each other.

'Only suggestion I got,' said Ruth, 'was one couple remarked how they doubted if there was any man alive who'd be good enough for Quinlan. Could be why the husband buggered off.' As if there was a need to respond to the look on Inga's face, 'She doesn't currently have a man of any consequence, by the way.' As Inga was about to move on, she added: 'Or woman come to that.'

Inga then looked at Ruth again. 'Any more sensible background?'

'Parents have put themselves up in a B&B while they visit her in the County. Roland and Margery Quinlan. She's a teacher at an Academy up in East Yorkshire and he's an estate agent. How he introduces himself, but the truth is he just works for one, which

101

means he's an office clerk who sits in the window. Two daughters, Carole-Anne of course and older sister Veronica's a child-minder she runs from her home.'

Anything missing from the body is always a question on the list of any murder. Quinlan was not dead, but it was always possible the killer thought she was, and would therefore act in a certain way.

Inga already knew her parents didn't have a clue and her so-called colleagues didn't even know she went jogging, so clandestine had she been about her activity. As a result they had not reported anything missing such as a Toronto Blue Jays baseball cap, or maybe a gold chain the attacker had taken as a momento as some do.

But then Inga was reminded how people don't always steal the obvious. She was able to recall the story of a 2CV parked in a London street being broken into. The perpetrator stole the Krooklok and left the car.

Back to the here and now she advised her troops how Quinlan had gold stud earrings in the shape of a ribbon bow, which she was still wearing when she arrived in hospital. Her mobile had been found in her bum bag along with the keys to her flat and car plus a yellow hankie.

Used her phone as a timepiece according to her mother and therefore had no need for a watch, and was never known to wear jewellery on her wrists.

DCI Luke Stevens' eTeam upstairs of course had taken charge of her phone and came up with nothing of any interest. ASBO up there had described the WhatsApp content as 'esoteric piffle' which was very useful but no real surprise.

Inga had expected nothing less from the likes of her, being on-trend with smart phone messaging rather than just plain reliable texting was no real surprise. Mostly to do with messaging about work and to a couple of weird groups.

'Any word on the streets Jamie?' Inga suddenly shot at him.

'Not found anybody who knows her. Bloke in her local SPAR shop place, he knew her from my description because she pops in from time to time but didn't know her name or where she lived. Just assumed she had to be fairly local.'

'What about the neighbours?' she persisted.

'They know of her, but nobody I've spoken to was aware of her name, none of them knew what she does for a living. Two suggested she might be a nurse.'

'Anybody seen her out running?'

'One or two,' Jamie admitted. 'But, they only mentioned it when I asked specifically. Wonder why she does it on her own rather than with a group?'

'Door-to-door's a waste of time.'

'I know,' said Inga. 'But it had to be done as specially as we have a local on board doing the close to home bit.'

'For the good it's done me,' Jamie sniggered.

DC Jamie Hedley was not at all sure how he should classify his meeting with Tamara Diagne and less sure whether he should mention it at all.

Two or three times he considered knocking on DI Larsson's door, walking in and confessing he'd spent a good hour or more in the company of Tez Diagne's daughter in a garden centre. Had it been a sleazy pub or a club in the early hours it would carry more weight was how he saw it. But who in their right mind has a conversation with a once drugged-up daughter of a notorious crooked nasty piece of work sipping coffee from china cups amongst the petunias?

He really had no idea how he should catalogue what it was all about. His big worry was how due to the surroundings, officers like the boss and Jake Goodwin would see it as nothing more than a date or the Diagnes' were up to something he should have spotted a mile off and steered well clear of.

On the plus side, Tamara had told him about what she claimed was going on at Cluny, but just how true was it? Was Tamara for real or was he being used and anyway had he said too much already? The two words *honey* and *trap* had crossed his mind more than once.

If he repeated what she had said about Cluny being just a front and it turned out to be totally false he knew the door would slam shut on his chances of more experience in MIT and he'd be back to all the shite of domestics in no time.

Was this in reality nothing more than all he had dreamt of all those years ago, laid on his bed at home dreaming of lovely gorgeous Tamara Diagne. Was it how DI Larsson would see it, and more worrying would be the sight of DS Goodwin leading the chorus of laughter?

By agreeing to meet her again was he digging his own grave with MIT? His worries were further exposed when she had insisted they meet in a pub in far-off Sutton-in-Ashfield.

To add to his concerns, when he'd suggested he do the decent thing and offer Tamara a lift to her chosen rendezvous she was adamant about making her own way there. Her response had somehow stirred a serious warning sign in his mind. She had been just too rigid, too intransigent in her dismissal of his offer.

For some reason during one of the courses he'd attended recently, an instructor had told a belt and braces tale although he was more dramatic with both a parachute and a lifejacket in a serious investigation.

The increase in serious concerns about what was going on and how it might well affect his career slid together nicely in his mind; forearmed and forewarned Jamie made sure he was there well before time.

The disembodied voice of the sat nav woman had got him there safe and sound. So early in fact he was able with the help of his warrant card to arrange to park his car at the rear amongst the staff vehicles.

When he spied her being dropped off by somebody in a Land Rover just outside the entrance, his worries were heightened somewhat, although he knew it could be quite innocent.

They brought each other up to date on their personal news, without Jamie giving away too many police secrets or admitting he was to all intents and purposes on the sidelines with regard to the Quinlan murder, although he had rightly been kept in the loop with observation of the Cluny Priory still ongoing.

Tamara was visually upset to hear as far as Jamie was concerned no action had been taken so far to close down the Cluny Priory. He was not at all sure if advising how the place was under constant observation was enough to dispel the way she felt.

She still appeared unwilling to take on board their need to investigate the attack on Quinlan before they could worry about drugs and a whole lot of untoward goings on.

Jamie sitting across from her in this chain pub restaurant of her choosing, was concerned initially how his lack of news had dampened the proceedings, but he soon realized she also had things on her mind she had a real need to talk about.

Tamara is the sort who eats mainly only with a fork, and she put it down. 'To be honest I feel cheated,' she started when talk got quickly round to her father. 'Looking back now of course I could have behaved differently. Nobody forced me to give drugs a try, except they were so available and virtually everybody I came into contact with were on them. They all appeared at that point in my life to be having a good time. I was in my teens, I was an absolute pain in the arse and to be honest compared with all these people around me I was having a really shit time.'

He chewed and nodded. 'Think I went through the same stage,' Jamie offered. 'Thought lads I knew in their twenties were living the life, and mine sat at home seemed really crap.'

As if it is always his way Jamie just never talks about his torments. The way he felt when his father walked out to move in with the strumpet from work, how he had been treated by Kerrie as a cuckold.

'Now of course I know how false it all was. Bit like clubbing, all looks wonderful from the outside and you then very quickly realize it's never all it's cracked up to be.'

'So you decided to join them?' With the restaurant more than half empty there was no one close enough to overhear.

'Pretty much,' she admitted. 'Not a day when I got up and decided I'll start snorting today, give it a go, brighten my life, have a real good time.'

'And of course it was all on tap.' He stabbed a chip with his fork. 'You didn't need to go down the shoplifting route to afford your fix.' Tamara just sat there with her glass of water held in the fingertips of both hands, smiling.

'Then of course other things kick in. Can't be bothered with food after a while, not when a fix is more important than anything else. Literally the only thing that mattered in the whole wide world.' She then sipped her white wine of choice. 'Enough of me,' she said and licked her lovely lips.

'Carry on,' Jamie urged. 'You don't want me going on about changes in the policy in respect of a sustainable reduction in sickness for deployable resources,' she smiled slightly. 'How's the Moussaka?' he asked to break the spell.

'Fine,' was all he got and realized his companion's attention was elsewhere.

'Can't believe what I'm seeing,' she said and Jamie waited as she surreptitiously watched other customers out of his sight. 'I know I've done my body no good with what I've been up to, but that's ridiculous.' Eventually she turned her attention back to him. 'There's a fat female over there with her two obese pals and it's obscene.' Tamara went back to her own food for a few moments.

When Tamara turned down his offer to run her home he could not quickly fathom an excuse to stay with her for the arrival of her 'lift'. A lift she explained from her cousin who just happened to be in the area on business.

Back at Gainsborough nick he was able to input the Land Rover reg number into PNC and the DVLA system only to be seriously disappointed.

Jamie discovered to his chagrin the 2001 diesel Land Rover Defender TDS90 belonged to a Spencer Nyman, was insured through Hastings, fully taxed and had a current MOT.

When he carried out a routine background check on this Nyman he discovered just one offence. Failing to give information relating to the identification of the driver of a vehicle, He had been fined £660, with a surcharge of £66 and with £85 costs, plus six points on his licence but it was all way back in 2016. He must more than likely be the cousin, just as Tamara had said.

17

In the end DC Jamie Hedley chickened out rather than taking the bull by the horns back at base. After a sweaty sleepless night tossing and turning things over in his mind time and again, he decided when the opportunity arose to pull Nicky Scoley to one side and take a chance with her.

The advantage of talking to Scoley was he concluded, all to do with her being female and less belligerent, less disciplined, less set in her ways and less likely to fly off at the deep end. At least that's what he hoped and prayed for anyway.

'Looking for a spot of advice, think I might have dropped a clanger just wondered if I could run something by you.'

'Go ahead.'

This was pluck up courage time. 'When I was at school there was this stunningly attractive girl all the lads used to drool over. I was a year below her and all I could really do if I'm honest was stand and stare. But she was like the school beauty and at my age at the time as you can imagine, girls and football were everything.'

'This advice about girls you're after?' Nicky asked with a snigger.

'No,' Jamie chuckled. 'This is background, so you get the whole picture.' He'd not bothered with his coffee as yet, just sat there arms rested on the table looking at the lovely butterscotch blonde. 'Be about three years ago now. I'm on lates and me and Davie Pendine are dragging in this waste of space been nicking booze from the offie and getting plastered. When we get in, there's this female being booked in by the Custody Sergeant. There was something about her I recognized. Anyway, to cut a long story short it's this girl from school I hadn't seen for years. What a mess,' Jamie blew out a breath and shook his head. 'She's stick thin, all scraggy and wasted, hair like rats' tails, filthy dirty, mouthy and horrible. Kept out of her way and thought nothing more of it. Recently right out of the blue with

107

being sent over to Gainsborough I bumped into her in Marshall's Yard, sort of had as quick chat and exchanged numbers, like you do.'

'Can we get to the point?'

'Different again. Really much improved. Not as good as she was at school, but certainly a real improvement.' Jamie stopped to sip his coffee. 'Next thing I got a Text about meeting up.'

'You said this wasn't romantic advice you needed,' Nicky chided and Jamie ignored.

'Here's the bad bit,' he took in a breath. 'Reason I wanted a chat this morning.' Jamie grimaced and sucked in a breath. 'Her old man's Tez Diagne, doing eleven for some sort of trafficking, drugs and illegals and generally being a real bad lot. Finish up doing about six, due out in a couple of years.' He grimaced. 'Knew I had to tread carefully, worried she's batting for the enemy and at the same time wondered why she wants to meet up.'

'And?'

Jamie sucked in noisily, and nodded. 'Yeh I did,' he admitted. 'I met up with her.'

'Did you tell anybody?'

'No,' was accompanied by a sheepish shake of his head.

'Idiot! That was the point you should have said something. Give you a chance to find out if any of us know what's cracking off, talk to your old colleagues in PHU. Did you?' Jamie shook his head. 'Your first big mistake'.

'And second was meeting her.' Nicky Scoley waited while he took a drink. 'Says she's clean, not touched anything for a couple of years, trying to sort her life out plus…' he hesitated. 'Trying to scupper her old man's set-up for when he comes out.'

Nicky's turn to suck in her breath through puckered lips. 'I know he's not a criminal mastermind, but even so that has to be more than a bit risky, especially for his own daughter.'

'Bad news apparently. Checked him out. Diagne's the sort who bribes, threatens and intimidates people and witnesses if they know what's good for them and then just disappear into thin air. He's bad enough. Or was.'

Nicky's turn to take a drink. 'Why she doing that? She give you a reason?'

'She can't have children.'

'What?' Nicky exclaimed at what she never imagined he'd utter. For the first time Nicky's heart went out to this former druggie, or so she claimed.

'All the drugs, sniffing instead of snacking, throwing ecstasy down her throat rather than eating food. Think she'd have had a skunk sandwich for her breakfast given the chance. In the end doctors have told her she's done so much damage internally she'll not be able to have kids. Too much cocaine, heaps too much heroin, starving herself, anorexia and all the rest.'

'She blames her old man then?' from Nicky was replied with a nod. 'And what now?' She could see the look on his face. 'Come on, out with it.'

'Way back when apparently, Diagne's dad got his hands on the Cluny Priory.'

'You're joking?' she gasped. 'How d'you mean?'

'Some drug deal went pear shaped apparently and he finished up with it as his pay off, so she reckons. It's all some sort of pretence, like a scam, they're not nuns at all they're distressed women.'

'For god's sake Jamie! What else d'you know?'

'Domestic abuse. They're all women hiding well away from violent partners, trying to turn their lives around and our Diagne uses it as a staging post, like a huge lock-up where he stashes drugs I guess for other people, and hides real people as well probably. Easy be illegals too knowing him. Plus all the stuff been ripped off, fallen off the backs of lorries. DVDs, tele's, phones that sort of thing.'

'You're bloody joking!' Nicky gasped. 'Why d'you do this? What you been sitting on it all for? Why weren't you on your feet at morning briefing? You'da been the star of the show. And the Quinlan woman? Where does she fit into all this?' Nicky closed her eyes and shook her head. 'Don't tell me.'

'The bit I don't know,' he shrugged and drank coffee.

'Why didn't you mention all this before for god's sake? You should have been straight into the boss.' Nicky gulped her coffee down as if she were suddenly in a hurry. 'You're not down in PHU now.'

'Hey! Don't forget I'm just the local lad around these parts, got called in then sent out to grass, like nobody wants to know me.' Jamie struggled for what to say next. 'It went from just having a chat with a female from my past who happened to be a crook's daughter for sort of old time's sake, to all this. Thought Jake would...'

'You thought what?'

'Well, you know what he's like.'

'He'll be bloody angry now and no mistake, you could be in serious trouble,' Nicky was shaking her head. 'She just come out with all this?' she asked. 'Or is this pillow talk?'

'No it's not!' was sharp. 'My guess is I'm probably the only copper she actually knows, all the rest have been like Jake, more interested in throwing her into a cell.'

'We can't ignore her.'

'Can I just say, if we get too involved with her then I think Tamara just might do a runner, says she can't be seen to be associated with us.'

'You think this Diagne's somehow involved with the Quinlan business?'

'No idea.'

'You sure?'

'Honest. She just wants to pull the wool from under his feet.'

Nicky was on her feet. 'Drink up and put your body armour on,' Jamie looked up at her. 'You'll need some protection when the boss gets hold of you.'

'I feel such a pillock.'

'You're more than that! No time like the present,' she said as she moved away.

He'd considered mentioning his clandestine activities spying on Tamara's arrival, but decided under the circumstances he'd already made himself look a useless goon without adding to his problems.

Tall brown haired muscly Detective Constable Jamie Hedley was absolutely in his element being part of the Major Incident Team. He felt he got on well with all the other officers despite lacking their experience, he had kept his nose clean, knew he was learning as fast as he could and making a serious contribution.

Until now. Now he was not at all sure what his future might very well hold.

Sat there hands clasped together facing DI Inga Larsson with long steepled fingers, elbows on her desk. She listened intently to what he had to say.

110

'I'm guessing the worst punishment I could hand out would be to send you back down to PHU, or have I got you all wrong?' He shook his head. 'Why in God's name weren't you banging on my door with all you learnt about the damn Priory? You knew we were trying to fathom it all out, you knew I'd been there with Jake and then with Nicky. We're here scratching our heads and you knew all this all the time,' Larsson said as she pointed at him. 'That's exactly why I sent you over there. Following this through would have been a real positive for you but now the negatives completely outweigh any bonus points you gain. This is MIT, we deal with major incidents as it says on the tin. With all due respect to PHU they're only dealing with acquisitive everyday crimes such as shoplifting. Why keep it to yourself?' she sighed and shook her heads as Jamie waited. 'What have you told her you shouldn't?' she demanded. 'Out with it.'

'Nothing. Acted as if I'd been farmed off out the way, told her the Quinlan business is all going on over here.'

'For you young man talk, talk, talk is your new by-word. Do you understand?' he nodded. 'Why weren't you in here or bending my ear about having a date with this little madam and asking what it is you could find out for us?'

'Didn't know what she knew at first. Just some girl from school way back as I tried to make contact with people.' Inga went to speak but Jamie carried on. 'Just started out exchanging numbers, then texts. How was I to know she knew anything about the Cluny place?'

'First time, fair enough,' Inga commented. 'But the moment you realized you might learn something about anything she would be willing to chat about,' Inga herself sighed with frustration. 'You could have asked how to play it. I seek the Darke boss's advice from time to time, you don't lose face or is that what was bothering you?' There was no reaction. 'Come on, out with it.'

'DS Goodwin has such strong opinions, such discipline not sure I should speak to anybody who's not a hundred per cent kosher. Guessed I'd be in trouble maybe just for even talking to her.'

'In that case why not talk to me the moment she got in touch. Tell me who she is, seek my advice.'

'Sorry.'

Larsson kept her thoughts to herself. 'Jake takes a bit of getting used to I admit, but you must know what a great copper he is surely,' she lowered her hands and leant forward. 'Use him, use me, use whoever you can to further your career. Steal what you can from our brains and put it in yours.' She looked away out of the window. 'But never keep stuff like this to yourself. Happens again and it'll be a lifetime of PHU or and I have to warn you, worse.'

'Sorry ma'am.'

'Let this be a lesson to you, do you understand? Do it again and we're talking verbal warning at the very least.' Jamie nodded. 'Don't blow it again, but,' she smiled slightly for the first time. 'There would have been no need for canaries if we'd known what was down the mine,' Jamie struggled to understand. 'Ask Jake and Nicky to come in, please.'

To his right DC Nicky Scoley whom he had confided in, and to her right his nemesis the person who he imagined could institute his ruination and to some extent be the very person he would like to be. DS Jacques 'Jake' Goodwin.

'First things first,' said DI Larsson looking directly at Hedley. 'You young man have a great deal to learn and you really should have spoken up much earlier and put us in the picture from day one. We don't go in for people flying solo, doing aerobatics to impress, not how we work. I ask for individual input, clear and precise thinking but all ingredients go in our mixture. We always make the cake together, but we all have to give it a stir. Do we understand each other?'

'Yes ma'am,' he said but was not entirely sure he did some of the odd remarks.

'Good. The floor's yours, this is your chance to wipe the slate clean, provide us every last snippet of information you can think of, give us a real fighting chance to get this case up and running instead of it dragging its damn feet.'

To their credit all three officers sat and listened to every word Jamie Hedley had to say without a smidgen of interruption.

'Are you saying all this nun business is just a cover?' Nicky Scoley asked. 'All this praying and sleeping in those awful bedrooms like cells is all hogwash you reckon?' Nicky wanted to know.

'Apparently. According to her that is.' Jamie blew out a breath. 'That's been the problem, was she telling the truth or was it just a pack of lies and I come to you with it and in the end finish up looking a complete pillock, packed off back downstairs for being a naïve idiot.'

'At least you'd have come clean.'

Inga sat back and smiled to herself. 'That's the delay,' Nicky said suddenly as Jake went to add his opinion. 'Why it took an age to call us, they had to make sure the place was spick and span, hide the stuff, get rid of anybody who shouldn't be there.' She looked at her boss. 'There was all sorts hidden away under our feet.'

DI Inga Larsson looked as pleased as punch just sat there behind her desk smiling and nodding.

'Thought that old hag was just pissing me about to be honest,' said Jake. 'Truth was she was getting all her ducks in a row.'

'That's why that Whyte Mulilima kid seemed so unsure almost scared about what happened. Chances are she wasn't telling the truth. She was never wandering about in the dark stark bloody naked.'

'That's why. She was trying to remember what she'd been told had gone on, why that crabby old Appleyard wanted to be with her all the time.'

'Probably does have to light a candle maybe, but none of the rest of it. What's the betting those rooms are just like show homes.'

'Told her I've not been there,' Jamie admitted 'As I said I'm being careful not to ask too many questions.' He hesitated. 'If I'm perfectly honest I don't see her being involved in attacking a woman, unless it was what she calls scum bags doing it for her old man then that's another story, but she may be our way in to find out what went on with Quinlan.'

'She's the best clue we have,' said Inga. 'In fact the only clue.'

'Can't see how on earth Quinlan would be mixed up with Diagne, do you?' Jake asked.

'NHS drugs?'

'Good thinking,' Nicky was told.

'She also sort of hinted about people as well as the frightened women, using the place as a refuge for a night or two. Could be illegals, people on the run.' Jamie shrugged.

'Crims B & B eh?'

'What about?' said Jake slowly. 'Just an idea, but what if somebody made a mistake down the line? They get slabs of heroin delivered, knocked off laptops, iPads and the odd immigrant, and somebody somewhere decided they'd take just about anything and reckoned it might be a good idea to drop off a body they didn't know what to do with? This maybe somebody trying to fit up old man Diagne possibly, this was a chance to get their own back. Revenge?'

'They panicked faced with a dead 'un and...'

'Except as it turned out, she wasn't.'

'Be fair,' said Nicky. 'Paramedics I spoke to thought she was dead, damn lucky she wasn't with her head smashed in.'

'You're right. That's why there was a delay and those silly old bags gave me a load of guff about having to pray,' Jake jumped in as he sat forward. 'Damn pity we didn't know all this at the time.'

'Panic set in is my guess,' said Inga. 'Do we normally store dead bodies...are they on the list...what do we do...? Must phone the police,' she stopped to chuckle. 'You can imagine what panic was going off with all those crotchety women?'

'And to be honest I'm still worried about Whyte Mulilima,' Nicky offered. 'We take it what we're being told is proper. These women dressed up as nuns are in fact women hiding away from their husbands, partners, lovers or whatever. Like a sort of refuge for women place. That's all fine and dandy and I respect people who've been treated like they probably have. But,' she hesitated and looked at Inga. 'It's no place for that poor kid. What's she doing there? She's never a battered wife.'

'Slave?

'Child bride for a paedo maybe?'

'Paedos plural to mess about with.'

'Jake,' said Inga. 'You liaise with PHU about taking a team in there and I'll liaise with social services, but not yet. Let's bide our time because we go bowling in there, we might well scare the women off and close down the drug storage but where does that leave us with our Miss Quinlan?' She took a sip of the dregs of cold coffee on her desk, then waved the mug at Nicky. 'Tell you what, how about a comfort break? Meet again in twenty minutes, get some coffee in and I'll get DI Leadbetter up from PHU to sit in and we can then crack through all this and come up with an initial plan.'

Nicky was on her feet quickly, and tapping Jamie on the shoulder. 'Coffee run, come on. What does Ronnie Leadbetter drink?'

In the end it was more like half an hour by the time they were all gathered together again, ready to crack on with Inga's plan and all watered. Some had even grabbed a quick snack during the break.

'Nicky,' said Inga. 'I know we're not social workers but I want you to look into Whyte Mulilima. I think you're absolutely right, she is the odd one out. Doesn't fit the bill of a battered wife and she's scared shitless, and according to the bitch in charge she's from Malawi or at least her parents are. You can start work on this as soon as you can, because if there is something odd about her, we need her out of there before we pull the plug. Could be she's totally innocent, but we have to tread carefully or other agencies'll be crawling all over us trying to shift the blame.'

'She just a tasty treat for scrotes who visit?'

'I'd put money on her being a trafficked illegal anyway,' said Jake.

The DS was aware how social workers as in any other profession come in all shapes and sizes, good and bad. The good Nicky knew from experience were more often than not older and certainly more mature. Had children of their own, sucked in more life experiences and are certainly world conscious. The young were forever in too much of a hurry, existing in a life of flashing images, putting career and mobile before anything else particularly the client.

'Use Michelle again while she's still got a bit of time. You can couple up on this, and you never know what you just might find out if you go in as the early bird. Stuff the rest of us would like to know about before we go in like a bull in a china shop,' she said and glanced at DI Ronnie Leadbetter, who returned the look with the hint of a smile.

'So, we'll hold back for now,' was him seeking confirmation. 'Give us a chance to do a whole load of probing and there's a few numpties who just might tell a tale or two. Now we know the place is not kosher.' Leadbetter turned his head to look at Nicky. 'You could be our advance party under the guise of looking after this girl,' he suggested. 'Don't take this the wrong way but some of those women just might spill a bean or two to a couple of young ladies.'

'You may well be right. But Nicky and I were there before,' said Inga. 'Didn't seem to make much difference.'

'But then we didn't know what we know now.'

'And this time Nicky you will know they're hiding something, in fact if what we're told turns out to be true, hiding a great deal. You just might see things differently than we did when we took it at face value and stupidly assumed it was some sort of holy retreat.'

18

Gordon Kenny had been fretting and worrying why it was all taking the coppers so long, in fact it had turned to serious concern. Then right out of the blue on the radio news on the half-hour there it was.

"The identity of a young woman found in the Cluny Priory near Gainsborough recently, has now been released by police. She has been named as Carole-Anne Quinlan from Gainsborough a thirty-six year old Impartiality In Action Lead Coordinator linked to an NHS service provision contractor. Police inquiries into the brutal attack are ongoing."

'Hang on there a goddam minute,' he shouted. 'Brutal attack! What about bloody murder?' he slammed a fist onto the table.

He'd guessed the smack on her forehead was enough to do her in. Why'd he not checked, found a pulse and strangled the silly cow?

Now he had another dilemma he'd never considered. Was that true, or were the coppers pretending? Was he supposed to react to that, blow his cover, come out all guns blazing and just kill some poor sod for fun just to show he's being serious? Gordon just sat there looking out the kitchen window asking himself if that was what they always do we never get to hear about in these murder cases

His tormented mind suddenly reminded him of the good news. If she's not dead then it won't be on his conscience. But, he does have the experience behind him for the next stage, all the elements he had been worried sick about have been dealt with. Didn't get the end result he was looking for with his practice run, but so be it.

Knowing his mum the way he did he was sure she'd not be happy about him killing some woman no matter what she'd been up to.

He'd always known it was a dangerous exercise using the dizzy dame for practice. It was all the mental issue he'd been suffering as an aftermath rather than the actual physical effort of ending someone's time on earth.

How Quinlan had treated his aunt still gripped him when he thought about her. The torment Ingrid must have gone through for years. How often would she see other grandmothers she knew out and about with their grand-kids? Proudly pushing a pram or a swing, buying sweets and treats. Going to sports day to cheer them on, buying their first bike and being at their graduation.

All totally denied his dear aunt by such a loathsome bitch. For why? What reason could she have?

Listening to Hawkwind's *Silver Machine*, he knew it had been a bit of a shaker with that Quinlan cow still being alive. Then in the way his mind always worked he had to try to reassure himself she really was still alive. What they said on the radio was the truth, the whole truth and nothing but.

This was the media. How trustworthy were they, how much unimportant garbage do they spew out on a daily basis? What lies have they been sued about over decades?

Now he was back to questioning his own ears. Otherwise he tried to tell himself they'd have said it's a murder enquiry surely. What was it they actually said he tried to recall? *Brutal attack*, sounds nasty but it's not the way they talk about death.

Gordon told himself it had to be good news from his perspective, and if it was would certainly take a weight off his shoulders. Absolutely not what he'd been expecting, certainly not part of his scheme of things quite obviously.

It had been on his mind since he slammed the iron pipe across her forehead, thinking about what he'd done almost constantly from that moment on, and he'd worried how long the thought of actually killing somebody would remain with him.

This was surely the very reason he told himself he needed a practice run. How would he feel after the act, how would it affect him, would he lose control and do something stupid? Now he knew. It had certainly weighed heavily upon him up to that point.

Gordon knew she'd not got a look at him, it'd been so fast and efficient just stepping fleetingly out from behind the big oak. Stupid bitch was mentally too far away, living in a world of Spotify or some other nonsense no doubt. With a bit of luck he hoped she'd still be struggling to come to terms with what happened to her. Chances are anything she tells the police will be nothing more than pure guesswork.

His mental state was not completely worry free as yet. He'd got a few questions and observations, apart from wondering what took them so long. Gordon wondered if the cops actually knew what a Impartiality In Action Lead Coordinator did for a living apart from waste taxpayers money? If they were anything like him they'd be more than a few coppers shaking their heads about such crap and no mistake. They after all do a proper job.

He knew she might have been living in Gainsborough of late, but she is certainly not from the town as the radio suggested. He found it acutely interesting how our police have taken so much time already and all they can come up with is what? Next to nothing which he found amusing as he knew a great deal more about the lousy bitch than they apparently could. Or did they know but had kept it away from the media?

Gordon decided to put the kettle on again and brew another cuppa and have one of those sugar free biscuits he'd bought, while he waited for the news to come round again. See if anything had changed. Be interesting to see if it was still merely an attack? Work for an hour could take a back seat.

Stood there leant back against the work surface he pondered about those nuns and knew they'd certainly not leave their door open in future. One of the things which had really surprised him at the time. Dumped her up against the chapel door and just pulled at the lever by sheer chance to find it open.

Has to be part of this hogwash about God's door always being open. 'Bet it's not anymore!' he told the red kettle.

19

Jamie Hedley had put any ideas of catching up with his old pals firmly to the back of his mind with everything going on.

After the meet with Larsson, Goodwin and Scoley he'd headed off to the gym in an effort to take his mind off work for a while. Go back to what he knew. A return to the weights, to keeping his body in prime condition as he'd been doing now for a good few years.

Social distancing was still in operation but they'd created three metre work boxes he was able to stay in to do his weights work. No running. No rowing and none of that Yoga business.

Wished now he had a before and after picture to remind him how his body building had progressed from the thin Mr Average to be somebody people would think twice about tackling, on and off duty.

Jamie would love to have the acute mind of Larsson but the sort of successful career DCI Luke Stevens currently running all the cyber teams had enjoyed. Not at all sure he was capable of handling encryption passwords and the sort of top notch software only found on the dark web.

Knew painstaking work had made the urbane DCI particularly successful in his pursuit of paedophiles, their images and videos. In one case he'd read about Stevens had been the one to spot a particular Claddagh Celtic Trinity Knot signet ring on the finger of a man on social media he had also seen in abuse photos.

Linking that ring to the paedophile site titled GalwayWay where he'd first spotted one the same, which had others in the team scouring Ireland for further clues, meant Stevens was able to take an entirely different direction completely.

In the end it resulted in the seizure of an encrypted laptop from a Kristopher Zucker – who had been using bitcoin cryptocurrency to sell videos of the abuse – when he flew in from Jersey. Hours of painstaking work undertaken by Stevens had landed this abuser of children with a close to three decade sentence. All done through total persistence.

Keeping Tamara's info to himself he knew was no way to emulate such a successful detective.

On his way home feeling more relaxed after his work out, Jamie was driving past Nutty Charman's mother's house and for a second considered about just pulling in, knocking on her door to check the lie of the land with her son. Nice woman Adele Charman, he'd always got on all right with her.

The thing Jamie always remembered about the Charman home was how anodyne it was, nothing was coordinated; something his own mother was insistent upon. Looked for all the world as if each individual item had been bought at auction without any thought to previous purchases. Good quality mind, but looked almost as if someone had set it all out in the formation of a room to add appeal rather than it being a home. Clash of colours, clash of materials and styles. Despite it all, what he could recall from his time in the Charman household was a warmth and a lack of pretension. Some of his pals at the time lived in real scuzzy houses, but not Nutty Charman.

Two days later he'd been told by a mutual friend he'd bumped into in Tesco, how Paul Miller who had never been called 'Dusty' like most are, was now working at the local Ford dealer.

'Hey Heders, long time, no see,' was the Paul he knew when he walked up to him in shirt sleeves. 'Where the hell have you been matey?'

'Down at the Spread Eagle waiting for you,' sounded ridiculous but to some extent it was true.

'More than dodgy that.'

'So I heard.'

'What they got you doing these days then?'

'With MIT now,' he knew from Paul expression he had to explain. 'Major Incident Team.'

Paul frowned. 'What's a major incident? That road traffic accidents and all that?'

'Murder, attempted murder and all that sort of thing and ...'

'Bloody hell mate! Thought you were just dealing with the riff-raff. Doing folk for dropping litter, fining me for having a party and the usual police bollocks.'

'I was,' he shrugged rather than react. 'Dealt with vulnerable people, missing people and these days loads of domestic abuse. Got moved up into a whole new world. Serious crime this mate. Not exactly on trial but got to be careful what I do as I'm sort of the new boy on the block. Steep learning curve let me tell you.' Best not to say he'd been used by the MIT team previously for short periods of extreme activity but then hastily returned to PHU each time.

'Like real murders you mean?' he checked as if he didn't believe what he'd been told. 'Dead bodies and all that gubbins?'

'Sure thing.'

'Bloody hell mate. Bet you've got a few tales to tell,' said Paul having blown out a breath in a half whistle. 'Hey, tell you what, few of us started this mad meals thing and you could join us, be like the old days and you can tell us all the nitty-gritty. Nutty comes when his woman lets him out, and it's Chris who finds the new places. It's a good craic and certainly a different world from the old Spread. We're going for a Romanian on Thursday, fancy joining us?'

'You go out for meals?' Jamie checked. A real step up from a pie and a pint.

'Not just any meal. Actually had a good scoff in a swimming pool,' Paul sniggered. 'Chris persuaded this guy he knows to let us put a table and chairs in the kiddies pool at the leisure and their café people came up with bacon and eggs. Right now he's trying to get an ice rink to let us do something similar.'

'With the water in?'

'No, ice!'

'I meant in the swimming pool.'

'Yes of course, water.'

'This Romanian,' said Jamie carefully, 'Is where?'

'New restaurant place just opened. Do a good pizza they tell me.'

Jamie chuckled at his friend. 'What's the point going to a Romanian place for pizza, and in the pool you should've had fish surely.'

'They'll do their own Romanian stuff that's why we're going. One of the rules is you must order the food of the country. Do veal goulash, breast of chicken pancakes and all sorts apparently.'

'Eating in a swimming pool,' Jamie returned to. 'How mad is that?'

'There's loadsa weird eating places, matey. Place in Egypt apparently where you are served by dwarfs.'

'What's dwarfs got to do with Egypt?'

'Just where it is. Chris found one in Brighton offering a bit of an eccentric Royal Family feel about it serving Sussex cream teas, all very British with tacky memorabilia stuff so he says.'

'When d'you say?'

'Thursday, eight thirty if you fancy it.'

'Just might manage it, depends on work of course,' said Jamie as he moved away and his phone rumbled in his pocket. 'What's everybody else doing these days?'

'Nutty's female's pregnant and his old lady kicked him out cause she thinks they should have got married first, now the poor sods are living in this hell hole of a pokey flat. Chris is seeing Penny Drysdale again, why in god's name won't he listen? We all know she's trouble, and Micky Aldridge is still drinking too much.'

'Nothing much changes then. You?'

'Still married, still only Ben and Bethany and looking to move somewhere more decent. Up to now's as far as it's got, just looking. You?'

'All to do with work means I'm over here for a bit, but I'll tell you what. I bumped into Tamara Diagne, remember her?'

'Bloody hell, she's a blast from the past and no mistake. What I wouldn't do to her! Wow! Last time I saw her she was in a right mess and looked like you'd catch anything.'

'Getting herself straight again, by the look of her. Been to the bottom, but now on her way back.'

'This work? You arrested her, d'you say?' Jamie went to answer. 'What's she been up to?'

'No, nothing. Just had to chat to her about something.' Jamie glanced at his watch. 'Better be off. Good to see you. See you Thursday, depending on work of course, and we can catch up some more,' and as he turned to walk away he pulled out his phone. It was not DS Goodwin wanting to know where he was and what was he doing, it was a message from Scott Casey. He turned back to Paul. 'Anything stopping me bringing a mate with me?'

'Anybody I know?'

'Bloke called Scott I met at the Blues, he's an author. Always on the lookout for snippets and locations for his books.'

'Don't see why not,' he shrugged. 'See you around.'

When he got back to his car Jamie opened the text from Scott asking if he planned to go to football on Saturday. Jamie replied as usual about work allowing he'd be at the Northholme and suggested he might like to join him and a few of his old pals for the Romanian meal.

Was this a new gag, this odd meal business, he wondered? Jamie knew somebody who had spent a long weekend in a tree house somewhere. Quite recently he'd heard about a couple he knew who were planning to spend a few days away on a double-decker bus. All mod cons, lounge, kitchen, bedrooms all on a stationery London double decker complete with hot tub.

He knew both options beat what a lot of youngsters get up to, spending their weekends peering at their phones, wherever they might be.

20

Gordon Kenny had moved his attention onto Rosemarie Mackenzie now he knew he could relax to some extent about the Quinlan woman.

Her parents weren't to know how Mackenzie's wife was likely to turn out, although they would of course have had an input in the early days. They are one assumes partly responsible for her being a timid little thing and as a result she had grown up to be prime meat for a crass bully like Don.

By the look of her Gordon had decided the name Rosemarie was as it turned out, about right for her. He'd always been interested in names. Some people he'd come across have totally inappropriate ones, yet others seem to have been given a moniker to fully suit their personality. Gordon had often wondered if it was similar to the way some people appear to become facially more like their dogs. How they somehow tend to develop in stature and character to suit their name, rather than the other way round.

If he was asked to classify this Rosemarie he'd put her down as a schoolteacher, probably one who teaches something a bit odd like Latin. She had an old fashioned geeky look about her, but he'd not actually bothered to discover exactly what it is she had done for a living.

Quite possible of course if he were to get to know her she just might turn out to be a very nice woman who has had all the stuffing knocked out of her by that berk of a husband.

One thing he did know was, she had an interest or rather a reason for leaving home on a regular basis, but he had no idea why.

It could be anything. A tiny three people reading group, Rosemarie and this Mavis Delaney enthusing over Cosy novels maybe, or could be avid crossword attempters or they do quilting together.

All the chopping and changing over the months had left Gordon unsure of the Coronavirus rules. Rosemarie always wore a pale blue mask walking to and from the Delaney's even though wearing them outdoors was not mandatory. Was she allowed to visit them? Were they related or had that all been relaxed?

There were so many things three people could be involved in and as it bore no relationship to the task in hand it was really not worth him speculating. By the look of her he had decided there is no way it could be anything even slightly unseemly. Worst it could be he had decided was her remaining true to form and teaching them Latin. The stick thin Delaney couple certainly look odd-ball enough for it.

Gordon was well aware, people often get involved in quite the most ridiculous and oddest of hobbies, and it is quite likely to be something really obscure. He'd at some point read all about people calling themselves 'preppers' who are obsessed with their need to survive a major catastrophe.

He had been amused by these oddities making plans apparently to escape such things as another financial collapse, a Coronavirus outbreak return or Donald Trump pressing the button. He'd also read about somebody who at one time actually opened a shop where you can buy all you'll need to escape something like the Zika virus!

If anybody suggests it's all in his imagination Gordon will just tell you to Google it!

What he found particularly reassuring about this Rosemarie Mackenzie, was he could plan around the regularity of her visits to the Delaneys. Same time almost to the minute, same day, always Thursdays. Perfect for what he had planned.

It was during his initial planning phase when he had discovered something else very useful.

He hadn't bothered with using an app or Goggle Earth to start with and had just concentrated on the comings and goings from the bungalow from the street aspect.

He was certainly cheered when one night he discovered the field behind their home. Knew straight away it would make life so much easier and then one dark night in early December he'd dared to venture over there.

A pal had asked him to look after his Spaniel for a weekend, so with Storm as an alibi he took the mutt with him for a walk. Surprise,

surprise in Mackenzie's back garden, a shed. A big shed which just had to contain more than a lawn mower, spade and fork hanging on nails, a few pots and a half empty bag of compost.

All along he had quite wrongly told himself Don Mackenzie spent his evenings indoors watching television repeats of 'Top Gear', foreign dramas with subtitles, looking at porn sites on the net, or reading. As it turned out he most certainly was not.

Don Mackenzie as he discovered, spent a great deal of his time in his shed. Gordon knew all about it being a silly 'man thing' but for the life of him couldn't remember knowing anybody man or boy who has had any use for a shed other than keeping gardening stuff in. Place for the strimmer, mower and the barbecue which like most folk they probably hardly ever use.

As it turned out Don Mackenzie spent hours in there. Annoyingly this meant it had been a complete waste of time him spending hours standing in the street watching the property from a distance. Yes, his observation had told him when Rosemarie went off out, and he also knew hardly anybody ever knocked on the front door in the evening. All along he assumed the ex-copper was a boring old sod just sat indoors.

Gordon knew how that nasty bitch Appleyard who was bleeding the charities dry at one time, didn't use her own name on the bank accounts. It had all come out at her trial and is all there in black and white for all the world to see.

The evil woman so he discovered had used people like his dear old mum. Even had the cheek to use her driving licence and the gas bill or something similar to open an account. Flouncing into the bloody bank pretending to be Lynda his mum. Just thinking about it makes Gordon wretchedly bloody angry.

What was it, three lousy years after his mum was released from prison for something she never did, and there's these battle hardened bloody cops all kitted out in their black raid gear playing hideously ridiculous tough guy roles. Hauling his little old mum out of her spick and span front room to a shit hole of an interview room to face trumped up fraud charges.

Knew only too well it must have been hell on for her. With her saying she'd be all right, no need to make a fuss is etched on his memory for ever. Told him how she was totally and utterly innocent and he wasn't to worry. There she was, little Lynda his mum just taking everything on her shoulders like she'd always done.

'Don't worry pet, I'll be fine.'

Bloody fraught with worry was how she was if the truth be known and Gordon is still damn angry at himself to this day for not taking her well away from it all.

His dear mum first came across arsehole Mackenzie when he was being a dick of a copper up near where Gordon was born and brought up. Then later when she was released he could understand her reluctance to return to the town she knew so well. The town where she met dad, gave birth to him and was then put inside for years.

There is just no way, his dear mum would ever just toddle off down those streets again without folk pointing at her, shouting abuse and in this day and age make her a huge figure of fun on social media. Her life would be an absolute horror show from morning to night. Bricks through the window, recycling bin turned overt, dog muck in the letterbox, graffiti daubed out front like they do, just for starters.

It was Gordon's fault entirely and he knew it. As her only son he knew he should have insisted he take her right away from people and places she knew. Away from those who would easily find fault and criticize. Give her a fresh new start in life away somewhere, anywhere.

He had to a certain extent of course when she was released, but he had an ulterior motive. He wanted to remain close to Mackenzie in order to deal with him as part of his long term plan. The plan he'd used Quinlan as practice for.

However, it was the worst thing he could have done. Cornwall, Midlothian or Carmarthenshire even would have been better for her, if he hadn't been obsessed with Mackenzie and his ghastly involvement.

When big hairy coppers went completely over the top and stormed into her rented flat in Hemswell she must have been absolutely bloody terrified. Sending her back to pokey to what must have been for her an absolute hell hole. Gordon can remember so vividly how those nasty bloody vengeful coppers very nearly kept her in custody that first night just to teach her a lesson

127

Although it had crossed his mind, Gordon knew topping a serving police officer is never a good idea, because it's then they'll go hammer and tongs at a case, when it's one of their own. Supposed to serve Joe Public first and foremost of course as their remit stipulates, but they're forever bleating about a lack numbers to deal with multi various problems. Pop one of the boys in blue into the mix and see what happens. They can find plenty of robust coppers then.

Of course with his mother still serving time and him visiting every single opportunity there was, he needed to remain close. The remainder of her family just blanked her. Only one of them ever visited her in jail, not even her brother, not a single one of her so-called friends. The one naturally was lovely caring Aunt Ingrid, her sister. What a sweetheart she was. Nobody else.

Families? Don't you just love them!

21

It was always a concern to Jamie Hedley when his mother appeared to forget things which were part and parcel of her daily routine. This time it was milk for her breakfast. One of the items she purchased on a regular basis.

Jamie decided he'd fetch some and trudged down to the shops rather than bother with the car and knew the walk would do him good according to all the warnings about obesity and the need for diet and exercise

'Thanks,' he said to the woman at the till, lifted up the milk container just as his mobile rumbled in his pocket. Outside he removed his mask, put down the milk and retrieved his phone.

YOU BE LONG? Infuriatingly was his mother texting.

JUST GOT MILK he messaged her. Surely she'd not forgotten where he was already.

TROUBLE AT FISH PYE'S

'What d'you mean trouble?' he asked when he called her up.

'Ben Matthews, you remember him used to be in the Scouts. Phoned me, said there's something going on. Lots of people turning up all the time, cars roaring about.'

'At Hector's?'

'So he says. Wondered if you'd have a look.'

'Brilliant! I'm on….foot. Back in a tick.'

Back home, Jamie slid the milk onto the work surface in the kitchen and grabbed his keys. 'He still live in Jockey Mead?' he asked.

'Far as I know.'

'Anything else?'

'Nothing,' she shrugged.

'Back soon.'

The cul-de-sac was as quiet as a grave, but two cars had passed him at speed along the road in. Maybe too quiet when Jamie pulled up, for there to be something cracking off.

129

When he reached the front door, it was slightly ajar with no light on, save for one dimly lit in the room to his right.

'Hector!' he called.

'Clear off...yer bastards!'

'It's me,' said Jamie poking his head round the door to discover an unholy mess in what had to be the old boy's front room. He switched the main light on. Sat slumped in an armchair was old white haired unkempt Hector Pye, known to all and sundry as Fish. 'You alright?' Hector looked away. 'What's been going on Fish?' Jamie asked aware he was anything but.

'I'm fine.'

'But you're not are you? I ask again. What's been cracking off?'

'Hello, hello anybody there?' said a voice behind him and when Jamie turned there was a small man brandishing a walking stick.

'What the hell you doing with that?'

'Sorry.'

'You'll be more than sorry. Now put it down.'

'Just saw you turn up, been a right shemozzle going on up and down the street. Young shits!' and the stick was still in hand.

'Who? What you on about?' Jamie demanded.

'Bloody yobs that's what, all here last night as well.'

'Doing what?'

'How many guesses you need?'

'Somebody needs to explain what's going on,' Jamie aimed at Hector.

'They nick your money?' this man joined in.

'No,' was grudgingly offered. 'Fuss about nothing,' Hector mumbled. He was hiding something and his look said he was embarrassed at doing so.

'Who made this mess?' Jamie queried.

'Musta been that lot.'

'What lot?'

'Been coming and going all night, bloody cars racing round.'

'And you are?'

'Lenny. Lenny Greenfield, number seventeen,' and he pointed to his left. 'Called round this morning but like now he's keeping schtum and who can blame him.'

'You had people in here?' Jamie asked but Fish just looked sheepish as this Lenny bent down to pick up a can.

'Leave it! Might have to get a team in,' and he turned back to Fish. 'How d'they get in?' he demanded of the old man. 'Who are they? Out with it for crissakes!' he bellowed.

'No comment.'

'Just stop it please, we don't need crap off the tele,' Jamie gasped. 'I'm trying to help you here, now tell me what's been going on, please.'

'Told me this morning one of them's his grandson.'

'That right?' Jamie asked.

'If you like.'

'Everybody alright?' a voice in the hall asked.

'In here,' Greenfield called out and another man walked in.

'Me son reckons it could be that Chunky Knapp,' which meant nothing to Jamie.

'Your son is who?'

'Does a bit of work at the youth club.'

'And you are?'

'Ben Matthews. Phoned your mum, knew no cop cars'd be coming out.'

'What d'you know? Looks to me like Fish is protecting someone.'

'Midnight last night, cars kept turning up and roaring off again. Same a bit earlier on.'

'Just littering the street and doing wheelies or is all this their mess?' Jamie gestured to all the rubbish.

'They've been in.'

'Why?' was loud and aimed at Hector.

'Missus says there's a spare room if he wants a bed for the night, case they come back. Probably got the kettle on already.'

'Hear you've had a bit of a morning of it. How the hell did you get involved in all that business?' Detective Sergeant Dennis Norton asked Jamie later in Gainsborough nick.

'Text from my old lady first thing, somebody phoned her to say something was going on at Hector Pye's place. Old guy she's known for years. Think one of his neighbours thought she'd get us out faster

131

through me than just dialing three nines and joining the queue.' Jamie grimaced. 'What's that all about?' he queried. 'It's insane. Not been back here more than a few days and people already phoning me mum when they need a copper.'

'How'd they know you're over here?' the head of local CID asked.

'You know what they're like with the jungle drums. Bet mum's told her friends. Jamie's back over here you know, be that woman what's been assaulted. Did you read it in the paper?' he mimicked his mother.

'And walked in on a right mess they're telling me.'

'Found Hector almost cowering in the corner.'

'Just cars racing about and these bastards trooping in and out all night, lads were saying. Any talk of loud music and booze?'

'Not from those I've talked to.'

'Parties are the usual cover, all a bit loud and rowdy and folk don't like to interfere, not like asking a neighbour if they'd mind turning the tele down with shits like them about.'

'Think they sensibly stayed put rather than risk facing them up. One of the old boys did turn up with his walking stick! You thinking this is Operation Antidote?'

'Been quiet for a good month or more as you know, but this has a different slant on it.'

'Still cuckooing however you look at it,' said Jamie.

'Some of the bad ones have picked on the vulnerable and hijacked their homes for days on end as you know. We had a few close shaves if you remember, got bloody close a time or two.'

'And the question still is, how d'they know people like Hector's on his own and vulnerable?'

'And, why didn't he phone us?'

'Got to be under threat of God knows what, to be honest I reckon he was just too frightened. He'd hardly talk to me when I first got there he was in such a state, traumatized to be fair. Anyway there's only a landline and forensics are saying the bastards musta pulled the plug. Sorry, but old boy like him's just not up to crawling on his hands and knees to sort it.'

'Been targeted,' said Norton confidently. 'Ones we've had before have all been old and vulnerable if you remember, one old guy that

Cosgrove fella was bloody blind. The bastards! Somehow they suss out a likely candidate, take over their place and run their drug dishing out and get pissed up. Means their own places are crystal clear if we kick the door down.'

'Clever,' said Jamie.

'How is the old fella now? Fish d'you call him?'

'Fish Pye,' Jamie sniggered. 'Been that since he was at school apparently. Neighbours are looking after him. Medics checked him over. No injuries, just put the shits up him I reckon. Frightened the poor sod to death and threated him's my guess. One of the women has offered him a bed for the night, but of course he can't climb the stairs, think they'll make up a bed on the sofa.'

As a result of Jamie spending half the morning at Hector Pye's bungalow had not managed to get into Lincoln as expected, but he'd phoned DI Larsson in order to explain why he had been otherwise indisposed, and not be at morning briefing.

Through his mother he'd been able to make contact with Hector's eldest daughter and people locally were in the process of helping to transfer him to her home in Newark.

The scruffy two bedroomed bungalow in Jockey Mead was now home to a CSI team.

'Has to be the closest we've got so far. Five minutes earlier you could have walked in on them,' Dennis Norton suggested.

'Thanks.'

'Trouble is, where next? What other vulnerable old folk are being targeted is always the unanswered question.'

'When he finally started to explain what had gone on I was hoping Fish might have overheard what they were up to next, but according to him they didn't, or he'll not say. Chances are he'd not understand their jargon anyway. Spice and skunk mean different things to different generations that's the problem. Just used his place as somewhere they could divi out their stash.'

'Good scheme when you think about it,' Norton mused. 'We're never going to raid a place like Pye's bungalow searching for drugs in a million years. Like now, by the time we work out what's going on they've moved on to some other poor sucker's home.'

'Why d'they have to make such a mess? Empty bottles, takeaway trays, fag ends and food all trod into his carpet, cans some half full and just a general mess.' His mother had said she'd pop round and lend a hand giving the place a good seeing to for the old boy while he was away.

'How they live that's the problem with dregs like them. Bet if you go to their dive, bed sits or whatevers'll it might stink to high heaven, but there'd be no weed, no coke anywhere near. Same with Knapp, expecting his place to reek of it, but no. Gotta be the new tactic. But the CSI lads are saying they've found a couple of wraps under the sofa at the old man's place. Guess that's not Pye's unless I'm reading this all wrong.'

'Anything from this Chunky Knapp fella except no comment?'

'No,' Norton shook his head. 'Was it Pye gave you his name?'

'No. A neighbour. Son does a bit of work down the local youth club and says this Chunky's always hanging around.'

'Bit old for him, but if there's some'at cracking off he's there.' Norton shrugged. 'In this case chances are he uses the kids as runners and knows where they congregate.' He sighed with frustration. 'Going no comment of course, but we've got two phones one of which they reckon's a burner. Might give us something.'

'Then they might not.'

'Hadn't you better be getting across to see Larsson?' Hedley nodded. 'By the way how d'you get on with her?'

'Sharp as a button but a damn good copper.'

'And tasty.'

'And that.'

22

Out in Ingham his discovery of Mackenzie's garden shed had Gordon Kenny taking an interest in the subject. He discovered a radio enthusiast at one time managed to call up astronauts on the International Space Station from his garden shed, so anything was possible.

He tried to imagine himself as a crabby old fool with a strange hobby in a shed, and wondered what hobby he could get excited about in his dotage. He decided by that time supposedly mature people taking nonsensical selfies will have gone the same way as Betamax and tank-tops so any hobby he chose would probably never be really dotty.

Gordon had settled on Mackenzie being in his shed and it was time to think about his wife again. He wondered to himself if she had ever said "your shed'll be the death of you" who is now very likely to be proved right. Something else which really gripped him. Mackenzie talks about Rosemarie as 'the wife', as some berks do. Something he'd noticed gays tend towards too on occasions. What a loathsome way to talk about anybody especially in this day and age.

Next issue he had to confront was what does this guy do in his shed, and is it the sole reason why he appears from other vantage points to just be sat indoors in front of the tele?

If it's a really decent model railway Gordon knew he'd find it difficult to drag himself away after, but if it's something mighty weird or has severe sexual connotations for which he deserves a slap, then he's likely to give him another one for luck to punish him.

He had thoughts of getting one of those SpyBubble contraptions. The sort where you can snoop on people's phone conversations, but that's not all. According to what he could gather it would mean he could read all his texts and those he sends. Big problem though. How in God's name would he ever install it on Mackenzie's mobile?

Would help though, knowing exactly what he was doing and planning to do.

In the end he decided it was worth a risk. Not a case of risking everything, but if it went wrong then he just might have to abandon the scheme for just a while.

If it did all go tits up he'd just pretend he was lost, chose the wrong house, say he was looking for someone maybe. As he had no plans to steal anything they would find it difficult to have him for burglary. Might throw trespass in his direction, but he's not at all sure the police are the least bit interested in such of silliness these days. Sadly lacking feet on the ground in this day and age in his situation is a bonus. After all as far as they were concerned he'd just say he was being nosey, so what could the cops do him for?

One of those sort of houses you often see on property improvement programmes. Where they pull down interior walls to produce a cave of a monstrosity for so-called trendy open plan living rigorously enthused about by badly dressed presenters. A concept Gordon had read recently was now considered to be past it's sell by date. People he now understood preferred closed-in rooms and he wondered if all those have had the transformation would admit their error and call in a brickie to make the rooms appear again.

Gordon chose to wait for this Rosemarie to go out, before he crept down the side of the bungalow into their back garden in the dark across the block paved patio and got a good look at the shed all lit up inside with dear old Don doing whatever was occupying his time.

Problem up to then always had been, the view from the field was just the back of the shed. No windows, no nothing. He could have been doing anything inside and Gordon had to know what, before he just burst in there. Find he's into firearms or old cowboy pistols and he could be in a bit of trouble.

He was gobsmacked. There as large as life was rotund Don Mackenzie shirt sleeves rolled right up in the odd way Yorkshiremen do, working on a rocking horse. A big wooden rocking horse large enough for a child to ride. Had the old copper really made that or maybe he was just doing it up? Stood in the dark watching him a shocked Gordon decided it had to be what he does as a hobby. Buys old tired and worn out wooden toys like rocking horses and does them up. He'd certainly make a few bob for a refurbished horse.

This was not one of these man cave places or even the combined man supping hideaway and lady lair some twerps go in for. More a pucker workshop than just a shed.

None of this planning and furtive behaviour was ever for Gordon himself. He's not into gratuitous violence for its own sake, just doing what he does for others and in particular someone very close to him. A woman who suffered on his behalf to whom he literally owed everything.

Gordon is of course fully aware that whatever he does can never make up for the torment his aunt and mother had been through. Frequently he thinks of the pair of them watching on enviously at other people's grannies out with babies and toddlers. How they both must have suffered the consequences of others nasty actions.

He can vividly remember the first time he came across Quinlan mouthing off, even at such an early stage she just got him really annoyed.

The bitch always had this smugness about her, and he'd marked her card as a possibility early on, but knew he had time on his side and there was no rush to choose the best candidate to die.

He hopes when all this is all finally dealt with people will understand why he simply had to do what he'd done. Why somebody had to pay the ultimate price. As he will tell you, we are after all responsible for our own actions.

Gordon Kenny hopes that by spending time in hospital herself as a patient these past few days, just might open Quinlan's eyes to what is going on around her. Hope she is in desperate need of a commode only to find there are not enough nurses to deal with the matter. If she craps in her bed it could well be good news for the NHS.

She was practice and now it was Mackenzie's turn, and this time there has to be no mistake. The guy was going to die.

By inbred strength of will and determination he had observed his primary target and his school ma'am wife for months. He'd put himself in danger to a degree with all this. Knew he could leave nothing to chance, leave no stone unturned and in the end all his sheer graft and dedication to the cause will he hoped, certainly pay off.

The Quinlan business actually did him a favour in demonstrating what could go wrong, and in the end did what 'practice' said on the tin.

Rosemarie, bless her harmless soul, was out at her friends and Gordon knew what time, almost to the second she'd be back home. Don Mackenzie was in his shed with this big rocking horse almost complete. He'd seen it through the window one evening when he crept round there once before. He wished he'd been able to stay and watch as this magnificent piece of work had developed from just lumps of wood he assumed and Mackenzie was at the stage where he was just sanding it down, probably a bit too thoroughly, a tad too much of a perfectionist it seemed. Anyway there it was just in need of the paint and lacquer and then all he had to do was add the saddle and reins and the rest of it.

Why he wondered stood there in the dark watching, had this skilled bastard not been a carpenter rather than a shit copper?

One thing Gordon Kenny had no way of predicting was how Mackenzie would react to him suddenly appearing. He could guess of course and that was something that had kept him awake for a few nights.

23

The Romanian meal on the Thursday as it turned out was seriously different. The old rundown shop the restaurant had replaced was now completely unrecognizable after refurbishment, and a couple of the people in attendance were faces new to Jamie.

Scott Casey had messaged him earlier about a place he'd been told about in Nottingham where a café was based in a shipping container.

Missing from the gathering was 'Nutty' Charman with a lame excuse, but everybody guessed it was his woman laying down the law. Her law.

Jamie had been on line to check the place out and at the same time looked up any other odd eating places and had scanned the menu.

He'd come across one with chocolate somehow finding its way into every dish, and a strange place which serves a confit duck leg on a sweet waffle. Alas, neither were near at hand.

Inside, the refurb of the former greengrocers shop looked as though it was not complete, but on the other hand Jamie decided it could well be what a restaurant in Bucharest would be like. Basic wooden retro chairs and gingham table cloths were a contrast to the dark wood interior. Alas the cutlery was to a degree too big, heavy and unwieldy.

He thought it was a pity the Eat Out To Help Out scheme had ended, but Jamie doubted whether the place had signed up.

Paul was there of course along with Jamie's old pals Chris Tiernan and Micky. Sitting opposite him was Scott Casey, with Paul's younger brother Warren to Jamie's right and at the end was a squat bearded bloke called Thomas who Chris introduced.

Paul's form of introduction of his brother Warren to Jamie he felt had been quite unnecessary. Aged about nineteen or twenty like Paul he was a well-built lad, but Jamie could sense he felt somewhat embarrassed by his brother's remarks.

'Sat our kid next the wooden-top, coz he's got some stupid idea about being a copper. Thought you could do something useful for a change rather than doing folk for smoking a bit of weed. Having a copper as a friend's bad enough, but we're not having one in the bloody family. What say you?' he asked the gathered throng who said nothing above a mumble. Jamie assumed this was all some sort of bravado with him playing the big brother role. Ignored his brother's facetious remarks, but certainly felt for the lad.

With the limit of six in any party gathering, the restaurant had provided two well-spaced tables for four. Jamie encouraged both Scott and young Warren to share one table with him.

Over recent times Jamie knew he had missed out on a social scene being without a woman. Too often groups tended towards couples, which is absolutely fine if you're part of one. When you're not it is as if you have some disease they might catch and he found very quickly after the Kerrie bust-up you can be sidelined almost instantly.

Difficult for Paul, Chris and Micky of course in that they'd known Jamie and Kerrie and two of them had also known her bastard fancy man Joey Foskett.

Just weeks after parting from Kellie, Jamie realized he'd not got an invite to Nutty Charman's birthday bash. Then found out later how his pal for a decade or more for some reason best known to himself had invited Kerrie and Foskett the shit, as a couple.

That had hurt, it really hurt. Loyalty and friendship just tossed aside and to add to the pain he felt, not one single person mentioned it to him or offered solace. Jamie had to assume they were embarrassed, that or more than likely couldn't give a toss about his suffering.

Be the mental health issues some men these days are able to talk about. Something Jamie had never been provided with an opportunity to do.

Some of the guilty as charged were now sat around a table with him.

Jamie found it interesting that night how after one drink, in fact lagers all round, they then all moved onto soft drinks, apart from this scruffily bearded Thomas. Not Tommy, Tommie or Tom, but quite definitely Thomas.

He'd read somewhere during the pandemic how during lockdown with so many men just not bothering to shave, the feature writer reckoned they were looking better. Looking better was a case in point for one or two, but Jamie agreed with the final acknowledgement as the beards came off, never better looking.

Even the ones who were getting a lift home didn't bother to soak their whole being in alcohol. Latte instead of lager these days was good and meant they also refrained from making old school remarks about men having a proper drink. Except of course this Thomas Steward character.

He actually became a bit of a pain in the arse this bearded Thomas. Had one of those gorblimey accents and Jamie couldn't for the life of him work out if it was real or just put on for effect. Same way some dimwits try to speak posh and end up looking complete prats.

The majority like Jamie had checked the menu in advance and ordered. This Thomas was just faffing about with the poised waitress in visor waiting.

He appeared to be distracted by everything and everyone coming and going as if he dare not miss a thing. In the end he relented and grunted an order without a starter.

There was talk about some places still insisting on serving meals on wooden boards or one place according to Micky on Welsh slate. Just so impractical in normal times but right there and then so totally unhygienic.

Fortunately white china plates appeared they all chuckled about to confuse the waitress.

Once all the basic questions Jamie had been expecting about CID and CSI had been posed and answered as best he could without giving much away, he felt more able to relax.

Most of their queries to be fair were based on watching too many cop programmes on television or movies at the cinema. He did wonder if people really think *Luther* is the norm in the world of law and order, but knew his own mother certainly did.

'That runner woman what copped it?' Paul asked. 'She one of yours?'

'Not actually mine, I work as part of a team and there're people higher than me involved of course and anyway it's all being handled by Lincoln,' was his attempt at a get out.

'Asking for it, what's the betting,' was this Thomas sniggering.

Jamie ignored the remark. 'I've had to find out about the Cluny Priory recently,' he offered instead.

'Cluny Loony!'

'Exactly. Investigating crime is not all about chasing people in cars, handcuffs and blokes in white suits. In that case we had to know why. Where does the name come from, who owns it now, who used to own it, why was she taken there? Sort of place you go past time and time again but never ask the questions.' he sipped his drink. 'Not just cops and robbers.'

'And?' Chris asked.

'Just nuns place, sort of stately home at one time,' he shrugged.

'Taken there?' said this Thomas. 'Thought the attack happened there. Sure it's what I read on me phone.'

Jamie was in a quandary, he couldn't remember what had been in the press about her being found. Was this some of the stuff the DI had held back?

'Whatever,' said a bored Chris Tiernan. 'Enough murders for one night, and no doubt Jamie'll tell us all about it when it's all done and dusted. So we find out all the harsh realities
 in the end.'

Jamie had not exactly warmed to this Warren sat next to him with an empty chair between as they all had, primarily because he was very quiet. With that Thomas idiot hogging the conversation and all the police talk it was easy to see why he'd chosen to take a back seat. He appeared pleasant enough though.

Jamie had gone for the Breaded Cheddar as did Scott and all the others having starters played safe with a form of vegetable soup.

Jamie then discovered he was the only one daring enough to go for the Moldovian Pork Stew with raw meat and other animal parts all fried together. When he'd first spotted it on line he'd double checked that Moldovia had something to do with Romania.

This odd-ball meals out business was a good idea Jamie had decided, in theory. In practice with the addition of this bumptious know-all goon and the quiet one sat next to him the gathering did lack the camaraderie normally associated with his long term pals.

'I'm interested,' Thomas Steward went on relentlessly. 'As I'm sure we all are. No big secret. All over social media and that and it'll all come out in the wash in the end anyway. So, what's the odds?' He gulped his lager and made a meal out of licking his lips. 'This is in the public domain fella. People like me pay your wages and don't you forget it,' he told Jamie. Paul Miller just leaned back in his chair and peered up at the ceiling. 'Spit it out for crissakes, what's going on up at Cluny Loony?'

Sounding bored. 'What's it to you?' Scott asked as Jamie felt it best to refrain from saying what was on his mind.

'Interested matey. Need to see if he's doin' his job properly.'

'Get off his back,' said Paul. 'I sell cars, but I'm not about to tell you how much trade-in Alan Wainwright got for his old Escort.'

'And you'll tell me how much the folk in Draper Street will accept for their semi will you?' was Mickey attempting to put a lid on the conversation and the grimace exposed a set of grey teeth and more than enough gums.

'Why? You interested?'

'No I'm bloody not!'

As if he was determined not to be sidelined this Thomas went on. 'What's all this twenty four hours business?'

Jamie responded somewhat reluctantly. 'From the moment we arrest someone we have twenty four hours to charge them or release them.'

'Why d'you need so long?'

'Think of all the enquiries we have to make, people to interview and…'

'Enough now!' was Paul. 'Where we going next time Chris?' was hopefully the respite Jamie was looking for.

'Has to be different.'

'We're limited by how far we can go surely. Poor old Nutty couldn't even manage it this far. What about a meal on a roller coaster or in the sea at Skeg, we could hire a motor boat.'

'Somebody must do Bird's Nest Soup, fried Crickets and Fried Tarantulas, and I was once told Latvians serve cold soup.'

'Know lots of places like that!'

'Next up,' said this Thomas. 'Gotta be that car place down south.'

'What you on about?'

'Good place they reckon that's all cars you sit in, great burgers they reckon. I'll get their website, let you know,' he told Chris.'

'My current boss,' said Jamie. 'Is from Sweden originally and she's keen on fermented herring.'

'Sounds lovely.'

'Think she'd have any ideas?'

'Probably about food, but the place is the problem.'

'Once went to a Punjabi place on holiday.'

'That's just Indian, surely.'

The evening fortunately for Jamie never returned to the murder although the berk Thomas tried to probe more than once, but was soon put in his place.

With his tendency to hog the evening for a period they had to suffer his enthusiasm for paddle boarding he claimed he did at Cleethorpes. Sort of activity Jamie saw as a poor man's surfing and this Thomas doing it could well be a sight for sore eyes.

There was of course a chat about Cluny Loony and a few dirty jokes about nuns, which was not totally unexpected.

It was good for Jamie when on the way out Paul Miller took him to one side with Warren for a man-to-man chat.

'Think we owe you an apology, think we read you all wrong. Not his fault but Nutty had this feeling you were now a sort of enemy. Sort of got above yourself. Didn't think you really wanted to know us anymore, he says you'd just tag on in the hope of picking up snippets of wrong doing maybe.' He slapped Jamie on the shoulder. 'Sorry.'

'No probs fella, just have to be careful what I talk about, current operations have to be taboo I'm afraid.'

'Makes sense.'

'That why Nutty never came d'you think?'

'Reckon so. Told Chris his wife had something on. But you know.'

'D'you see me as the enemy?'

'Don't talk daft, matey. If we're looking for a tosser that Thomas fits the bill.'

'You can say that again,'

144

'What's his angle? Wants all the warts and all police gen seems to me.'

'He'll not get it from me, so he can pack it in.'

At one point so annoyed had Jamie become he had seriously considered nipping to the loo and calling Control to tell them about the five pint man he was with, who was more than likely expecting to jump in his car at the end of the night

'If we don't pack him in first. I'll have a word with Chris,' said Paul brightly. 'All on line anyway these days. Being an estate agent's a dead duck.'

'Where we eating next d'you reckon?' Jamie enthused.

'Forget that car place. I'm not doing a hundred mile four-hour round trip just for some stack 'em high burger. I mean, c'mon,' he said shaking his head. 'I'll warn Chris to steer clear.'

Perhaps not reporting Steward had been a good idea after all. Doing it would have most likely have placed him firmly with the enemy. Perhaps when their relationships were more firmly re-established he could do things like that without recourse.

'Problem is finding odd-ball places. Only one I've heard of round here is at The Deep in Hull. You can eat in a tunnel and watch all the fish at the same time, so I've been told.'

'Have to ask about. Need to see what there is.'

'There's quite a few bizarre places but not round these parts,' Paul advised. 'One is based on a rainforest with waterfalls, lightning, even tropical fish as a back drop. Another place I looked up, you eat in complete darkness where you get served by blind waiters.'

'Medieval banquets,' said Jamie as it came to mind. 'Might be worth a bash.' He grimaced. 'D'they still do them I wonder?'

'There's a cockney eating experience place, but it's down south, and one where circus performers go through their routines while you eat. Found a restaurant on a bus on line too.'

'Beats going for just another burger.'

Paul looked left and right and dropped his voice. 'You giving Diagne one?'

'Don't talk wet!'

'She your latest bonk?'

'Oh pack it in!'

'Bit thin still and pasty faced when I last spotted her'

'You've changed your tune,' Jamie chortled to his old friend. 'What was it you used to say, you don't look at the mantelpiece when you're poking the fire.'

'But there are limits.'

'Just coz she's ginger?'

'Don't talk wet,' Jamie told him firmly. 'And no I'm not. This is work.' What he was doing and what he'd like to do were two quite separate issues.

'Should you be talking to the likes of her, knowing who her old man is?'

'Tez Diagne is inside for your information, and this is not some hot romance this is business, police business.' His phone rumbled, and Jamie pulled it from his pocket. Another text he didn't react to and slid the phone back. His mother whittling on about how long he'd be.

'And you wanna be wrapped up in all this stupid paraphenalia?' Paul asked Warren stood there.

'Sounds interesting.'

'Like watching paint dry. Where's any sense of achievement?'

'When we lock 'em up.'

'Lock up the wrong ones most o'the time seems to me. Cock-up after cock-up, as far as I can see. According to the papers anyway.'

'Paul,' came a call from Micky stood talking to this Thomas and he wandered off.

'Stick it in your pocket,' Jamie said to Warren handing him his business card. 'Give me a call, we'll have a chat.' As he walked to his car, his phone rumbled and he opened it when he'd got in and sat down. Code Red.

24

All Gordon Kenny's planning was finally over. He'd parked the car up, spied dear Rosemary toddle off for her evening with those friends of hers as he'd done a good few times, and slowly made his way along to Mackenzie's place.

Last chance saloon had arrived as he stood for a moment down the side of the property in the darkness. Decided it was now or never for his dear mum's sake, no going back and certainly no regrets, no matter how things might turn out. Spoke to mum, told her he was doing this all for her. This was it, time had finally come for somebody to pay the price.

For once in his life he was grateful for late autumn and the darker mornings, evenings in particular and night. This was a good one, as dark as dark can be.

He knocked on the shed door, loud enough for Mackenzie to hear but not too loud so the nosey neighbours would remember it of course.

Gordon was as nervous as he had ever been in his life. His old ticker was racing along at nineteen to the dozen, thumping hell out of his chest. Guess it would have been a bad time to have a heart attack. Just about to plunge the syringe into Mackenzie and suddenly he'd got a pain in his chest. Not good but it must have happened to some poor soul. He checked his watch, pulled the balaclava down and knocked

'Come in,' he heard, and it was probably a combination of nerves and just instinct made him turn the door knob, pull and he just stepped in.

He was lucky, the ex-cop wasn't stood there with a couple of pals facing him with truncheons in hand. Mackenzie was bent down slightly holding sandpaper over a wooden block in his left hand and his other resting on the horse's back. When he half turned, glanced and stood up Gordon simply stabbed the syringe into his shirt pocket pressed down hard, instinctively grabbed at the cream shirt at the neck, pushed the lump of the man who overbalanced dropped his sandpaper and was on the floor beneath the horse. Gordon stood back enough to pull the reinforced Smartie tube from the pocket in his cargo pants, flipped open the top and carefully in gloved hand slid the dangerous syringe in, clicked the lid shut and hid it away.

Mackenzie was scrambling and fighting to get up with hands losing their presence, going numb and feet he tried to scramble up with would not respond. The harder he fought the faster the neurotoxin worked on him as eyes alert and understanding he tried to speak to shout as he sunk down onto the wooden floor.

Really was so very simple, but not something you should try at home!

Mackenzie hadn't said a word, and now couldn't as paralysis took complete control. All Gordon can remember now was his face when the syringe slid in as simply as having a flu jab. Shock, a "what the hell's crackin' off here?" sort of look on his face. Any worries he might have had about him lashing out in defence just never materialized.

No time for emotion as he took one last look down to him on the sawdust strewn floor with the horse ready to topple over. He'd not bothered to offer his victim a mere whiff of sentiment or sorrow as his one and only life ebbed away in front of him laid by the magnificent horse now towering over the bastard.

No time to stop to look around. Back out the way he'd come and closing the door quietly on the man now just lying there aware his future had mere minutes remaining.

Another thing Gordon can recall was how much sweat he was drenched in when he stepped back out, heart thumping and racing and breathing hard and fast. Like everything else he was well practiced, but nothing had prepared him for the actuality.

There in this garden at the far side of the shed out of the light, he checked his watch, went through a routine he'd practiced time and time again. At home he'd got undressed and dressed in the dark, even out in the garden at night half a dozen times down at the far end by the old compost heap.

To avoid having to scramble hopelessly about in the dark he'd bought a pair of those night vision goggles, and like everything else had paid cash. Gone to the store – amazed to discover there was a big supplier actually in the county. Cost him a few quid for this pair of Pulsar Edge he'd seen on the net. Going there to buy them was a bit of a laugh with him wearing the false beard in case of the omnipresent CCTV.

Behind the shed with the goggles still on and adjusting to the green-hue quickly stripped off what little black clothing he was wearing and stuffed it all into two of those dark green rubble sacks one inside the other, he had crumpled up in backpack he'd nicked off some geezer at the gym one morning. He'd not bothered with niceties like socks or underpants, but he was wearing long rubber gloves and a balaclava. The other bin bag he'd carried with him contained clean clothes, even down to socks and shoes and all this he quickly slipped on, stood no more than a few feet away from the nasty shit he'd just murdered, in the dark with a bit of help with light from the shed.

What he had remembered to do in readiness for killing Mackenzie was to locate suitable attire to wear as the plan was to enter the property as one man any witnesses would describe and emerge as another. Easy thing would have been to go for stuff from M&S, Next or Debenhams. Clothe himself in the sort of clobber a wife would buy for Christmas.

In the end he had discovered a range of sweats, jeans and tops by a label he'd never heard of before. Bought them from a couple of back street shops with no CCTV and paid cash of course.

This was his well-considered way of avoiding disaster just in case somehow he managed to snag his jacket or left fibres for the coppers' forensic guys, they'd not be able to link them to him.

Fortunately Gordon had never been brand aware, like some wassocks, but he does have a degree of pride. If the boffins check all his gear back at home they'll find nothing matches the murder night attire.

Same went for the black boots he'd got from a small charity shop, any footprints will never match anything he owns such was his dedication to detail.

He removed the rubber gloves and in good amplified vision with the goggles checked all around and stuffed them in his backpack.

Last but not least from the pocket of his jeans he removed a small ring box, opened and just dropped the contents onto the trampled grass.

Over the fence with clothes, footwear and goggles in the bag on his back, onto the field at the back of the other bungalows. Striding out as time was of the essence of course, then he scampered quickly along a short lane and reached his car, adorned with false number plates stuck on top of his normal ones.

Planner Gordon knew he must have left some sort of DNA back there in amongst the grass and weeds by the shed but night vision or not there was no way he'd ever have kept it pristine.

Equipment such as the goggles would have been much easier to buy on line as almost everything is these days, but he didn't want any of it to be traceable, so paying cash had always been a priority. His one concern had been with so few people using cash in this day and age he might stick out, but so be it.

The jet-black clothes, rubber gloves, bin bags, rubble sacks he'd paid cash for all at different market stalls or stores in different towns in three counties.

Even he was impressed by the time he was in his car about how well he'd got undressed and dressed, but they do say practice makes perfect. Doing it in the dark at the back garden at home seemed ridiculous at the time but now it had proved its worth.

Time was important to him but had not rushed. Knew the clever dick pathologists would work out time of death, but whatever it was there was a need to appear to be miles away at that time. Time of course was also his friend as he conveniently knew exactly when dear Rosemarie would return home, as if like clockwork.

The clock in his car told him he had well over an hour and a quarter even if she was home a bit early by some miracle of fate for once in her life.

There were at that juncture two important issues to face. One was his need to dump the syringe with its deadly remnants. Although in essence the planned route was far from straightforward he knew exactly where he was heading. Nothing had been left to chance you see. This trip he'd done four or five times, once in daylight initially and then the others at night.

What he hadn't done before of course was park his car where he'd left it that night. Gordon knew it would be asking for trouble with some nosey sod telling the coppers how he'd seen a silver Skoda parked up there three or four times and by chance had made a note of the number. Knew exactly where he wanted to leave it, but never had in practice.

The roundabout route was thoroughly annoying, but of course absolutely necessary what with all this CCTV and these ANPR cameras here there and everywhere he'd checked out and in police cars.

By this time heading north he was really up and running down the other side, almost literally to some extent. No actual posse behind him as far as he knew, but they'd get round to it all in time that was for sure.

Once away from the intensity of the act itself he knew his major priority was to get shot of the dangerous syringe for starters.

His research had been so intense he had somehow discovered there's a restaurant in LA where Pig's Blood Sundae is on the menu! They use so he'd read on line in the library, chocolate ice cream made with blood instead of egg yolks. There no accounting for taste.

Nothing so stupid for him, all Gordon had done was to consider creating his own version of Black Pudding, which of course anybody investigating all this will discover contains pigs' blood. The recipe for the delicacy is quite straight forward and as an aside he found it quite delicious for breakfast as part of his take on a Full English one Sunday morning.

The recipe of course is on his laptop just in case the clever-dick boffins start poking their noses in should the worst happen. Not just there on its own, but along with a number of other recipes he'd jotted down to create a deception.

Plan was to take a flask of it with him and pour it on Mackenzie to confuse the investigation, but as with a number of other ideas he'd ditched that one week previous.

He simply could not imagine anything would go wrong after all this planning over time, but he worked on the premis of it being better to be safe than sorry as tedious as it may have been at times..

There was a particular reason why he then stopped half way between two villages, turned the lights out on his car and walking swiftly back to the gateway of a big house where he had previously spotted a large Cordyline plant sat proudly in a huge old milk churn.

He retrieved the Smarties tube containing the syringe from his cargo pants in the backpack and simply pushed the Smarties tube and its deadly contents into the soil and pushed it well down. How long he wondered and smiled would it be before anybody discovers that?

All he had left now were the clothes he worn to kill Mackenzie. Not overly contaminated but they had his DNA.

One thought he had in the early days of all this planning was to drive well away from the area. Maybe head off up to the M62. He had been regularly tempted to just drive north and west, but then even considered pointing his car down the A1 to the south and cheekily leave his rubbish in folks' bins down there for them to dispose of for him.

Gordon Kenny had decided in the end how some roads are far too busy day and night and it'd be just his luck if a couple of bored coppers stopped him for no good reason just to break their monotony.

Both ideas had been thrown aside when he realized he would need a real damn good reason for being wherever it was when questioned. Heading to where he knew through work would most likely bring him into focus with people he'd know or knew of.

Gordon knew if he chose somewhere in particular, he needed a rock solid reason for being there, a reason which would if need be, stand up in court.

They'd both seemed good ideas at the time. Drive well within the speed limits, be courteous, and make sure he wore his seat belt – who but a complete imbecile wouldn't – and most important, don't stop for fuel.

Only worry of course were the other road users, the dopes allowed behind the wheel full of drink or drugs who might just come flying round a corner and blow all his plans and his car sky high.

Stick to B roads as long as possible to avoid the cameras was the plan in the end, and was exactly what he did. Not a long haul straight up north from Ingham and towards the steel town of Scunthorpe.

Just using B roads it took him rather an age to get anywhere near his next port of call. Gordon had gone north to East Butterwick and turned east across onto the road to Messingham. Having already ditched the first sack he was then heading eventually for Scawby Brook.

He'd scoured the area in daylight of course to find the best place to just pull up before it all became too urbanized.

Had to be careful which bin he chose once he was in Scawby Brook for real, as like all towns and cities even little next to nothing places have their fair share of low life. Not the sort of character you want to come across at night when you really need to be left completely alone to get on with important issues.

Hiding a cheap and nasty backpack was never the sort of thing you need to be doing whilst at the same time keeping a look out for some scruffy unshaven scoundrel with a can in one hand and a roll-up in tother watching your every move and wondering what's in it for him.

A month or more previous he'd parked a car a good way away and sauntered into the area he'd chosen for a look around. Chosen the day he'd had his car in for service so drove right into the area in the courtesy Nissan.

 When it came to the real thing he then only had to park up with the lights off and walk fifty yards or so around the corner, open the lid of a grey refuse bin quietly lift out a black sack, back pack in and bag back. That time of night in a quiet village there was never anybody about and certainly no chance of any coppers patrolling in this day and age.

If he were stopped for any reason he had all his excuses ready to explain why he was in this area of North Lincolnshire.

Of course his research had told him which streets would have their bins emptied on what day. Had to be a bin he could just turf a heavy duty rubble sack into, but quietly.

25

From the Scawby place it was a simple case of turning right back on the road to Brigg, but at the next mini-roundabout Gordon turned left. There was of course method in his madness route; he had to avoid Brigg like the plague.

When you've covered the route as many times as he had you'd know what's hiding round the corner. At one chosen place he stopped just off the road long enough to remove his false number plates. Threw one in a hedge, drove a mile and tossed the other into a field. They were really of no consequence as he'd copied the digits off another Skoda he'd seen when he was working away weeks before.

With each and every aspect of this business he'd done his homework meticulously. Locating somewhere appropriate in Scunthorpe was such a case.

He'd had a bee in his bonnet about place names for some years. Down in the south places have names like Wisborough Green, Southwater and Sunninghill and by the sea they have delights such as West Wittering, Goring-by-Sea, Langton Maltravers and a place named Beer. He'd not visited any, but from what he'd gathered from Google they all appeared quite posh.

Why he'd often wondered does the north have less salubrious names? Scunthorpe known locally as Scunny, plus Burnley, Blackburn, Blackrod, Bury and Burscough was a quintet he often brought to mind. Burn, black, black, burn, bury and a good cough, all reminding everyone of the dark satanic mills of their heyday.

Using back roads he eventually made his way across to the M180 at a steady pace, not too slow or fast, down to the Doncaster North motorway services and his first encounter with CCTV he was aware of.

Being where he was had no hidden dangers. In his world he knew he could religiously admit why he was there. No need at all to attempt to avoid cameras, indeed they were almost a joy to behold with him back in his everyday world miles from Mackenzie. Check of his watch told him Rosemarie'd be about home by then.

The services provided an opportunity to attempt to smarter himself up a bit with the scruffy clothes he'd chosen simply for post event. Used the toilet, washed his hands just like a regular customer in warm water openly in a sink with lashings of the liquid soap stuff and big mirrors to check.

Whole time he was in there doing his ablutions just a couple of guys, probably HGV drivers strolled in, didn't say a word, did their business and left.

Once done he was masked up and back going about his normal business as he had been doing for quite a few years. No need to hide anymore, no need to be worried shitless or constantly looking over his shoulder.

Gordon would not normally eat at that time of night and his customary food choice would see him steer clear of burgers, but who was to know his likes and dislikes? That is until he found the Burger King outlet getting ready to close up for the night.

He'd been in no mood to eat for hours with the stress his actions had created, but this was now the flip side of the coin and Costa beckoned. Ham and Cheese Toastie he'd enjoyed before at various sites with his customary English Breakfast Tea. He added a Salted Caramel Muffin to give his blood sugar a boost. With only a few people about and having discarded his mask to eat, he decided to stay a while to give more people an opportunity to be able to recall his presence.

Gordon gave in eventually to the desire for another pot of tea. He doesn't drink coffee. Considers it leaves this nasty taste in his mouth and he's sure other people get a horrible whiff of it when they get close. He did however add a naughty slice of Banana and Pecan Loaf to his bill.

Friends had suggested he try a coffee served by one of these irregular artisan coffee makers, yet others had suggested to relieve the bitterness they conjurer up, he'd need to take salt to calm the flavor. He was still not a coffee partaker.

All though fairly empty he was able to people watch and one woman intrigued and annoyed him. She had what he assumed was a coffee, hot enough for steam to be rise from a nasty cardboard nonreusable and probably non-recyclable cup. With it her companion delivered a glass of what looked for all the world to be ice, she then chunk by chunk dropped into the hot coffee.

As a non-coffee drinker he was confused. Was this what people call an Iced Coffee? If it was, he'd never imagined it would start off hot. Whatever, it was still all very peculiar.

As he tried to relax over his cuppa he did feel a degree of sympathy for Rosemarie Mackenzie and what she would be going through by then. He was assuming of course it had been her who had been the first to discover her Don dead in his shed. Fortunately as you could set your clock by her, Gordon was miles away from their group of bungalows on the outskirts of Ingham long before she'd raised the alarm.

Sat there in the warm he was assuming of course once she has regained her equilibrium after first the shock and then the grief that follows, Rosemarie will be able to make more of her life without the control freak. A demise with a prize awaiting just around the corner: freedom from the chains than bind.

He decided, sat there with a full stomach after a more than decent breakfast just people watching, how the big wig policeman in charge would have been told by now about what had happened. He'd read it can be mistaken for a heart attack or stroke until they do the bloods.

Gordon sat there with cup in hand wondering how long it would take for one of the cops to realize it'd not been something they see every day.

His mind jumped from one concern to a worry about next to nothing, to serious doubts, all of which he knew he'd have to deal with. That business with Quinlan if he was honest, now appeared to have been a mistake as it had in truth not really prepared him as much as he had expected. The silly bitch not being dead had in effect been bad news.

Next Gordon was asking himself as he sipped tea if he had been so wrong to take the law into his own hands? After all who else would bother?

Police deal with the bad guys and increasingly mental health issues. Paramedics and nurses handle the sick and damaged. Who looks after the innocent apart from over paid legal tossers? You get

Police assistance whether you can afford it or not, and everyone most certainly gets more than their money's worth from the NHS.

If you're innocent, the first question is how much.

Gordon smiled to himself. No, he told himself he had been absolutely right, he'd given his all for free to a mother who deserved it. To the one who had done her level best to give him as much as she could possibly afford. He knew of no other mother who had ever given as much.

Whatever he was suffering sat there was he assured himself, nothing whatsoever anything like his dear mother had suffered, been tormented with for years and years.

Within days, he was expecting one of the rags who call themselves newspapers to come up with some daft name to call him.

They'll go mad of course. A bunch who couldn't it seemed give two hoots for mouthy Carole, but kill a nasty copper and they go berserk. Be too late for the papers today, but the news channels will be running it already no doubt.

As tempting as it might be, he knew he had to retain his discipline and remember to call on his normal newsagent at the usual time and to buy only the paper he normally would. Gordon Kenny knew full well it would be very tempting to scoop up a copy of each of them who have published the story. Fortunately he was too cute, too in control for such a mistake.

Another thing he'd really had to be disciplined about was his mobile. He was fully aware this killing business is not as simple as it first appears. Not the messages themselves, but the location would be a big give away. He had been told at some point how there's now an app you can get that will change your location. Could have bought one of course and set it to somewhere like Sheffield and then carried on making calls when he was in Ingham and Scunthorpe and nobody would know.

Except he was cute enough to realize the techy wizards would know he'd downloaded an app. The geeks the police employ nowadays rather than take on foot patrols would unravel and unencrypt it all in no time and pinpoint exactly where he had been and when.

In the end Gordon Kenny had decided to buy a cheap-jack mobile off Hemswell Market one damp and dreary Sunday morning. One of those you can just make calls from and sends texts. Has no GPS or any of the smart phone gubbins. Bought the battered old phone for a few notes, then went to an Auto Jumble to pick up a knocked-off SIM card. One inside the other and in no time had an unregistered phone. His pucker smarty-pants Samsung he had left in a hidey hole where he would claim he'd been when he lost his phone, if stopped.

Time to dump the crappy one and start afresh. Gordon took the SIM out sat at the table and bent it about a bit, wandered off to the loo again for a pee, wrapped it in a wad of toilet tissue, plopped it in and pressed the button. Gone but not forgotten.

The coppers' spooks can do all the techy business they like but the phone won't move. Hidden, protected just waiting for him to collect.

He had endeavored throughout this whole lengthy process to remain detached, telling himself this was someone else's doing. Compartmentalizing he decided the brain quacks would call it. Not allowing his anger to spill over was an absolute priority and since then he had patted himself on the back, metaphorically of course, for having done as he was told, by himself.

On the way out in the car park fully refreshed and to a degree relaxed he just checked about for no nosey folk and dropped the phone what'd probably been nicked anyway, into a drain hidden from CCTV by a Vivaro van.

Fed and watered, happy, free and ready to go and get on with a life that would never be the same again.

26

'A Neil Raine the next door neighbour of a Rosemarie Mackenzie phoned in to report a suspicious death. The dead man in question is her husband...' DI Inga Larsson hesitated, sucked in a breath and continued slowly: 'Former Detective Inspector Donald Mackenzie,' she quickly scanned the room. 'Doubt whether any of you knew him or worked with him, but you may have heard the name,' she hesitated when nobody spoke. 'Detective Sergeants Jake Goodwin and Nicola Scoley are already on scene or damn close to it along with Sandy co-ordinating, the local doctor and the Crime Scene Investigators. DCS Craig Darke is on his way in, because the dead man is a former colleague of his, so be warned, watch your step. He'll have this done by the book, no cutting corners. I need this place setting up for a full scale murder inquiry and will need a temporary incident room organized out in Ingham somewhere.'

'Need a team for that?' DS Raza Latif asked. Just the sort of reaction Inga welcomed of course, but was worldly wise enough to know crafty Raza was offering in order to get out of the string of more mundane tasks heading the team's way.

'Thanks for volunteering,' she smiled to herself. 'Get yourself out there and find us a decent location as close as you can. Village Hall, community centre whatever. No need for a complete incident room setting up, just a base we can all use for local interviews and the like and CSI can use for local access. They'll be there some time by the sound of what we've been told already.'

'What do we know so far then ma'am?'

'Looked like heart attack when the Interceptors got there, but the doc noticed a bit of blood on his shirt. Looks like he's been given a jab of something. Actually took place in this Don Mackenzie's own garden shed. His hobby was making rocking horses. Like big rocking horses kids can ride on apparently; absolutely fabulous things so the boss was telling me, should have done it for a living rather than

159

messing about being a copper and have some lardy deciding to get his own back.'

'What we think it is. A revenge attack?'

'Well it's not someone looking for rocking horse shit is it?' She looked back across at DS Latif. 'I've messaged Jamie to go straight there, he can give you a hand finding somewhere.' She glanced down at her monitor. 'Control say there's a village hall, they'll get the caretaker there as soon as, for you to liaise with. On The Green at Ingham apparently. You'll find it easy enough.'

They'd start from the centre of the maze. That shed place in his garden, she'd just got pictures of from Connor. From there one by one the extras being added to her team would be tasked with assisting in the evaluation Mackenzie's inner circle of family and friends including ex-colleagues. Move out slowly and carefully to those his wife could identify he had seldom contact with. Then there were those he'd sent down over the years, now released from long term and seeking revenge. Looking for that one broken down damaged adult.

Closest DC Jamie Hedley got to the actual incident itself was being allowed into the back garden, lit by the lighting rigs on their tri-pod stands, and there almost hiding the shed was the big blue incitent CSI had set up, but he was kept too far back to see any more than the movement of shadowy figures.

There was no requirement for him or Raza who had wandered off in an attempt to find someone local who might point them in the right direction. Jamie had hardly got his bearings when DS Goodwin in his blue and white hooded over-suit was at him.

'Get your hands on as much tape as you can and shut off the field,' he insisted as he pointed over the fence and into the darkness beyond. Jamie could only just make out a fence let alone what might be beyond it. 'Uniform are sending enough lads to shut every entrance. Only one way in down a lane to the left apparently, and a gate off to the right there,' he pointed into the darkness. 'Nobody in, nobody out, d'you hear me?'

'I'm with Raza, boss wants us to sort a briefing location.'

'Not with all this to sort first you're not!'

'Raza's heading for the village hall waiting on the caretaker, on my way to lend a hand.'

'Just get your arse and a roll of tape into the field, what we don't need is some bloody nosey old git who insists on taking his dog for walkies and ruining the evidence. Now go!' Jamie turned and headed back to the side of the bungalow. 'And keep the ghouls and dickheads with cameras away too!' rang out after him.

A peeved Jamie trundled off leaving the flashes of the CSI photographer's camera behind him.

What a pity he'd gone for that meal. Decided to go rather than spending the evening back at his flat in Lincoln catching up with a few things and sorting through his mail. Maybe had he been in the city he might well have been handed a better job when he reached the scene or an even better one back at Lincoln Central.

His role in life or so it always seemed was not to be involved in the interesting elements, the dead body, the blood and all the clues.

At this stage in his career he had to endure all the mundane and to some extent leave the exciting bits to others. All he could hope in his relative junior role was how one day in the not too distant future he'd get the nod, get an entrance ticket to the main feature, the nitty gritty world of dead bodies.

He stopped long enough to text Raza with news of what he'd been lumbered with. Response told him Raza had managed to establish the whereabouts of the caretaker. In Lincoln going out for a meal, so it could easy be a lengthy wait.

As much as he would have loved to have just had a peep at the sight inside the shed, when somebody said it was a strange one. Jamie knew the CSIs had hardly started and didn't need him dumping annoying forensics detritus all over the murder scene, and mixing his DNA with the killer's. Just have to accept for now he'd be on the outside looking in. Again.

Anyway he knew if it was unusual it might just churn his stomach, and he had to be realistic and do the best he could with whatever task he was allocated. He'd get to see Connor's photos back at base in the morning anyway. Reeling out POLICE – DO NOT CROSS blue and white tape? So be it.

'What you doing Jamie?' DS Scoley asked when she suddenly turned the corner of the bungalow and was there in front of him.

'Shutting off the field with tape, but I'm also s'posed to be with Raza trying to sort out the incident room location, but they reckon the caretaker's buggered off into town.'

'Need the field cutting off. Foot marks go right up to the fence apparently, got more lights coming in and a bigger generator, we need to scout every inch to see which way he went.' She moved aside to let him pass. 'Tape in CSI's van,' she said and pointed down the road apiece. 'Just keep everyone away from the fence, might have a footprint forensics can send off to the National Footwear Reference Centre to get the manufacturer. Looks like only clue we've got so far.' Nicky slapped Jamie on the shoulder. 'Good lad.'

DC Jamie Hedley was a bit underwhelmed by the fact he'd had to admit to those seeking gossip about the incident, how although he'd been on site, he probably knew less about the incident than people who had never left the confines of MIT back at Lincoln Central.

He'd done his job, he was proud of the fact he had kept the field at the back of Mackenzie's garden with the help of a few bobbies bussed in for the event, free from any sort of human life. Yes there had been a dog walker or two who were initially somewhat annoyed but on receipt of explanation did calm down a tad.

There were of course the usual surfeit of odd balls wanting to poke their noses in, a few scruff bags with their mobiles desperate to step over the blue and white tape for a pic for their Twitter account, or to send off to *BBC Breakfast*.

At one point DS Raza Latif had come looking for him when he was in need of a hand to sort out the village hall, but when he discovered Jamie was doing a grand job controlling a widespread team he withdrew his criticism. Especially when he realized there was no chance of a free cuppa stuck out there in the middle of a field. With a bit of luck when the caretaker turned up he'd put the kettle on.

It was DI Inga Larsson who eventually gave him and others a further insight into the situation over at Mackenzie's bungalow, with her first briefing in the village hall, once she had persuaded the caretaker he had no need to remain there earwigging constantly, at one in the morning.

'According to the Doc it appears he was injected with something. She'll obviously know more when she opens him up this afternoon of course but in the end we'll not know for certain until toxicology is done and we know how long that can take.'

Inga was intrigued by the initial analysis of an attack considered to be calculated rather than frenzied. He'd been totally caught unawares it was assumed and in effect dead or probably close to before he hit the floor.

'Know its early days,' said DCS Craig Darke, 'but I don't suppose we have any suggestion of motive as yet do we?'

'Think if we look at who has just received a get out of jail card we might have a clue.'

'Asked for all his old case files to be sent over, boss' Jake Goodwin advised Darke, Larsson and the assembly. 'They'll be going through them back at base as we speak, with any luck. Looking at those at the end of a long stretch first.'

'Do we know if he was involved in anything else? Any scandals?' Inga asked Darke. 'You knew him better than anybody we have, sir.'

'Has to be a link to his past, somebody hell bent on revenge for the years they've spent in nick. Others will have been out and about for ages. Can't imagine there's any kind of rocking horse war.' There was just a hint of a snigger but it was torn away when he realized he was making fun of the dead.

'He always done that?'

'Woodworking yes,' Detective Super Craig Darke responded immediately. 'Rocking horses are fairly new, so I understand. Being such a big project I think he started doing them a bit before he retired, has the time now or rather he did, to spend on them. A lot of people struggle for things to do when they retire, but Mackenzie had a ready-made interest. God knows what I'll do when my day comes.'

'Not the sort of thing you want to be halfway through, when a Code Red pops up and you can't get back to it seriously for a week or two maybe.'

'Exactly right.'

'At least it's not a stupid man cave,' Jake suggested to make Inga snigger.

'Back home they'd translate that as a toolshed,' she advised

'Which is spot on.'

She shook her head. 'That's what Swedes call this man cave business of yours,' she advised. 'What we don't know at this stage of course is,' said Inga wishing to get back on subject. 'Was Mackenzie expecting a visitor or visitors?'

'No forced entry.'

'Did whoever it was knock on his door perhaps, or was the door open and our target just walked in, wham bam all done?'

'Got it from the wife,' added Jake Goodwin. 'Mrs Mackenzie said she'd left him working in his shed, didn't say anything about expecting visitors.'

'But we didn't ask her specifically,' Inga posed and Jake shook his head. 'Question. Was he expecting anyone in particular and if not, who does she think just might have called round? Regular callers maybe, drinking pals, old coppers he worked with, that sort of thing.'

'Someone he obviously upset. Person who ordered the horse maybe?'

'Add the idea to your list please Jake,' said Inga Larsson who then tapped a finger on the solitary map of the area stuck to the wooden off-white panelling by tape, with her pen. 'As far as we have been able to make out in the dark, trodden down grass trail runs from the shed door sharp left round the side almost to the fence, then stops. Area there is well trodden and the CSI guess is, he had the bloody cheek to take his time there for some reason, it's well-trod down.'

'Takes some bottle...'

'Or,' she shoved in. 'That's where our perpetrator hung about waiting beforehand.'

'I was going to say wouldn't you want to get the hell out of it a bit sharpish?'

'What reason can there be for stopping there?'

'Unless it was where he gathered himself before the attack.' Darke suggested. 'Probably right. Plucking up the courage maybe.'

'If he did, means it was an amateur jobby.'

'Could also be because he was disturbed, stayed hidden behind there.'

'Possible Mackenzie nipped indoors and this was our man waiting about until he got back?'

'Possibility and...'

'Already had a visitor maybe?' Inga nodded at.

164

'Tells me this was well planned, not some spur of the moment argument getting out of hand,' Darke popped in before Inga could continue. 'Mackenzie said it'd be a Palomino and whoever it was asked for a bay colt.'

'D'we know who ordered the horse?' Jake queried.

'Not up to now, they're going through his things, but his wife's in no state to talk to as yet.'

'Doc's given her something so she'll be out of it for a while,' the DI managed at last. 'Get it from her in the morning.' Inga looked concerned for Rosemarie before she went on. 'So far CSI have come up with precisely nothing on the other side of the fence and although the search teams have pretty much combed the whole of the field and have come up with all sorts of rubbish, it doesn't look as though there's much of a clue. Be easier in daylight of course.'

'Why did they bring in all these smoking bans? Fag ends gave us so many clues in the old days not to mention DNA, now we have bugger all.'

'Except the scrunched up coke can.'

'Cola actually.'

'Killing Mackenzie's never random, this is not a Lottery lucky dip, not with whatever was used.' She scanned the room quickly. 'Want two teams to dedicate the next twenty four hours to searching for all there is to know about him.' She glanced back at the board. 'Go back to when he was born, where and who to. I want all there is to know about him, about where and when and who with. Forget he was a copper, don't hide the truth just coz he was once one of us,' she said despite the boss's presence. 'I want to know and I need the whole grizzly story.' Her head spun to look at Sandy. 'Don't look at me like that!'

'Sorry ma'am, just…'

'Just what?'

'Well,' he hesitated. 'We dropping this Quinlan lassie, and going hammer and tongs to this old timer?' He shrugged his big shoulders as if he'd given in. 'Guess in this day and age anything goes. Be looking for his boyfriend next.'

'What else do we have about her?' she asked everybody. 'What exactly do we know about what happened to Quinlan and why?'

'She could easily have been his piece on the side, boss.'

'And pray tell me how did you jump to that connection?'

'She being Mackenzie's piece on the side is not too far-fetched, nor is her jilted boyfriend sticking a syringe in an old man she was seeing on the quiet.' Larsson had heard enough and went to speak. 'Her fella's a nurse and nurses are good with syringes. Ma'am,' he added to annoy her.

'P'raps he had an issue with Mackenzie being a copper,' said Jake. 'Kids down in London stick knives in each other over bloody post codes remember!'

'And drugs.'

'Bit of a fantasy,' said Inga. 'But what else have we got? I need the mother, the why's and wherefores. Has Quinlan got anything to do with Rosemarie Mackenzie? Is she her secret daughter or is she his big secret? His illegitimate, his legal but dumped, the one maybe he had adopted, maybe even the one he handed over for cash to illegals. Here's one for you. Is Mackenzie connected to the priory at all? You get it, I want it…warts and all. But,' she added and paused. 'Linking the two together is at best pure guesswork. The moment we get a snippet of proper evidence we reassess.'

'She her foundling?'

'Good thinking. Quinlan's thirty six and the woman's in her sixties.'

Inga Larsson could not believe what she was hearing. All these theories were based on nothing whatsoever. She put it down to tiredness, it had been a long day.

'If Mackenzie was into hard core deviant porn on the quiet,' said Nicky Scoley glumly which Inga almost laughed at, 'we can't afford to do the force a disservice or do our best to save the force's blushes by keeping stuff quiet...'

'I said,' an annoyed Jake Goodwin jumped in. 'Something just has to tie these two together.' He glanced around. 'Remember serial killers are made and not born. Somewhere in their lives they've suffered a massive trauma, quite often abuse physical and sexual which is responsible for the way they are.'

'I want their family trees,' was demanded. 'Full blown, all the who do you think they are business,' said Inga. 'Who were his parents or still are his parents, I want to know where they came from and any other kids they had. Has his wife had a kid Mackenzie

166

knows nothing about? I need his Police record torn apart cover to cover. Reprimands, anything, every bollocking he'd ever had here and up in Yorkshire. I want all about his wife and her fancy friends, his pals, who he worked alongside good and bad and I need his snouts and a list of skurks just out of nick bearing a grudge.' She looked at DS Woods added to the team. 'You head the pair delving into this Quinlan woman, and Raza you go back over Mackenzie with a fine tooth comb and take Sandy with you.' She hesitated momentarily. 'I take it neither of you knew Mackenzie.' Shaking heads gave her the answer she was looking for.

Inga just sat there as the on-the-spot briefing ended and they all trooped off back outside. Too many of them at times allowed her to do all the talking, expect her to always choose the path to go down, pick right from wrong, left from right.

Now Darke. 'Have to admit you're right,' he stated to surprise her. 'Just go easy and remember the PR. Truth will owt of course, but we need to be mindful of his wife.' *And the reputation of the force and Chief Constable.* 'I'll head back.'

She had a body count now of one and a near miss she was convinced she was not at all sure were connected. Inga Larsson kept reminding herself she'd be a long way from being at home caring for Thérése when it came round to breakfast, but knew her young daughter was in good safe hands.

If this was indeed a serial killer albeit with one botched job if that's what it was. Inga knew profilers would be called in, and she was a trifle surprised Det Supt Craig Darke had not mentioned them already. He'd been at her briefing, he could add one and one together.

If profilers did nothing more than point her in the general direction of the type of person who might have committed such atrocities, it would be a bonus. They'd look at things from a completely different viewpoint.

A clue to where he might live and what circles he worked and relaxed in would prove useful as well. In fact even though it might well turn out to be all its, bits and maybes it was a lot more than they had gathered up to now.

167

Any day soon a knock on her door and there would be stood a clever dick with a DPhil from Oxford or somewhere posh, full of smart remarks and theories.

Inga Larsson was experienced enough to know the chances are had this been a normal run of the mill murder it would most likely have been committed by a family member.

A family issue of course was still a possibility, and as the sun began to come up she knew before long in daylight CSI would source at least a degree of real evidence. If they didn't she knew she might well be in serious trouble.

By morning, the family route had drawn a blank, and as ever it was a case of waiting. Waiting for CSI for real evidence and for Mackenzie's wife to be able to provide valuable information about his and her own family.

Next up she decided was a list of people known to the first victim. That too was not over lengthy and when they'd drilled down into close personal relationships they had discovered a void where lovers should normally reside.

Carole-Anne for one she concluded, was clearly not in the least bit popular.

Most of those who had at least admitted to knowing her then confirmed what those who came previous had said. They accepted and tolerated her because their role required them to do so. None admitted being smitten by her, of being in awe or having a high regard.

Be interesting to see what comes in about Mackenzie.

27

Carole-Ann Quinlan walked slowly into a designated 'clean' room at the Lincoln County Hospital, to be met by DI Inga Larsson and her DS butterscotch haired Nicola Scoley both already sat there, masked-up waiting patiently for her.

Only sign of the trauma she had endured in the hands of person or persons unknown was a large white bandage wrapped and secured covering her head above her eyes completely.

Inga Larsson went through all her normal niceties, asking after her health, enquiring about her needs, mentioned her parents and said how charming they were and then introduced DS Scoley. Once all the procedural customer service gumph was over and done with it was time to get down to business.

'Can you please run through the events from your perspective for us please Carole-Anne?'

'How many more times?' she threw back with a look of displeasure and an exaggerated sigh.

'Just humour me if you wouldn't mind.'

Carole-Anne sighed deeply again purely for effect. 'I have a strict fitness regime like we all do of course, and part of my designated system is a regular run to provide me with the obvious cardio vascular benefits.'

Larsson had switched off almost the moment she started. Still tired from the night before she was in no mood for her nonsense. Why didn't the stupid woman just say she was running along the grassy path to the common and out of nowhere she was wacked on the head, lights out, can't remember a damn thing?

'Can we go back a bit,' Larsson suggested when this female took a breath. 'Did you see anybody, perhaps someone walking their dog, other joggers, couples out hand-in-hand for an evening stroll? Even stargazers?'

'Not at all sure I'd take notice if I had. My concentration as you'll appreciate over rough terrain, has to be absolute and actually it just happens to be something people admire about me, my ability to be immersed totally in a subject with an unusual intensity.'

'You saw nobody at all?'

'As I was saying, with my level of...'

'Do you run that way very often?'

'Sorry, I was just explaining...'

'All very good,' Larsson interrupted again. 'But we're interested in who might have attacked you. Things like how fast you ran, your cadence, lead leg preferences and the influence Tirunesh Dibaba has had on your life are really totally irrelevant to our enquiries.'

'Yes but...'

'Did you see anybody is what I'm asking...?'

'Excuse me!' Quinlan shouted and for a moment Inga almost just ploughed on then thought better of it. 'You ask a question, at least have the decency to listen to my response.' Her index finger was being pointed at Larsson. Big mistake. 'You'd not last five minutes in my world.' She really should not have done it but the DI purposely yawned and folded her arms, then turned her head to show disinterest. 'My fitness regime is an important part of who I am. I need to be on top of my game, I have a large team to run and support and obviously to compliment my endeavours I need to be fit, and being a vital cog in the health industry it is most important for people see me as being obviously the way they themselves would wish to be. One of the major issues in this day and age to my mind is unfit nurses. Fat lumps just waddling about is part of a major project of mine we have need for the NHS to introduce. Leaner and meaner is the future. If in the end it means reduced numbers then so be it. If it means we recruit from abroad because of their better diet, so be it. A so-called caring profession cannot be the mainstay of the world in which I operate any longer. You,' the finger pointed again, 'and people like you need to learn to admit when you're like a fish out of water as you obviously are right now.'

Inga Larsson remained calmer on the outside than she felt. 'We are in a hospital, but let me make one thing quite clear to you. When I was young my parents took me on holiday to Canada. Whilst there we joined a railroad journey where the train was attacked by make-believe bandits. Fortunately the good guys came to our rescue on horse-back, and what the sheriff said applies right here and now, and you need to understand that.' Larsson hesitated just long enough. 'I'm the law around here.'

'Please don't try to...'

'Enough now!' Inga took her chance before she had to listen to any more of her antagonistic nonsense. Less nurses sounded like a wonderful idea. Not. 'Tell me, have you seen anybody in the area when you'd run down there before?' Inga asked. 'Old man walking his dog, local kids up to no good, nuns, courting couples.'

'It's a simple enough question.' This Carole-Anne looked aghast at Nicky's tone. It had all the hallmarks of "How Dare She?"

'I can't say I have, but...'

'Please try harder,' Larsson insisted.

'You're not my mother!' Larsson ignored.

'What's the next thing you remember after the bash on your head?' she threw at her. Larsson sees the public as an additional policing resource she wished the UK would adopt. But without including this silly bitch.

A sigh before and after 'Waking up in here,' were for effect. 'Look,' she said firmly. 'I'm heading along, heading for this sort of overhang of trees, creating a tunnel.' She lifted her arms. 'Next thing I'm in here.'

'Not in the priory?'

'No.'

'Do you know somebody called Rita Appleyard?'

'No,' was indignant. 'Why, should I?'

'No reason why you should, just a name to crop up in our enquiries. Wondered if you might know her, heard her name mentioned, come across her in your work even.'

'What role does she perform?'

'Looks after women.'

'Are we talking medical profession?'

'Not exactly, unless you include care.'

'I tend to restrict my area of specialization to health issues, it's too easy to become sidetracked and lose emphasis on the important matters open to debate.'

'I take it you had a major role with the pandemic.'

171

'In my role of course it was almost 24/7 back then. Still have a major input to some extent of course. Not all over by a long chalk, but the sheer intensity and long hours I worked for weeks and weeks are fortunately a thing of the past, but we constantly have to be wary of the possibility of a rise in cases of course. Before you can turn round with the way some elements of society are behaving it'll be masks on and back to intensive care to deal with a spike.' She hesitated. 'Running happens to be my way of getting back to the fitness levels I normally enjoy.'

'How about the name Don Mackenzie?' Nicky asked. 'Does that mean anything to you?'

'Look,' said Carole-Anne forcibly. 'I don't think people such as you have any real concept of what it was like at the sharp end. Let me assure you,' she went on pointing. 'As bad as you might think it was, in fact it was ten times worse than that, physically and might I remind you emotionally. Something none of us who experienced it will ever forget.'

'Don Mackenzie,' was repeated.

'The one got himself killed?' she asked with a sneer as if he was a no good lump from a sink estate.

'Former Detective Inspector Donald Mackenzie who just happens to have been murdered.'

'You seriously think I nipped out from here and bumped him off last night?' Carole-Anne shook her head slightly and pouted. 'Sorry no. Reckon the nurses would've noticed. You're not having much luck are you?' she thought amusing. 'Who's next on your little list then? Anybody else I don't know?'

Larsson had to be very careful how she reacted to the sarcasm. 'How about his wife Rosemarie?' was answered with a shake of her head and the smile remained to which she added a snigger to do her no favours.

'What about Cluny Priory?' Scoley dropped in.

Carole-Anne sucked in noisily. 'Don't remember anything about it. I was out of it remember as I've already explained. Or have you forgotten already?'

'Have you been there before was what I meant? Have you ever had any reason to go there, perhaps through your work?' Larsson spoke more calmly than she felt as was quite normal for the Swede.

'Why would somebody in my position ever go anywhere near somewhere like that. They told me it's some sort of nunnery.'

'Who are they?'

'Nurses,' was offered all with half closed eyes and a grimace. 'Here,' she added as she was splaying her long thin fingers and stroking the back of her hand close to the canula.

'If you think about it, there has to be a reason why you were found there by one of the young nuns. Unless we're much mistaken, surely even you can understand there has to be a link somewhere down the line.' Inga glanced at Nicky. 'Hardly the sort of place you choose at random.'

'If you were just dumped somewhere for absolutely no reason, why do you think anyone would choose a location that bizarre?' Nicky joined in.

'You tell me. You're supposed to be the experts,' was supported by another smirk of sarcasm.

'I'm sorry,' said Inga in response to the supercilious tone. 'But surely you're the one who would know if you have had any connection with the place.'

'There isn't.'

'Do you happen to know any of the nuns by any chance?'

'Politics and religion are real no-go areas as far as I'm concerned. If I made my personal thoughts known on either issue, I'm sure you'd not be best pleased especially if I started on one constant in life, police brutality.'

'Feel free,' said Larsson, arms folded.

'No thank you,' disappointed both women. They would have enjoyed listening to more of her nonsense.

'Admitting you know a nun is hardly a major religious issue.'

'I've said all I'm going to say.'

DI Inga Larsson pushed herself up to her feet. 'Thank you.' There should have been a few lines about thanking Carole-Anne for her help, even though she'd been anything but.

'By the way,' said Scoley down to her. 'We've destroyed your cannabis.'

'We'll see ourselves out.' No goodbyes, no handshakes.

The two detectives didn't speak as they thanked the Sister walked off from the ward and out onto a corridor.

'What chance the coffee might be acceptable?' Inga enquired when she spotted a sign.

'Could do with something. Anything.'

'Cappuccino?'

'Do you really need to ask?'

'Even if it's dire?'

'Whatever,' she smirked.

Seated opposite each other close to the hospital entrance with coffees in cardboard cups annoyed Inga intensely.

'How's Terése?' Nicky asked.

'Doing well, after a dodgy start if you remember, turning into quite a character.'

'Think you were lucky with your timing. Could easy have been in Maternity when the virus was rampant.'

'Time you and Connor came round again.'

'We'd like that. I'm sure he'll take more pictures for you if you like.' Pleased Inga who mouthed a thank you.

'Silly really how it worked out. Everybody's on lockdown and I was on Maternity Leave which was pretty much the same thing. Just made life that much more awkward.' Inga took her first drink. 'Talking of the virus, it's almost as if that nasty piece of work is creating animosity for the sake of it,' said Inga. 'Please,' she said in hushed tones. 'Remind me. Did she actually suggest she's a nurse? All that 24/7 and long hours business?'

'If I didn't know better I'd assume she was. I'd think she was one of those all masked up putting their lives on the line we all clapped for. Thank goodness we've got Sally to set the record straight.'

'I've a distinct feeling all that hogwash tells me exactly why somebody gave her good smacking. No more than she deserved. How dare she after everything that's gone on for the past year? All that effort and dedication. Not to mentioned deaths,' Inga sighed. 'Also explains why she's divorced. Imagine living with somebody like her.'

'No thanks,' Nicky chuckled. 'Wonder what it is makes her such a despicable angry woman with such provocative attitudes, and why she tells lies?'

Inga grimaced and sipped. 'Didn't actually say she's a nurse to be fair.'

'Not in so many words but you mentioned the pandemic and then she tried to suggest she'd worked like some of them on the front line, how the long hours had been exhausting working in all that PPE.'

'And if it hits again she'll be putting her mask back on,' Inga just shook her head.

'I don't think.'

'With any luck we'll not have to speak to her again.'

'Wishful thinking,' Inga smiled. 'Why is she so angry? Not our faulty she's in here.'

'Think she's a vegan?' said Nicky.

'No idea.'

'It's just things Quinlan had in her mucky flat, like babaganoush, tofu and asparagus tips are never what the healthy amongst us would eat given a choice.'

'Tofu is only a posh name for curd made from soy beans and from what I can remember tastes of next to nothing.'

'One chef I saw once gave it a thumbs down and reckoned it was nothing more than just solid soy sauce.'

'Time we were off, we've got more important things to deal with' Inga said with a smile and got to her feet, stopped and turned. 'I think wake up and smell the coffee is one of the most ridiculous sayings ever invented,' made Nicky grimace. 'The vast majority of people make their coffee by adding milk, and as soon as you do the smell goes. So, in most cases you simply can't wake up and smell the coffee.'

Nicky just stood there amused and watching as Inga turned back and walked off.

'Detective Superintendent Darke and I have concluded, under the circumstances we will postpone Operation Blackstone,' did not exactly come as a surprise to the gathered throng, this was just as close to a formal announcement as DI Larsson was going to give.

In front of her the team and a few added extras who had been answering calls, making others, sifting through information and identifying possible actions, gradually looked up. They lifted their heads, some still with phone to ear. 'With the death of DI Mackenzie our resources are stretched so we need to leave the place alive and kicking for a little while longer.'

'This postponed or cancelled altogether?' DS Raza Latif wanted to know.'

'Postponed,' Inga came back. 'PHU have traced a number of vehicles going to and from the target unit and will continue to do so. With the Mackenzie matter now added to our problems we need to keep an eye on what's going on. We go in and the chances are the whole place will just implode and our sources of information may well go with it.

'Nicky,' she said across to her young detective. 'I need you to continue chatting to social services, but as before we don't say where Whyte Mulilima is, just in case a plop from their team does something really stupid.' She looked across to DS Jake Goodwin. 'We need to keep the Border Agency out of all this too, we don't need them screaming detention centre for her.'

'Just a thought, boss,' from Nicky Scoley. 'People trafficking's always a possibility.'

'Leave it all to you,' from Inga was acknowledged with a nod from the bobbed head. 'Might just be another lead into all sorts of goings on. May well have been sold a pup with all the forced marriage business.'

'Had occurred to me too.'

Inga was back to her iPad in hand, shadows under her eyes were a give-away. 'Something else we need to consider, no matter what they may find in Don Mackenzie's background, I don't care what comes crawling out or what the higher ups might think, we need to know what his connection is with Cluny Priory.'

'You think…?'

'I think we need a link between the Quinlan female in the pew and a dead Mackenzie in his shed, what think you? Was he a born again Christian, a Jehovah's Witness, Seventh Day Adventist, a Mason do we know? If he is, what's the chances there's a religious link?' Then, 'Go on,' said Inga at the sight of a MacLachlan grimace.

'Corrupt Masons can be real bad news.'

'Nuns, religion, Jesus, carpenter, rocking horse…'

Inga was there first. 'Mackenzie made rocking horses,' she smiled and enquired. 'Makes him a carpenter you think?'

'Richard and Karen were Carpenters too!' to lighten the proceedings may have been the intention but undermining a serious thought process from his immediate superior was not a good idea from a usually far more astute Sandy MacLachlan.

'Be something like that. Serial killers tend to be odd-balls and have bizarre reasons when it all comes out in the end. Almost impossible I understand to think like a serial killer, so don't bother.'

Inga knew slowly but surely a pattern would start to emerge from a process of elimination, usually of suspects, and it was always possible religion might well play a part when they got to the truth. All the atheists, conscientious objectors, the non-believers and crackpot bigots crossed off a list and there remains the killer.

If only it was that easy.

Inga had always loved a challenge. Moving from Sweden had been her first in life, then tackling the British education system and their incessant exams. Having overcome such hurdles, studying law had all been to her a bit of a breeze.

Now she faced another, and this one already had the makings of a real struggle. Inga stifled a sigh. Perhaps being woken at all hours of the night by Terése no doubt sickening for something had not been as bad as she imagined compared with this quandry.

Inga always had reason to believe how the inevitable intrusion felt by her close knit team when their ranks were bolstered by others was taken by them as an affront to their abilities particularly by Jake. His mood changed, he was less relaxed, certainly less 'cool' and he became short tempered. The upside of course being he was trying so much harder.

The silly sarcastic quip about The Carpenters was not the Sandy she thought she knew, but there was nothing to be gained by saying anything. She knew he'd probably regretted it the moment it left his mouth and she had no need to make an issue of the matter.

'Rosemarie Mackenzie. Is she a church goer by any chance?' Jamie asked. Inga waited as people metaphorically scratched their heads. Here she was doing it again, all her talking and her team were letting her.

'Best we've come up with so far is a weekly visit to a couple she knows and they knit for charity mostly for refugees who arrive on boats. That's where she was when the knife came out to play.'

'Knit what, just out of interest?'

177

'Just stuff, probably easy bits like scarves for refugees and such things.'

'Knitting covers for illegals top of the range iPhones what's the betting, although we're told they're so bereft of possessions.' Jake's sarcasm had again reared its head.

'A-ha. Could be religious,' Sandy inserted. 'Could be knitting for missionaries to distribute.'

'She was a legal secretary back in the day. No mention of religion.'

'Chap who ordered the horse from Mackenzie has been checked out,' Raza offered. 'Lee Shaughnessy, lives uphill. Finally tracked him down. His wife said he's away on a week's course in Colindale in North London, and when I spoke to him it's where he was when Mackenzie copped for it. Plus he gave me three names as alibis.'

'Another one bites the dust.'

28

Gordon Kenny knew he had to behave as normal as possible. He still had work to do and as planned had headed off out to visit a market town. Included was a steam railway he'd forgotten to visit on a previous trip there.

There was not very much Gordon could do about his situation, apart from walking into the cop shop and putting his hands up.

As it turned out it was the wrong time of year for a ride on a train unless he'd gone at the weekend on what a poster said were Covid free trains. Even the station coffee shop was closed but he did manage to spot Queen Victoria's personal coach he was particularly interested in.

He'd first heard about it on a television programme which had alerted his interest and told him previously the coach had been fully restored in order to provide a taste of 19th century Royal travel.

From there he headed into the town itself to sup at a twee tea shop full of ladies who lunch, for tea a slice of jam sponge and made a note in his diary to return to the railway in the spring.

People don't like change of course, but despite which change happens. He knew men who could remember when fizzy pop lager and clubbing was all the rage. Now the world seems to have a gym on every corner, all offering something for nothing, but only the very best will survive. Cycling and walking are the big things now with government pumping money into both after the virus. More cyclists in London now than motorists, but some dodos will still refuse to leave their four by four at home. Still worried about the need to tackle charging rhinos on the ridiculous school run no doubt.

His primary reason for going to the gym before he set off out, apart from recording his presence and being seen, was to have another thoroughly good shower to establish a pattern of behaviour. The morning after he'd washed away any remnants of his Ingham exploits down their plughole being careful to obey their social distancing rules rather than his own, he put on another fresh set of clothes.

No matter how much time Gordon spent in their showers he knew it will never ever wash away his memories. Some of his thoughts he is aware are likely to torment him and be those he'll have to confront time and time again throughout the remainder of his life.

The technology such places install will of course have recorded his attendance down to the very second, but personal eyes on was an add-on he knew would provide serious evidence if and when required.

He knew his criticism of gyms is based around the standard of the crap one he attends, and was aware how he might well have a different viewpoint were he to move to somewhere decent. Somewhere pucker might give him a serious and more suitable programme to work through, which he really had no need of or time for at present.

One day he'd decided he'd take his health and fitness a tad more seriously. Join a decent outfit like a David Lloyd Club rather than one of the here today gone tomorrow second division places doing little more for him than providing an alibi.

Choose the sort of complex that's more than a stark place for pumping iron. Make use of other facilities like tennis he'd played at school for a bit, and swimming plus an opportunity maybe to try a spa.

There were always Spinning classes going on he'd steered clear of and they'd tried to get him into High Intensity Interval Training. All things he could have a bash at in the future when he had less on his mind.

He has never been one to make use of personal trainers as he once had one going on about lactate thresholds and gait analysis. When in return Gordon asked for his advice on advance stride assessment systems and foot plant rhythms. The dope apparently had looked at him gone out. He decided the route and power system was way out of the muscle bound's league.

When the day arrives when he no longer has a need to attend, what he will miss most? Not in any particular order but probably the smell in particular in the male changing areas, the muscle creepers and all the vanity you have to wade through.

He was sure a decent facility would be more spacious and provide somewhere he could relax and enjoy.

Try as they may, the gym had never managed to con him into trying some ultra-expensive muscle-building protein jungle juice. Probably a placebo anyway. He reckons it's simply some sort of gunge downed by big blokes with ridiculous tattoos on their muscles who in truth would struggle to carry shopping home for their missus.

Sort of thing most people try just once, a bit like avocado and Morris Dancing.

There he was idly jogging away on the damn treadmill that day and got to thinking once more about the one who got away. That Carole-Anne bitch.

Every time her name comes to mind he cannot but help thinking of Ingrid.

It was Ingrid's birthday last week and once again Gordon had been vividly reminded of how intolerably she had been treated. Her only crime as far as he could see was wanting to be Matilda's grandmother. No desire greater than to want to hold the child and treat her like any wholesome loving granny would.

When all this murder business is well and truly out of the way, he'll have no need to go to the gym simply to prove his existence and location. He'll be looking for a range of workout options to suit him instead.

29

It wasn't the first time and Inga knew it would not be the last. Virtually every member of the team was mocking her by pretending to read a newspaper with the intensity of concentration when she walked into the Incident Room first thing.

Inga knew her name was in all the papers along with Mackenzie of course and Craig Darke.

Might well on this occasion have been a reaction to the team's little joke, but every now and again she does it. Almost as if it is planned to catch everybody unawares. Something totally unusual, out of the box and all smothered in blue sky thinking some would say.

Nine o'clock sharp, on the dot Inga Larsson stood out front iPad in hand ready to go. This day she just nodded almost imperceptibly at Lizzie Webb seated alone in the group of four chairs forming a sort of front row and they swapped places without a word being exchanged. All looked rehearsed but likely as not it had not been.

This was one of those occasions, the curved ball with collator directing traffic. Lizzie Webb a mere (some would say) civilian and a female to boot.

Cleverly done to keep her team at the top of their game. Inga Larsson never changed her attitudes and those around her knew what to expect. Every day the same DI in front of them at briefing time. Consistency would create detectives who are themselves consistent in thought and deed. Then right out of the blue do something off the wall, to show individuality still had a part to play in the teamwork she insisted upon.

'We have a link between Mackenzie and the Cluny Priory,' was a striking statement for Lizzie Webb to open with. 'You might well deem it as tenuous but it does create a chain all the same. Alas, so far we have not been able to establish any connection between him and our Carole-Anne Quinlan.'

With that Lizzie just whipped off the top sheet of her flip chart beside her.

'Family tree if you like,' she said pointing to the name Donald Templeton Mackenzie in a box at the top. 'We've been through all his major cases, and we threw the names of all those he put away for major crimes into the HOLMES system.' Lizzie stopped to sip coffee from a mug on a side table to whet her lips. 'One of those he put inside was a Lynda Kennedy.' Lizzie Webb nodded down to DS Jake Goodwin sat two rows back at his work station.

From his monitor Jake read. 'Lynda Kennedy stabbed her husband to death in the family home in 2003 a case where as luck would have it Don Mackenzie was Senior Investigating Officer.'

'Next,' said Lizzie. 'We asked HOLMES for links between this Kennedy woman and any names we've come across so far including Carole-Anne Quinlan, and rather than link to her, which is what we were hoping for...' she hesitated like one of those thoroughly annoying reality programmes. 'Up popped our pretend nun Rita Appleyard.'

'This Appleyard woman,' said Inga as her audience muttered. 'We all know about as being the chief nun or prioress she introduced herself as at Cluny Priory. What we already knew was this Appleyard was done for embezzlement of charity funds held in bank accounts she had opened in the names of members of staff at the charitable trust for whom she had once worked. One of those coincidentally was this Lynda Kennedy who by chance happened to work for the trust after she was released on licence.' She looked around the room just to make sure she had everybody's full attention. 'This Lynda Kennedy had previously been inside for murder,' Inga Larsson just popped in and a stony silence prevailed for a moment or two.

It was Jake's turn. 'Lynda Kennedy subsequently committed suicide by stepping in front of a London to Edinburgh Virgin train in 2016 near Retford. In the end of course she turned out to be totally innocent and Appleyard went down for it.' If nothing else they all heard the sharp intakes of breath and whispered four letters from many.

'Subsequently an inquest report,' said Inga reading from her tablet. 'Stated that having served time for killing her old man which was regarded at the time as being totally out of character, she was seen to be getting back on her feet. She had suffered very badly in prison so we understand, living hand to mouth with the garbage we all know they perpetually have in there. Then suddenly when she's trying to put her life back together, out of the blue we're knocking on her door and dragging her in to answer charges of embezzlement. Those of course turned out to be completely untrue,' Inga sighed. 'Just all too much for her, poor woman. Thought of going back to prison must have absolutely terrified her is my guess.'

'Added the Kennedy story to give you some idea what we're talking about with Rita Appleyard. Absolutely no scruples.'

'Are we to assume Mackenzie had nothing to do with the Appleyard case?' DC Steve Joblin one of the extras now brought in from the Prisoner Handling Unit to lend a hand, checked.

'Correct,' said Jake. 'Appleyard did about thirteen months of a thirty month sentence.'

'But Mackenzie could still have known her or known of her?' Jamie Hedley popped in.

'Most likely.'

'Could have gone to Cluny Loony maybe?' DC Matt Hoyles another interloper suggested.

'Unlikely,' Lizzie Webb responded. 'In fact I'm just checking dates,' she said as she thumbed through notes. '2010 Appleyard went down, I'll check the actual offence dates when he may have been around, but he'd retired by the time she was released.'

'But we do have a link,' said Inga as she turned in her seat to see more of those gathered. 'A bit flimsy I'll admit between Mackenzie and her, because Quinlan finished up dumped in Appleyard's church. Not a coincidence, or is it?' There were more than half shaking their heads.

'We have put Quinlan into the system, in fact into all systems,' said Lizzie. 'She comes up blank, not even a parking or speeding ticket.'

'How about you extend the search,' Inga suggested. 'Might be worth a try to add kitchen utensils as an added extra.'

'Always aware of course,' said Lizzie thoughtfully. 'If you input garbage it is exactly what you'll get out. All the nutters who've killed their missus with a potato peeler will just plop out.'

'Ma'am,' said Raza Latif to bring the conversation back. 'Why dump her there, unless it was for a specific reason?' he wanted to know. 'Do we think it might have anything to do with her not being very popular?'

'An understatement,' said Nicky Scoley. 'From what I've been told they hate her guts. Just the sort of female boss who gives women in management a bad name. Did she get what was coming to her, has she upset anybody in particular, has she sacked someone maybe and this is he or she getting their own back? Quite possibly,' she added answering her own question.

'How about this is connected to her bragging about being involved in Covid-19 cases, when she absolutely was not?'

'Somebody'd dearly beloved died and hears she's claiming all sorts you think?'

'Always possible,' and received a nod from Nicky. 'But we have to ask, why in Cluny Priory?' Inga asked.

'If she'd just been dumped in a lay-by, then there'd be no link to Appleyard and through her to Mackenzie.'

'Nicky,' said Inga. 'What about chat lines, on-line dating or just fishing for the man of her dreams on line?'

'Might as well be chasing moonbeams seems to me,' Jake chimed in.

'Luke Stevens' analysts on his on eTeam have looked at it every which way,' said Nicky. 'Nerdy as heck they might be but they've had her laptop, her work PC and her phone. Last I heard from Orford and his techy-wizz team, Quinlan is all work, work, work and look at me, me, me. Be the sort who are absolutely gagging to be liked morning noon and night.'

They all knew about Orford. Bespectacled nerdy Adrian Simon Bruce Orford's names spelt out ASBO and he was without any doubt a computer-geeky saddo of the first order and butt of many a fine joke. But having said that, seriously damn good at his job.

'You want to poke your nose into the encrypted part of the internet,' said Jake Goodwin. 'Inveigle your way into the dark net using secret forums, then ASBO's seriously your man.'

'Problem is now,' said Inga. 'Our Miss Quinlan is being discharged and we're told heading off up to Bridlington to stay with her parents on the coast, so face to face again is not on right now, unless we have something serious to discuss with her.'

'I'd rather not,' Nicky slipped in. 'If you don't mind.'

Over the years Inga had spent many a lonely hour entertaining herself with the psychology behind crime, particularly the violent genre.

In those quiet times in her old flat overlooking the Brayford above and beyond the joyful revelers, the eaters and drinkers and intoxicated students, she had read more than a few theories about detecting serial killers.

This was long before she had met Adam by chance as part of a murder enquiry.

She'd read how really successful detectives had in a number of cases - some very high profile, managed to get one step ahead of the perpetrator. First job apparently was to look at the location of the crime scene. Not all the detritus the finger-tip search always produces, but where and when.

All very well with obscure dumping grounds and deserted locations. A woman clinging to life sat in a pew discovered early morning and an ex-cop stabbed to death in his own shed in the evening.

If they truly were linked, was this the early sign of a serial killer? If it happened to be the case Inga knew from conferences she had attended on the subject there would be a trigger. A bully of a father possibly, an alcoholic mother, taunting beast of an elder brother or bitch of a wife would be behind it all.

Something somewhere in the killer's distant past had set the hares running and now people were paying the price.

What on earth could the link possibly be? How could they begin to be ready and plan for the next one based on such information? Or was it indeed a clue in itself? Had the places been chosen at random specifically to confuse? Did the killer know Inga would be looking at a link between the two locations and therefore had made them completely unconnected on purpose?

Did it mean the killer was cleverer than her? Choose odd-ball locations to create doubt in her mind, and thereby hide any clues to the next place.

Dare not mention it in present company, but did the killer know her, did he know how she performs and acts under certain circumstances? Were her systems that predictable?

Back in her poky office, time for photographs to appear on line from the CSI photographer Connor. Pretty much as she had seen with her own eyes that night, until she looked closely at Connor's photo of a gold ring and in particular the close up of an engraved inscription on the inside: CA+A. She called CSI to ask about the ring which she was advised had been discovered in the grass at the rear of the shed.

'Excuse me,' she called out when she looked at the next slide on her screen. 'What's Quinlan's husband's name?' she waited as it occurred to her this could well be the real evidence of a link between Quinlan and Mackenzie. Maybe just maybe some of the frivolous suggestions had not been far off the mark.

'Alistair,' Nicky Scoley called out after scanning the board and Inga ushered the DS to join her.

'What is a ring with that on it,' she pointed at Nicky's partner's picture on screen. 'Doing in Mackenzie's garden?'

'Can't be...no she was...what's going on?'

'You tell me,' said Inga as she sat back and one by one she encouraged the team to troop in to check out the photograph.

An hour later Nicky Scoley was head down banging her fists on her work station. 'For God's sake!' she shouted as she lifted her head and blew a breath up across her face. 'Wondered what happened to that,' she said. Looking across at Inga she sighed and shook her head. 'When we talked to stupid Quinlan yesterday she'd already realized her ring was missing.'

'Why didn't she say something?'

'Assume she'd asked the nurses but why on earth not ask if we had the damn thing?'

'That's a connection, must be.'

'And the best bit, when I asked where she lost it she said she didn't know as it's always on her finger,' Inga had screwed her eyes shut. 'Says it's what you do to show you're divorced put the wedding ring on the other hand.'

'Since when?'

'She's a bloody strange one.'

'More than bloody that,' Jake added.

'When I asked her, she still claims she doesn't know who Mackenzie is, never heard of him until it was on the news, no idea where he lives.'

'Do us a favour eh?' Inga said to Scoley. 'Get photos off Connor, nip up to Gainsborough and ask Rosemarie Mackenzie if it means anything to her at all, just to cover all bases.'

'But the inscription…'

'Can we just double check, please?' was insisted. 'Darke boss is watching remember. Cover all bases.'

30

With DS Jake Goodwin riding shotgun Larsson took Jamie Hedley into a small committee room at the far side of the building on the pretext of discussing something well away from prying ears and eyes.

To be fair she did her best to make it all look less formal with coffees all round although she did not go so far as to provide cake or biscuits. After general chit-chat about the case, Inga suddenly got down to business.

'Did you know Quinlan had taken drugs before the report came in?' she demanded.

Jamie Hedley looked completely bemused and confused, and gave the impression the question had caught him by complete surprise. What was the look from Jake Goodwin all about?

'You maybe, erm,' he offered to Inga Larsson. 'DS Goodwin maybe,' he dared. 'Or…' he frowned and sucked in a breath noisily.

'Not us. Who?' Inga threw at him. 'I'm asking you a simple question. Were you told she'd taken ecstasy? If so, who was it?' she demanded and tiredness provided her voice with a note of exasperation. 'Give me a name,' she almost shouted, a quite unnecessary action in such a small room. 'Come on, out with it,' was sharp.

'Can't remember…but…' Jamie just sat there utterly bewildered at the tirade from his boss. This was not at all what he was expecting. He wasn't making it up. 'I'm sure somebody somewhere said she was drugged up…'

'Out running when she was in that state? You serious?' Goodwin demanded, although he knew from reports she could well have taken the stuff the previous weekend. 'Might be a plodder, but don't be silly.'

Jamie Hedley had his head slightly bowed and cupped in both hands. 'I'm just saying the reports said she'd taken stuff and perhaps somebody mentioned it early days. With so much going on, I can't recall and I've not been here. P'raps it was someone back in Gainsborough,' he shrugged slightly. 'Maybe?'

The drugs Quinlan had in her system when she was attacked he felt he already knew when he read the report, or had he just got hold of the wrong end of the stick?

Why him, why was he having to face all this? What about the others, surely they all felt the same, knew the same. He guessed they'd been told but he'd had to read the report.

'Come on,' Goodwin insisted.

'I can't...remember,' he admitted.

'It's what we're paying you to do.'

'Well think!' was close to shouting.

'I am,' he admitted as sweat began to run down him. Jamie's head came up and he raised both hands in a gesture. 'So I didn't, sorry my mistake, got confused, sorry I just....'

'Shows how wrong people can be about someone. As you know I've got two team members away on courses and PHU put your name forward to help out, as and when.' Inga stopped to shake her head. 'Offering you to us must have been a gag to get rid of you. First you cozy up to that Diagne female, know all about the Cluny place but don't say a word, now this. Climb the ladder? That's a joke. Wonder you've got the gumption to climb out of bed.' Inga folded her arms and sat back.

'Yes she did have drugs in her system,' Jake said firmly and pointing a finger at Jamie. 'Could easily just be remnants from days previous. Did this come from the Diagne woman you're sweet about by any chance? You been taken in by her?'

'She know something she shouldn't?'

'I don't know what to think!'

'Are we seriously suggesting this Diagne woman gave Quinlan a good bashing for no reason?' DI Inga Larsson just pushed out a weary breath and allowed her head to roll from side to side. 'What she doesn't know about ecstasy, coke, heroin and all the rest of the skunk she deals in and probably laughing gas too, isn't worth knowing, and you,' she pointed at Jamie. 'Let her walk all over you.'

'Ecstasy is on the increase,' said Jake very soberly. 'Now the drug of choice amongst the young and they're marketing the stuff like people do with mobile phones, right to the vulnerable who'll fall for it all. Upped the active ingredients and moved into bars and even coffee houses. Mainstream in most European cities these days.' He stopped momentarily. 'And who do we know who's into it in a big way? And who had all sorts stuffed down her throat?' He sat back. 'I rest my case,' he said.

'But according to you she's off all that?' Inga posed to Jamie.

'Fat chance,' was Jake. 'She's causing chaos maybe,' he said. 'You're wallowing in obfuscation and she's laughing her socks off. We're talking to you when we should be bashing her door down.'

'Hang on ma'am,' said Jamie to his boss using a tone he wouldn't normally dare to consider appropriate such was his mood. 'We'd already found Quinlan before I spoke to Tamara. I was only over there because you sent me.'

'Oh Tamara now is it?' Jake laughed and Inga smiled. Law and order was the fulcrum around which his whole life appeared to revolve and Jamie almost reacted to the remark. This was Goodwin on his hobby horse, this was what it was all about. 'How about if Quinlan's one of her dealers or a runner or some such nonsense?'

'She didn't know Quinlan,' Jamie almost shouted but managed to control himself. 'Diagne heard about it on the radio or on line or somewhere.'

'Or so she led you to believe,' was Jake sarcasm he added with a grin. 'And like a bloody fool you took it on board. Stop being so bloody naïve man!'

'Somebody definitely mentioned she'd probably taken drugs, After all every car they stop these days smells of cannabis' Jamie offered. 'Could be anybody.' He squeezed his temples with his hand as if the action would push out more information. 'P'raps not part of a report, just somebody somewhere mentioned her being a druggie maybe. Did somebody assume that, or made a casual remark and I misheard and took it as being real, assumed she had.'

'Not from round here,' Jake struck back. 'We didn't mention drugs until the report came in about her urine. Who apart from Diagne woman have you been boozing with?'

'Nobody really,' was all Jamie could offer. 'Not *been* with anybody if that's what you mean. Just a meal with a few old friends and…'

'What about one of them?' Jake butted in.

'They were onto me like people do, wanting snippets of insider information, all the gory detail like the ghouls slowing up on the motorway to gawp at accidents or take selfies. Didn't say a word, just stuck to the line we've given to the press like I'm always told to.'

'You know these drinking pals well?' Inga posed.

Jamie grimaced. 'Bloke there I've never seen before, maybe.'

'Who?'

'God knows.' Jamie plundered his memory bank furiously with no luck.

'Who would know?'

'Mates I've met up with and …Thomas,' was suddenly coughed up by his memory bank. 'Some guy called Thomas.'

'Tell me about these mates of yours,' Inga Larsson insisted. '

'I knocked about with the same few friends for years. Then with a few big investigations I got involved in with PHU and the courses I did before I joined you, I missed out on our weekly quiet pint for a good few months. Pubs were shut with the virus. Then I moved up here, we've been busy time has passed and with everything going on and moving I've sort of lost touch. Went down to the Spread Eagle one night to meet up with them as usual. Wondered if one of them might know what's going on at Cluny, only to find they'd moved on coz the place is going down the pan like so many already have. Be a care home before you can turn round.'

'And if they weren't there how come somebody mentioned Quinlan being on drugs? Who else you been about with, met up with. Or was it you brought up the subject?'

'Weren't at the Spread as I said, then I just happened to be driving past a motor dealer one of my pals works at and decided on the spur of the moment to stop to have a word. He told me they'd got fed up with the Spread and were all meeting up for odd-ball meals these days and…'

'Odd ball meals?' Inga asked with a helping of curiosity.

'What's one of those when it's at home?' jumped in a sniggering Jake.

'They set up meals out in odd places, quirky things like in a swimming pool one time, actually sat at a table in the kiddies' pool.

Go to places doing different foreign food, not the usual Chinese and Indian or burger rubbish. So I joined them last week for a Romanian.'

'Not very odd-ball is it?' Jake chuckled sarcastically. 'Romanian.'

'There's a place somewhere abroad who serve chunks of meat you eat with your fingers, and there's even one for women only apparently. Problem round here is there's not many. Found out this week there's a restaurant in Moscow staffed entirely by twins and there's a place down London where they only serve cereals.' Jamie had to chuckle. 'Called Cereal Killer.'

'Very funny.' Jake looked at Inga. 'Fancy a meal out boss? Got Puffed Wheat on the menu, probably best cooked medium rare,' he obviously considered amusing.

'This what you're doing?' Inga enquired. Was this seriously what one of her team was doing in his spare time?

'Just started, but as I say there's not many round here.'

'And this guy you mentioned?' from Jake brought him back down to earth. 'This Thomas.'

'Not met him before one of the lads brought him along. An estate agent, and seemed a bit of a berk to me. Got on my nerves like, kept asking questions about the Quinlan case, might have been him said she's on stuff.'

'And he is who exactly?'

DC Jamie Hedley pulled out his phone while the other two both sat looking at him with Inga sipping the last of her coffee. He phoned Paul Miller and found the whole experience embarrassing with his two bosses hanging on his every word. Wanted to sound casual for Paul and he in turn wanted to chat being unaware of Jamie's situation with the pair of more senior officers sat across the table.

'His name's Thomas Steward,' he told Inga when he put his phone down, and Jake scribbled the name down. 'Works for Irvine Carruthers the estate agent. One of the other lads brought him along, no doubt knows where he lives, want me to…?'

'Job for Sandy,' said Jake Goodwin. He glanced at Larsson. 'Get him to have a word,' Inga nodded her agreement. 'Anything else?' Jake threw at Jamie. 'What else d'you know, what else you been telling these mates?'

'Diagne told me her old man has got cannabis farms on farms,' he sniggered. 'Cannabis farms in barns on farms she reckons if you get my drift.'

'Why d'you keep everything to yourself?' Inga demanded.

'All I know. Didn't want to start asking questions and she gives me the heave-ho. Could have just been her spinning me a yarn. I've only met her twice.'

Inga saw the look on his face. 'Go on, tell me more.'

'I'm the new boy on the block.' He glanced at Jake, then turned back to Inga. 'She tells me some cock and bull story, you organize a raid and it's all a load of cobblers with her at home laughing her socks off, what a ....will I look?'

'But you could've still told us,' Jake advised. 'We're a bloody team or haven't you noticed?'

'D'you know where?' was answered by a grimace and shake of his head. 'Brilliant.' Inga looked at Jake. 'Job for the drugs lads,' and she picked up her notepad while they waited. ''That'll do for now,' said Inga suddenly. 'We'll get Sandy to take this on as a little job and one for Robbie Tudor to give PNC a whirl. See what Sandy can come up with on this estate agent fella, see what his past comes up with.' The pair of them were on their feet, jackets swirled round. 'You remember who mentioned drugs I have to be the first to know,' she told Jamie still sat at the table. Inga stooped to lean down to Jamie. 'Not a word to anybody about this. Understand?' Jamie nodded. 'In the meantime I've got to think what I do with you.' The pair of them were out of the door and off downstairs.

Jamie Hedley just sat there for a few moments as if he had been hit by a whirlwind. He picked up his mug for the first time and the coffee was cool and from the canteen, better than nothing, but only just.

Here he was struggling to hold down a temporary post in MIT whilst all around him coppers were cracking all sorts of cases. Murders and people causing mayhem and even stuff like that EncroChat top-secret comms system operating all over Europe had been penetrated months back.

Tonnes of drugs, guns and mega million in cash all discovered under cover of that lockdown. What was he in trouble for? Forgetting who told him that woman could have been on drugs.

What did Jake have against him, was it just his link with Diagne?

Knew he should have said something about his troubles, but would they really be interested in his problems?

To even get where was today at the bottom of the CID pile he'd had to endure the need to revise from set law texts and sit exams which tended to feature criminal scenarios. This he had been required to carry out whilst still out and about doing his shifts on the streets of Gainsborough.

His current boss Larsson he knew with her top law degree had only done the fast track three month training stint, without the need for years in uniform as he had.

Jamie realized all that he had achieved by getting into CID could very well suddenly be in tatters and there was a likelihood he'd be back on the streets. With that would come the real possibility of having to live back at home.

A call took Inga Larsson upstairs to the eTeam. One of the techies explained how when Quinlan was in hospital unconscious, Jake Goodwin had provided the geeks with her mobile to check for a possible stalker or social media abuse. With her unconscious he was unable to seek her permission but even so on his instructions a list of her calls had been produced by her service provider.

The vast majority of those calls had obvious connections to her work and family, with nothing untoward to deepen the mystery and the phone had been returned to her belongings in hospital.

By sheer chance when Nicky Scoley had carried out a search of Quinlan's apartment she discovered a phone in her kitchen drawer hidden seemingly on purpose, underneath two grubby tea towels.

In bed that night, in his old bed where he'd spent a good thousand nights Jamie got to thinking to himself which was part of his problem.

Having lost his partner and child to another he realized he never talked to anybody other than to Jamie Hedley any more. Just nobody to bounce ideas off, to simply have a natter with, chat casually to. At work yes, but all work or news related but nothing whatsoever about him, his life, hopes, dreams and fears. His worries.

To an extent Jamie was aware what he considered to be his life and his future had to some degree just collapsed in on itself.

He sat up in bed looking all about in the dark. This was it, this was what his entire life amounted to, a life he'd now probably cocked up good and proper.

31

DI Inga Larsson shunted Jake Goodwin into her office the moment they were back with the Major Incident Team.

'I've got some news for them all, but first. How about we put Jamie to the test? Get him to get what he can from this woman of his about the cannabis business. In the meantime we get intel on the farm owner and maybe organize a night search.'

'You going the whole hog with some two-bit cannabis raid? Haven't we got more important things to do, boss? We pull in a chopper and they come back with a load of guff about it being full of dozing cows we'll not be flavor of the month around these parts.' Inga went to speak but Jake had more to say. 'Not him please!' Jake retorted. 'Do we really want to risk the cost of a copter with thermal imaging cameras on just Hedley's dubious say so?'

'Not all guns blazing. Get the drugs lads to do a long distance snoop. Have a creep round at night, use a drone. Are the lights on, how warm are some of the barns?'

'You want me to get him to ask lady Diagne?'

'Do that first.'

'If you want my honest opinion,' Jake was giving it whatever. 'Hedley's more used to dealing with shoplifters to my mind. Was his move here a step too far? It's a giant leap for someone tied to his mother's apron strings to go from burglary to dead bodies.'

'You thinking he's a mummy's boy?' Inga chortled.

'What I've been told. Why, don't you?'

'Truth is Jake, what he's doing makes sense. He's only living back at home on a temporary basis while we're on this case. We've used him before and remember he's been divorced and got a kid.'

'And that makes a difference?' was smirked.

'He's helped out before and in the past he's done really well. Why I asked for him this time,' she told her Sergeant and with that threw her door open and strode into the middle of the incident room. 'All change!' she shouted to stop the whole team in their tracks. 'Just come down from ASBOs little empire. Guess what? Looks like our little madam just happens to be up to her eyes in drugs.'

'Who we talking ma'am?' a confused Jake checked as he reluctantly sat back down as others whispered.

'Quinlan, that's who!'

'Surely you mean Diagne and her old man,' Jamie dared.

'You had Quinlan's phone put through the system for all her back calls, remember,' she reminded Jake. 'Nicky,' she looked at. 'You came across what looked like a burner phone in her kitchen as well as cannabis and Jamie here got himself involved in a cuckoo set up with some old guy his mother knows.' Inga Larsson hesitated as they all waited. 'Guess what? As strange as it seems it looks like they're all connected. According to ASBO and his geeks the algorithms in the program cross match and three phones have pinged up some of the same numbers. The vast majority are on Quinlan's burner and on one belonging to that Knapp they're sorting out downstairs. He's a notorious PHU suspect and is certainly involved in dishing out drugs, now doing it in old folks' front rooms or so it seems.'

'That means…' was as far as Nicky Scoley got.

'Exactly. Now we know why Quinlan was attacked,' and the self-satisfied look was very evident on Inga's bright face before she broke into the silence. 'She's been a naughty girl, looks likely she upset the overlord and got punished. Jamie,' she turned to and pointed. 'I want you to concentrate on Diagne.' She spotted the look on Jake's face. 'I know it's a long shot but suddenly out of nowhere we have this Quinlan woman taking a bashing, that old man you know…' she pulled a face.

'Fish Pye.'

'Thanks. Being used by the druggie bastards including fatty …er…'

'Chunky Knapp?'

'Thank you,' she responded to Jamie with a grin. 'Chunky Knapp on her phone plus we have this Diagne woman taking an interest in you, or rather probably taking an interest in what she thinks you know. Here's the big question. This a Tez Diagne set-up while her old man's inside do we think? This him ruling the roost from his cell?' Inga posed and looked around the room. 'Quinlan tried to rip him off once too often maybe, and one of his scum boys has come down heavy on her.' She pointed at Jamie again. 'That's your priority from now on, keep close to Dennis Norton over at Gainsborough and see what they discover about the cuckoo set-up and play sweet nothings with Diagne.'

The look on Jake Goodwin's face told he was not at all happy with her plan.

'Ma'am,' Jake said as he got to his feet and ushered her back into her office. 'You sure about this?' he asked Inga as soon as he closed her door firmly.

'What's the problem now?' she demanded. 'You know some other way to get in with Diagne?'

'No, but...'

'But what? Who else can chat to her, who else knows the old Pye guy well enough he might tell what he knows, and how much experience does Jamie have to be able to deal with the ins and outs of something like the Mackenzie case? I'm giving him what he has experience of, what he's used to amongst people he knows,' she hesitated. 'Amongst people and a place he knows, and living with his mother pro tem sounds like a damn good idea to me.'

'Just don't think he's up to it. We've still got that issue with the drugs remember.'

She pointed at her sergeant. 'One thing you need to understand Jake is, our priority has to remain the murder of Mackenzie. But luckily for us Jamie's living with his mother because he knows Gainsborough. Remember, if he wasn't over there we'd not know about this cuckoo business, a possible link to Quinlan, and we'd have missed out on the link with Diagne. There's no chance he can bump into her in Marshall's Yard if he's hanging round the Brayford.'

Next day Jamie was pleased to be away from the MIT Incident Room and spend his time back in Gainsborough. He was tying up a few local, what he considered to be quite unnecessary odds and ends for Jake Goodwin first up, then had to check on Hector Pye. Late morning things took an even better turn when DC Nicky Scoley called to ask him to join her for a spot of lunch.

It had all started according to the DS with the murder of a pig man out near Market Rasen, when Nicky and the DI who is now her boss had recourse to interview a local woman for background information at niche tea rooms she owned.

It was the start of a series of meetings they enjoyed from time to time, in the main normally at the end of a case. Just the two of them going over events, and was as such a Swedish arrangement Inga called a fika. Coffee, cake and chat. Usually back home when she visited she'd have a treat, probably a sweet saffron Lussekatter bun her mother would have come up with.

Somewhere in the back of her mind Nicky had wondered whether the boss was in truth using such a close arrangement to ask favours of her, as she was unaware of any similar relationship she had with other officers under her command.

Now she had asked the question. Inga Larsson needed to know what was wrong with DC Jamie Hedley. "Be a good girl," she'd suggested. "Buy him a pint and see what you can find out for me. He comes well recommended by PHU, and he is just what I'm looking for but there's something Jake's not happy with."

Nicky knew there were stories being put about, in the main she gathered from others in the Prisoner Handling Unit who dealt with low level crime who were apparently just very jealous of the opportunity currently being afforded to Jamie.

Were the stories true or were they just nasty gossip some people appear to wallow in at the discomfort of others?

A table outdoors at Costa in Marshall's Yard with a toasted sandwich and Americano each and Nicky just allowed the conversation to meander naturally for a while. She knew she had to tread very carefully, not appear to be prying and yet also not go back to Inga empty handed.

Talking to Michelle who had also heard bits and pieces she hoped now she had a clearer picture of what the issues might be.

'You ever been to a quirky restaurant?'

'Quirky?'

'Something off-beat away from the norm of Chinese or Indian.'

'You mean foreign food?'

'Not entirely. Went with a few friends to a new Romanian place, but there are all sorts these days.'

'Such as?'

'Discovered one that used to be public toilets' made her pull a face. 'One serves no meat, no gluten, no sugar and no alcohol.'

'And they get customers?' she chuckled.

'Apparently. Came across one serving an ostrich egg as the centre piece of a big anti-vegan fry up.'

'Where's that?' Nicky asked.

'None around here, most of them are down in the smoke. D'you like avocado?'

'Not really.'

'Pity. There's a place in Amsterdam which sells only avocado, even have avocado burgers.'

'How odd.'

'Not as odd as the price. Fries are six quid!'

'And there's me thinking Connor and I might try one of these places.'

'Coming over here so I read,' made her chuckle.

'You still live at home?' she enquired very casually although she knew was not exactly right.

'Yeah sort of, but only while I'm on this.'

'No woman?' According to the grapevine she understood he had moved out and set up home with some female at one point. There'd even been a suggestion he was divorced.

'Bin there done that,' he responded and Nicky kept her gaze on him. First there was a sigh. 'Didn't work out,' he added after a few moments.

'That's a pity.'

'Not all it's cracked up to be,' he told her. 'Just,' he said as he shrugged. 'One day it's fine, next day it's all gone for a ball of chalk. There's a new boy on the block so to speak. If you get my meaning.'

'Must have been hard to take.'

Was this what Inga felt affected Jamie at times, when he appeared to lack concentration? Mind too full of what might have been and what he'd been through.

'Tis when your mates take the piss all the time about being a cuckold and they're socialize with your ex and her boyfriend lover.'

'You serious?'

'Yep.'

'What's that all about?' Nicky asked and guessed this was where his problems lay.

'I'm on nights and she's laying some cheepskate. I get home and it's like just a normal day. Months it went on, bloody months but I'm not to know somebody's been warming the bed before me.' Jamie grasped his head with both hands and peered down at the table and seemed to Nicky to be in trouble.

'You okay?' she asked with concern and held his arm gently.

'Just still gets to me…thought of it, there's me…' he sighed deeply. 'Sorry,' he said after a few moments of silence as his hands dropped down and his head came up. Hints of tears in his eyes.

'Excuse me for asking,' was gentle and closer. 'But what's the situation now?'

'She's still in the house, moved the low life in she's shacked up with, and I'm giving her a tidy sum to pay the rent.'

'She's living with somebody and you're paying the rent?' was gasped.

'About the size of it,' he shrugged sat there with his hands around the cup.

Nicky imagined any such break-up must be like grief. Everything the poor sod had hoped, had planned and worked hard towards just destroyed on a whim.

Folk more than willing to offer gossip, contrived updates on how his ex was doing would have been painful and was probably how the PHU lads had got hold of scurrilous titbits. People with big mouths sticking their oar in with unnecessary and often vile gossip.

'Got really bad at one time with her running up debts in my name. Had to change bank accounts even had a solicitor record I'd changed my signature on a specific date to stop them forging it on credit agreements.'

'You must be joking.'

'All quiet now, though.'

'Where d'you live normally now?'

'One bed apartment back in Lincoln. Newark Road.'

'Oh I see,' she said and Nicky sipped her coffee. 'While you're doing Gainsborough, I take it you decided it's easier with your mum?'

'About the size of it. Boss wanted me over here with all the stuff going on with Cluny. Difficult to respond quickly from the city and saves on petrol hammering it back and forth. Means I can socialize if need be.'

Nicky doubted she would be able to inveigle a great deal out of him, but if the stories were true he really had been taken for a ride.

'Any thoughts of getting back together?'

'Two chances. Fat and no,' was all he said but the blonde knew from her job not to jump in feet first.

The story the PHU lads were rather keen to tell was the unseemly fact of Jamie having been duped into getting Kerrie pregnant, or assumed he had. Truth was or one rumour going the rounds at least happened to be, about the child quite possibly not being his.

'What d'you think of MIT?' Nicky asked to change the subject. Did he know how his sweetheart had conned him she wondered sat watching him sip his coffee. Was this decent looking guy living under the misapprehension he was in line for a card on Fathers' Day?

'It's good, sort of what I thought it'd be. Interesting and exciting even, but hard work.'

'And some.' Nicky drank a bit more.

'Great deal of satisfaction, and a good boss. Trouble is the way things have worked out with all the twists and turns I'm not sure I can keep pace with what's going on. One shock after another. Being over here makes it difficult to keep up with what's going on back at Central.'

'Keep your eye on the ball, you might not get another chance like this.'

'How d'you mean...?' Jamie asked before he supped once more as if his coffee was a crutch. 'Been borrowed before but only for a particular case each time.'

'Your chance to put yourself in a good light. If I were you I'd give it one hundred percent. Next time we need someone new, you never know your luck. More than likely it's going to be an average being moved out and one good one in.' Nicky drank the remainder of her coffee. 'What other...quirky places you found to eat?' She and Connor had a regular meal out at different places and something off the wall might make a real change.

'One with circus performers going through their routines while you eat. Found one being operated inside a prison where they are using it for inmates to gain experience before their release.'

'Inmates work there?'

'Apparently.'

32

Since he's got rid of Mackenzie, Gordon Kenny had been to the gym every morning before he started work. During his planning stage he'd noticed one of the fitness places was said to be open 24/7 and wondered about joining in order for him to nip in there after he'd done for the fat git. In the end Coronavirus popped up and gyms were closed as part of Boris Johnson's lockdown.

Decided in the end routine was best, provide more acceptable evidence and history of his lifestyle. He did however go to his normal gym once they were allowed to open again after he got back from the M180 and breakfast, but only really to record his attendance. He was in no mood for a serious workout but it had provided him with an opportunity for a thoroughly good shower.

He was pleased he was able to take advantage of a thorough clean because increasingly that particular gym annoyed him. That day probably due to his inner worries the tatty posters just got to him. The stupid *Eat Big, Lift Big, Get Big* and the *If You Fail To Prepare You're Preparing To Fail* garbage he really wanted to rip from the walls and replace with how most people operate: *Work out, shower and get out*.

Some of that nonsense plastered on the gym walls reminded him too much of the pointless posters in hospitals the likes of Quinlan were responsible for. All the remnants of social distancing rules and enhanced cleaning procedures in the gym he appreciated. They'd installed all those sanitizing stations and some aerobic classes in good weather had been set up in the outside yard. Classes reduced and machines separated all of which made little difference to him. He'd not gone there to improve his six-pack.

Thoughts of the place aside, he knew the police would go over the top with all their hogwash about 'one of our own' and 'no stone unturned' and 'brutal killer'. The Quinlan female had to have been pretty close to death but there was none of that business for her he noticed.

Gordon guessed they'd be in best uniform lining the streets for his funeral. Even those who hated his guts and there'll be a good few of them you can bet your life would be press ganged into attending.

He was aware how the police frequently wonder why they have a poor image in some quarters, then they pull a stroke like that. Putting their old pal before the public, before abused kids, before old ladies being assaulted or having their piggy bank stolen and in this case before a woman out jogging.

What about the rest of us he wondered? Is this promise only when you're a constable? He's aware it's not what they mean but it does appear to be a very strange way to phrase it. Unless of course it really is what they do mean, they'll serve the Queen to the best of their ability all the time we're constables, the rest of you can look after yourselves.

One thing did make him chuckle was how the local media went on about the rocking horse as if it were a live animal and not just something Mackenzie had knocked up in his shed. About par for such a rural county.

When he'd read that in the paper, Gordon bet some folk are stupid enough to send in bales of hay for it, or guessed one of the red top tabloids might have given it a daft name.

Then he'd had to plough through all the crap about how good a copper he had been, unstinting service for Queen and country, devoted to the service they come out with.

He was to some extent becoming mighty frustrated with the lack of action by the police. Hoped they hadn't dismissed Cluny Loony just as a place somebody dumped a young woman. Possibly been taken in by all the pretence of being some sort of holy place where angels fear to tread.

They give up their worldly possessions apparently in order to link to the vow of poverty so he understood, and spend a great deal of their time in silence. How does that help the world he wondered? Gordon simply could not imagine what they hope to achieve by all this, as despite what they think they are doing, the world around them just gets worse and worse.

204

Why had nobody noticed Appleyard's not a real nun, or is she such a good con artist she can fool anyone she meets. Anybody but him of course.

Gordon had to assume it could partly be his fault with Quinlan not being dead. Perhaps they would have upped their investigation had she been a goner. Possible under those circumstances they would have pulled out all the stops, even considered how Appleyard just might be part of something, even responsible for it. Not what they'd do is it? Go onto that PNC business to check out a nun. Be some stupid protocol to ensure they check with the cardinal or a monk or whoever first.

Gordon had been considering how all this business going on will put the frighteners on Appleyard, make her decide things are getting too close for comfort and provide a real opportunity. Persuade her to move out of her comfort zone, lose her protective coating of nuns and go back out into the real world.

Gordon had never expected to go further than two, but seeing as he didn't manage it with Quinlan, he had been wondering about the possibility of Appleyard being his new number two?

He knew he'd have to think up something really special for her. What about tying her to the rail tracks like they used to in all those old black and white movies with a damsel in distress. In this day and age he could use his phone to video it all and put it on *YouTube*.

Laughed at how ironic it would be if Appleyard were a damsel in distress. He would however draw the line at playing the part of the handsome geezer who turns up to drag her free from the oncoming huffing and puffing steam train just in time, himself.

He amused himself at work with thoughts of creating the whole scenario. With all the business of dressing her up in a large white billowy dress. Knew he'd be able to check exactly the sort as such dramas must be on the internet somewhere, but whichever way he played it in his mind, there was always the but.

The driver. The train driver. An image to bring him plummeting back down to earth.

The one who drove his express over his dear mum probably has it on his conscience all the time. His nightmares would inevitably involve him desperately trying to stop the train in time. Asking himself at night what he could and should have done differently.

Gordon knew it would never be fair to lumber another totally innocent hard working guy with that on his mind forever and a day.

Knew he needed to come up with something less frivolous. Create some sort of spectacular ending for her, something outrageous to send the cops into a spin with his audacity.

He'd noticed a female cop got a mention or two in the paper along with Mackenzie of course and some Detective Superintendent. He'll be the big cheese, ordering folk about, thrusting his rank up and under everybody's nose.

Did think it a bit strange reading of a female copper in the paper being foreign. Had what looked like a foreign name. Be Danish or something similar or married one he decided, easy be on some liaison visit was his guess, wasting more taxpayers money.

Good news for him of course, being from a different environment she'll not be up to it, not understand UK laws and systems. Struggle from day one and the poor soul had probably been lumbered with sorting out the mess.

Thinking back to the train driver, Gordon himself was to some extent wracked by a high degree of worry, when tormented by flashbacks of the really vivid moments. The softness when he just plunged the syringe deep into Mackenzie is probably something which will remain with him for all time.

Knew for sure the deed was now done and there was no going back now, no way to undo the damage he had inflicted on another human being. Had to be done of course, there'd been no getting away from it. This has been his revenge and Gordon was more aware than most what they say about that.

Indeed it just so happened he'd read somewhere about it being a dish best served straight from the fridge. Psychologists suggested that delaying retribution provided the best results for the wronged person, and he was in the majority for once in his life.

All this time he had have carried his anger around with him, like a backpack to restrain and at times overwhelm and remind him constantly. He had lost people dear to him because of the abuse of others like Mackenzie. The mental scars may never heal properly, his emotions were once again all over the place but he left the physical hurt for others.

There was this particular moment his mind kept recalling, how Mackenzie tried to catch his breath as if it would do him any good. Now and again something inside would suggest to Gordon he should feel sorry for him. Why? Did he ever feel sorry for the one he'd loved more than any other? Did the bastard ever give a damn about anyone other than himself?

Only one he had thoughts about was Rosemarie Mackenzie, who he assumed would slowly be coming to terms with what her Donald's death meant to her.

Knew from experience the poor woman'd have to silently suffer the host of insincerity from folk offering condolences with worthless attempts at concern. Be those two-faced bastards almost demanding her to recall the shock and horror she'd suffered upon opening the shed door

People may not agree with what he'd done but if they were ever in his shoes they'd not abnegate their responsibility to those who have suffered in these people's hands.

33

ANYTHING HAPPENING? was the second text Jamie Hedley awoke to next morning. Not a message to drag him from his slumbers, but one he came across over the breakfast table.

There was a distinct look of disapproval from his mother that he should be looking at his phone at the table. Not something he normally did, in fact quite possibly it was the first time he'd ever done anything bordering on such downright bad manners as it was in her eyes, right in front of her.

He'd put it down to stress if she asked what had got into him, with everything going on, and eyes watching him. The one from Tamara was the only one he read, just knew the other two on his phone could wait.

During the course of the day he was attacked by two more messages from the redhead. YOUR VERY QUIET and BEING IGNORED?

Sat in his car at the close of play, he returned her calls. Explained without going into detail how action was being taken and reiterated what he had already told Tamara about not disturbing the situation bearing in mind the attack on the Quinlan woman was still ongoing.

HALF MOON RETFORD 8 BE THERE

And he was. Like an obedient puppy dog who couldn't get enough of his new toy, there he was slipping onto a seat opposite Tamara Diagne.

He'd done what he'd managed previously. Got there very early to see her arrive. Same Land Rover pulled in, looked like the same guy driving but this time in a dark red t-shirt, filthy dirty scruffy jeans and what looked like Chelsea boots followed her in and he'd spied him sat in the corner of the bar next door.

Jamie looked at the redhead somewhat differently, apart from being desperate to know who the guy was. What was Paul's problem with her colouring? Add a bit of weight here and there and she'd be back to almost her best, and yes given half a chance away from work he would.

Jamie went through it all again, about all the enquiries going on, the need to keep Cluny operating plus the added complication surrounding the death of Mackenzie.

Tamara Diagne laughed at him. Loud enough for at least two people leaning on the bar to turn their heads.

'How stupid of me,' she chuckled. 'He's a bloody copper, so of course he's been given the red carpet treatment. Sorry can't deal with your issues today missy, all the cocaine and corruption'll have to wait, we've got to find who topped our old drinking buddy.'

'Be fair,' Jamie retorted. 'He's been murdered.'

'And if somebody had stolen his bus pass he'd still get preferential treatment,' Tamara tossed back and swiftly took a good swig of her white wine. 'Part of your problem, you can't catch real crims coz you're too busy bowing and scraping to a load of bloody big wigs who are probably on the damn fiddle anyway. Like judges travelling on an old folks rail cards and claiming first class.' Jamie looked at her. 'As they do,' she emphasized. 'And don't tell me I'm wrong!' she said pointing at him.

'That's not fair,' said Jamie quietly again. 'We want to catch whoever it was attacked the woman and stopped your old man's fun and games all at the same time.' He pulled in a breath. 'I keep telling you. We rush into Cluny all guns blazing, we'll stand no chance of figuring out what happened to that Quinlan woman. Who did it? Is it safe for young women to walk about of an evening or is there a maniac on the loose? We want to know what went on, she and her mum and dad need to know and now of course to add to it we want to know if it's connected to the death of Don Mackenzie.'

'And all the time I'm stuck out here like a sore thumb. How do I know who might have seen us together? Be me old man's sneaks keeping an eye out for me and what I'm up to. He don't trust nobody, in fact I don't think he even trusts himself.' She looked all about. 'I shouldn't need to hide away in a crap hole place like this bloody place.'

'See you brought a friend.'

'And?' she said sharply and wiggled her head.

'We're old school chums, that's why we're having a chat. What d'you say he's here for?'

'Gave me a lift, as it happens.'

'Didn't see your mask.'

'Yeah right!' She sniggered. 'Be serious! Not quite what some spazzy hired by me dear old dad will think. He'll see me and a copper and thick he might be, but even some of the dimwits working for me the old fella can add one and one together and get close to two.'

'And how d'you explain the driver, when you know I could have given you a lift?'

'That'd sound good, getting a lift off a copper too. Next question'd be why not go to a pub in town?' She sighed out a breath. 'So what's happening now?'

'You can't expect us to get the PHU lads to charge in there and put a stop to whatever's going on, blow the whole thing sky high and...'

'PHU?' she posed.

'Prisoner Handling Unit. They deal with all sorts of bits and pieces.' *Including people like you* he wanted to add.

'But you know what's going on,' Tamara insisted, put down her glass and leant in to Jamie. 'You don't need to go anywhere near Cluny to stop the postal corruption and stuff like that. Just stop it at source...'

'What are you talking about?' Jamie threw at Tamara.

'These delivery drivers working fiddles on the side,' she said as if everybody knew what they were up to.

'What delivery drivers?'

'Few years back now. You musta heard 'bout it. Think they were subcontractor drivers working for Parcelforce and were being investigated. There were suspicions about them stopping at specific places on their routes that were not real addresses and handing over specially marked parcels to blokes just hanging about.'

'What's it got to do with us?' Now this was dangerous water for Jamie. When he'd first started in PHU they were dealing with an offshoot to all this corrupt delivery business. Now he had to listen to what she had to say and bring to mind what he knew at the same time.

'Cluny,' was all she said before she raised her glass to sip again.

'Cluny?' he repeated to give him time to think if nothing else.

Tamara Diagne just sat shaking her head and sighing. 'Who's going to report some Parcelforce lorry stopping off at the priory place? Not what people do is it, ring customer services to make a complaint about nuns having stuff delivered?'

'Are you serious?' he asked hoping she'd have more to offer as he wracked his brains for the name of the mastermind. He remembered how they'd come across a link to a guy running an illegal pharmacy where he imported tablets and repackaged them. Something in the back of his mind told him Temazepam was involved but he could be wrong.

'What's so good about Cluny?' she asked, then answered herself. 'Nobody ever asks the right questions. Who do you know has ever asked what happens to the collection every Sunday in your local church? Do you know what the vicar does with the cash the congregation stumps up? Does anybody? And if somebody somewhere does know, how do they know the cash he hands over is the amount they actually take? Nobody asks questions, nobody gives a shit. It's not the done thing dear, it's not British. It's all hobnobbing bollocks that's what it is.'

'Let me get this straight,' said Jamie slowly as he digested what she had just spouted. 'You're saying corrupt drivers are stopping off at Cluny to deliver. What exactly?'

'Anything,' she said as if it was obvious. 'Drugs, cheap medicines, alcohol, fags, nicked iPads, any stolen rubbish that've not come through the Royal Mail.' She smiled. 'Pays for the driver to take his kids to Disneyland a time or two, I bet.' Tamara put her red head on one side. 'Not actually knock on the door, think the deal is they stop off down the road, some geezer's waiting takes the package and then probably just wanders into Cluny across the fields more than likely with it and the driver goes off on his merry way.'

'You think the nuns do that?'

Tamara shut her eyes for a moment. 'Maybe they do deliver to the door I don't know, but isn't that your job, aint that what you lot are being paid for?'

'Are you saying legitimate company's vans are being used by these bent drivers? Don't they know what's going on?' Jamie knew in the cases PHU had worked on, the legitimate couriers knew nothing about it. Often packets were picked up on a quiet road out of town and delivered down some back street.

'Not necessarily. Think my old man's set up a couple of courier companies who don't really want to deliver anything legit.'

'But they do?'

'Bit difficult if somebody phones up and says can you pick up this parcel or two, not easy to keep turning work down. You know how stories get round. Talk about some lot always being too busy to collect parcels, what's up with them? So they do a bit of proper work, pick and choose what they want to get involved in. Pays the overheads of course. Got a people carrier and do trips to and from the airports as well to make it look legit.'

'Our people who've been there said it was quiet as a grave.'

The sigh was back as Tamara looked to the ceiling for help. 'They don't deliver to Cluny in broad daylight, driving up to the door. They're done special, usually at night and infrequently so nobody gets suspicious. Main stay of course is the drugs and DVDs, one's where there's a big market.' She stopped and looked back up to the ceiling. 'And a big mark up,' she chuckled and grinned

'Why didn't you mention this before? Could tip the balance,' he admitted to her. 'Might make Cluny and Mackenzie the priority, they might with this in mind, just let the Quinlan woman slip into the background. Took a bit of a battering but how many others get that on a Friday night anyway?'

He so wanted to slip Quinlan, old Fish Pye and drug distribution into the stream, but knew it was best not to at that stage.

'I can't...'

'Hang on a sec,' Jamie interrupted. 'Was your old man involved in any deal with Mackenzie do you know? Any of this black market stuff, like running an amphet delivery firm linked to Mackenzie by any chance?'

'If he was I've never got wind of it.' Tamara took a sip of wine and sat with her fingers on the stem of the glass and talked to the wine. 'In fact my mum asked if I'd heard of your Mackenzie bloke when it was on the radio, so I don't think she'd ever heard him mentioned.'

212

'This Quinlan woman who was attacked and dumped at the priory. D'you really not know her? What about your mum?' What about her dad, dare he ask that?

'No idea. Even now I've heard her name she doesn't mean anything to me. Sounds like some rum job she does from what they were saying on the radio, don't begin to understand what it's all about.'

'This your dad?'

'Doing what?'

'Sorting out this Quinlan woman,' he risked.

'Never heard of her till she was on the radio, and he's inside remember. What's she got to do with anything?' Quite a lot probably.

'What has she got to do with anything?' he asked. 'Did you know she was on drugs?' Tamara just shook her head. 'I mentioned it at work and the boss wants to know how I know. She had a right go at me.'

'Why you asking me?' Tamara threw at him. 'Why d'you think I'd know stuff you don't?

'Just wondered in case you knew and it's where I got the idea from.'

'How would I?' she asked. 'My best guess is it's something to do with my old man and Appleyard. You can bet she's up to her neck in something and somebody paid a few bob to get this woman hidden away.'

'But she was sat in the chapel and the nuns reported it, eventually.'

'Nuns? Yeh right,' she chuckled. 'Gotta be somebody's bloody cock-up and you can bet they're paying for it.' Tamara sniggered. 'Stroke or no stroke my old man'd have their guts for garters.'

'But it still doesn't tell me how I knew she was downing ecstasy.'

'Don't look at me. I don't even know the silly bitch drugged up or otherwise.'

As the conversation slowly drifted away Jamie wondered why she had wanted to see him, apart from again urging him to get the full might of the law onto Cluny Priory.

In the end he drank down his lime and lemonade bade her farewell, went to his car and drove home. Wondered about stopping down the road apiece, parking up and waiting for her to be driven past but decided it was too risky.

Spending time with Tamara Diagne was now becoming a road to nowhere apart from hearing about deliveries to Cluny, and during his trip home it dawned on him how he could have spied on her and this driver had he not been in his distinctive Renault.

Was this her bloke? Was this scruffy herbert a Tez Diagne sidekick keeping an eye on the boss man's daughter for him? Did she think he was on her side even though he could very well have been planted on her by her father? Was he just a paid get-away driver?

Maybe he was and she couldn't drive.

More questions than answers, but by the time he got home Jamie had one for himself. DI Inga Larsson suddenly wanted him back across at Lincoln Central for morning briefing next day.

34

'Sundeep Amin,' said Inga Larsson as Jamie Hedley began to relate to his boss what his redhead had told him.

'That's the one!' he exclaimed.

'Got a few months inside I think it was. Been done before if my memory serves me right, for something he was up to in Scotland. Flooded the place with illegal prescription drugs. Probably why they wanted independence, they were all high on some of his gear,' she offered with the hint of a grin.

'Think you're right, be when I was in PHU. All to do with prescription medicines in especially identifiable packages.'

'What Amin was done for, but it was literally anything you can order on line, and these days it's big business.'

'You say was.'

'Probably still is, bearing in mind hundreds of these delivery people are joe public moonlighting to earn a few extra bob to pay the mortgage.'

'Don't think her old man is necessarily into prescription drugs, he's more into the stuff with a higher mark up. But the principle's the same. My guess is the courier company Tez Diagne set up probably delivers bits and pieces around and about to give a false image. The bent drivers are all working for the legit delivery companies, or sub-contractors who are a law unto themselves, probably make arrangements to hand stuff over to some guy waiting down one of the back roads, then they walk it into the Priory, possibly over the fields.'

'Nothing comes back on Diagne and these days with him inside, back to his wife or daughter. We stop any of his deliveries I'm told they're always legit and never go anywhere near Cluny.'

'If you're working for DHL for example, being legit they'll be monitoring where you are and what time you're everywhere so I'm told. Be no good one of their drivers taking a detour to Cluny for their sideline in ecstasy, spice or whatever.'

'Some of them you get an email telling you how many stops away they are.'

'Sub-contractors? Don't tell me anymore' Inga blew out a breath in frustration. 'Had one of them come to sort out our broadband, couldn't fix it, said we'd lost a lead and left us high and dry. When we phoned up they agreed to send another engineer with the proper cable.' She smiled. 'Same fella turned up of course acting as if he was doing us a favour, managed to find the cable and got it all going.'

'Two jobs is double the money.'

'You're so right,' she responded. 'Absolute rip off,' she said nodding. 'Goes on all the time so I understand.' Inga looked at her DC. 'Why didn't Diagne's daughter tell you all this before?'

'How am I to know ma'am?' he tossed back. 'Probably thought when we turn the place over we'll discover what's been going on. Lads doing ANPR come up with anything?'

'Any pucker delivery vans are all above board, properly licenced, taxed and insured, like Diagne's vans they'll all check out. They only get zabba-dabba-do if they're not. Number plate recognition's next to useless if they're kosher.'

'What if you were to ask her why she'd suddenly come up with this little nugget?'

Jamie Hedley sucked in noisily. 'Think this is her trying to force our hand. She's dead scared we'll not do anything because we're more interested in the Quinlan attack and Mackenzie's death. Worried sick one of her old man's cronies will find out what she's up to, so she's set the ball rolling.'

Inga nodded. 'Makes sense.' Then looked at Jamie carefully. 'Why doesn't she just scarper, go abroad to Spain where all the other crooks hang out before he gets out, give her time to set up a new life?'

'Always possible she's planning something, but I think her mother has control of the finances,' Jamie smiled and put his hands up. 'Just my guess. Always possible Mrs controls all the Diagne money. With him in nick, somebody's got to be looking after everything, laundering money, cooking the books. My guess is they want to scupper his businesses first, leave him with next to nothing to come out to and all his low life have cut their losses and found a new scam. Not leave now, leave all the cash behind and when he comes out he can quickly raise a few bob through his business or dip his hand in the till, put a team together ready to chase them across Europe.'

Jamie Hedley stopped when his boss was calling somebody behind him into her office with her hand.

'Just a quickie,' said Lizzie Webb. 'No connection whatsoever between our Don Mackenzie and Rita Appleyard, except she's been in trouble with the police time and again and he of course was a policeman.'

'And our Carole-Anne Quinlan?'

Lizzie frowned. 'There is no connection anywhere for her. Too good to be true, divorced and she has no current relationship with anybody we've come across, no parking tickets, no speeding, you name it she's a complete blank. Just works for this Think Tank business.'

'Thanks Liz.'

'We au fait with the Think Tank concept?' she asked as she turned back. 'They're some sort of research and policy institutes most of them with in her case with health as their main topic.'

'Too good to be true eh? Nobody's that clean. Thanks Liz,' she called after her and Inga Larsson grimaced at Jamie Hedley. 'Except for her spare phone and the info her call provider came up with. Think it's time I had a word with the boss, see which way we play this.' She hesitated. 'Which way would you play it just out of interest?'

'Pardon?'

'Which way would you go now?' Inga asked. 'Continue to chase a serial attacker and killer who might not actually exist, or go for bringing Diagne's reign to an abrupt end and in the process see what we can find out about the women in Cluny and hope somewhere down the line a link just pops out by sheer chance?' Jamie went to offer his ideas. 'Sit down,' she said suddenly. 'Here's your chance to come clean. Out with it,' she told him in no uncertain terms as Jamie sat down. 'There's something on your mind all the time as if you're

217

not with us,' Inga pointed at him. 'Come clean, as long as it's not your love life.'

'Was once,' he mumbled into his lap then peered up. 'Sorry ma'am.'

'Let's not worry about that for now,' his boss hesitated. 'How about talking to me about it, tell me what the problem is.'

'D'you know about me and Kerrie?' Inga nodded although her knowledge was brief. 'Think latest idea is I'll be paying towards the mortgage on this new place she's after. Renting now, wants to up the stakes to buy.'

'You're paying her rent? Why?'

'Won't let me see my daughter.'

'She told you that? Sounds very much like blackmail to me.'

'Bragging about it anyway so I've heard, on social media.'

'Don't tell me you read all that crap?'

'Did at one time, got a bit too much at times. Not now though,'

'Do you know what and where?'

'Think so, but I could find out.'

'She doing this legally do you know?'

'No idea.'

'Get me as much info as you can, I'll get Lizzie to do a bit of digging for me, see what she comes up with.' Inga gathered together the papers on her desk. 'We'll get this sorted, no problem, and,' she peered out into the Incident Room. 'Just between us.'

'Can't lumber you with…'

'Please?'

'Thanks ma'am.'

'And cheer up,' she smiled and then took on a serious look. 'You're doing well, don't let outside events override everything else. Bits and pieces have gone awry but I know it's not easy.' Jamie went to leave. 'One thing though. Do not meet this Diagne again for any reason whatsoever without telling me in advance.'

'Right. Thanks ma'am.'

'I know it's none of my business but take my advice, get a DNA test done. You could be coughing up all this money for nothing.' Something he didn't want to even consider. 'Problem?' she posed and he responded to with the merest of shrugs. 'Out with it.'

'Probably me. But all the time I remain with the status quo I still have a child.'

'And you're worried a paternity test will blow it all away?' He nodded. 'You can't go through life living your life like this and you'll certainly not achieve what I think you're capable of with this perpetually hanging over you. And another thing it makes you vulnerable. Got to say I'm pleased HR are involved and they tell me you've changed personal issues legally as protection. Just need this DNA check.' Jamie grimaced at. 'All the time you're still paying rent, all the time you believe the child is yours you're paying through the nose for nothing more than a what if.'

Jamie Hedley was by nature a worrier. When things were bad over the drugs business with Quinlan he feared the worst and suffered sleepless nights. Now he was worrying again for an entirely different reason.

Something somewhere worried him about the driver Tamara used. He couldn't put his finger on it, but there was just something not quite right about the guy.

He'd put the Land Rover through the DVLA system and had come up with nobody of any consequence, but at least with his address he had somewhere to start. In the pub when he was chatting to Tamara he'd caught the scruff watching him for no good reason from the other bar.

Who was he Jamie wondered endlessly, where did he sit in the Diagne organization while the boss was lying in his cell bemoaning his fate?

A few days later all masked up Jamie found himself ensconced as a passenger in a small Fiat 500 as Warren Miller drove to the edge of the city.

He was under strict instructions from the boss. This was not an official operation in any sense of the word. He knew for absolute certainty how he must not involve young Warren in anything which just might put the lad's future firmly back as a car mechanic for ever.

The lad was his driver, nothing more, nothing less. Trying to spy on this Spencer Nyman in his own car was fraught with danger. If Tamara was with him she could well recognize his motor although she'd not been in it and no doubt so too could Nyman. In Warren's little motor he felt comparatively safe and masks would help hide his identity.

For over half an hour young Warren Miller was able to experience what life with the police can be like so often. Tediously boring. They just sat there in his little Fiat sucking rhubarb sweets the lad had in a side pocket, watching to their left in case this Nyman emerged.

'Exciting eh?' Jamie chuckled.

'Better than the *One Show*.'

'That still going?'

'What's he done, this bloke?' Warren asked as he nodded his response.

'Not actually done anything as far as we know. Car's all in his name, taxed and insured and everything.' Jamie knew he had to be really careful with what he said. 'Just need to know what he's up to.' He just glanced across at Warren. 'Told you this might bore the pants off you!' No mention of Tamara and how he thought about her, and in a peculiar sort of way, cared for her, concerned for her. 'You sure you want to do this for a living?'

'You do.'

Jamie didn't tell him this was not official, this was not actually work it was just him on a whim approved he felt somewhat reluctantly by the boss.

Jamie felt to a degree embarrassed with the way things had turned out and was just considering what to do next other than getting Warren to drop him back home when he saw lights blink on the Land Rover parked on the drive a few doors down the road.

When Nyman pulled into the car park at the Harvest Moon on the Glebe Estate which was at one time a farmhouse, Jamie told Warren to drive past, turn round and park on the road.

'That's him,' said Jamie as Spencer Nyman slid from his vehicle and made a big issue of hugging a tall thin man who had emerged from a dirty filthy Mitsubishi very much against social distancing rules. Could he not afford the car wash on Outer Circle Road? The pair watched as they ambled together into the pub once the silliness was over.

'Now what?' Warren asked.

'We wait.'

'For what?'

'To be honest I don't know.' He felt really good inside seeing Tamara was not with the bloke, and wondered to himself if that was what in truth it had all been about. Checking up on the men in her life maybe. Pleased as punch she was not waltzing into the pub arm in arm with Nyman.

'Want to know what they're doing?'

Jamie grimaced. 'Don't think so. Not sure I want to go down the waiting route for them to get pissed up and call in the Interceptors.' The moment he'd said it, the idea of Nyman being banned came to mind and perhaps it just might be an idea. Would mean Tamara would need a new driver, a job he could volunteer for.

'What you thinking?'

Jamie daren't admit even to himself. 'He's a driver but there has to be more to him than that. And he's clean yet the person he drives for is muddled up with all sorts of nasty business.'

'Want me to see what they're doing?'

'Don't be silly.'

'Why's it silly?'

'This is just to give you a bit of experience. Just show you this is not like an episode of *Luther*. Plus remember, I'm responsible for you and none of this is official.'

'But if I just wander in there, where's the harm? It's a free country.'

'Can't imagine what you're likely to see.'

'You never know.'

'Nothing stupid now,' Jamie insisted as Warren moved to extricate himself from the seat belt. 'For God's sake don't talk to them, in fact don't even look at them. Just nip in and nip out.'

Jamie Hedley was anxious for five minutes, but when it became ten he was starting to become apprehensive. Concern turned to criticizing himself for his utter stupidity once again. DI Larsson didn't know he was using a totally inexperienced 19 year old police hopeful as a get-away driver for the evening, but she was aware he planned to get someone to save him having to use his own Renault.

He didn't need this. Worries about the paternity test the boss had almost demanded were still with him. Could be the final nail in the coffin of him, Kerrie and his baby.

'Now what?' he asked himself out loud sat slumped down in the car with a black woolly hat pulled down. Without thinking he just got out of the car and walked slowly towards the pub in the vain hope of seeing something. He passed Nyman's Land Rover and then the black Mitsubishi. Why he often wondered do people have cars with an open back? Be useful for builders he appreciated, but with a wife and kids? Mentally noted it was a 14 reg and just strolled around as casually as he could and leant against the pub wall at the side wondering what on earth he should do.

All of a sudden behind him round the front he heard voices, so walked away. From behind a Transit he spied it was Nyman and the tall bloke at the Land Rover going through the double hugging silliness.

He waited for Nyman to pull away and just had a peep round to see which way the other one was going. He pulled away as well, and headed off like Nyman towards the by-pass. Instinctively he checked the number plate again and confirmed the number in his brain.

Now for Warren. What was he doing? Where was he? He considered going into the pub to find him but just as he got to the door it dawned on him how Tamara could be in there. Jamie strolled back to the Fiat, then sat inside making a note of the number of the Mitsubishi.

Suddenly Warren in his big grey hoody was at the driver's door and sliding onto his seat.

'Where you been for God's sake?'

'Playing *Candy Crush* on my phone,' Jamie looked at him. 'They were out back where the smokers go to have a fag. Got mesen a coke and sat playing with me phone.'

'And.'

'Can play with me eyes closed to be honest. Definitely something went on, loadsa whispering like. Bloody sure of it, under the table sort of surreptitious like passing something.'

'Do we know what?'

'No. Tall one shoved it in his pocket, whatever it was. But I brought this with me,' and Warren pulled his hand from the big front pocket of his hoody and presented Jamie with a glass ash tray.

'That's theft young man,' he chided and sniggered.

222

'And evidence, officer.' He chided cheekily. 'Roll up belongs to the big fella, filter's the one the tall guy smoked.'

Jamie chuckled. 'And what d'you suggest I do with this?'

'Check for DNA, might even get finger prints off the roll up. That'll tell you who both are and that.'

Jamie just had to laugh, at what the lad had done. 'I already know who the big bloke is.'

'I'm sure forensics can come up with both names.'

'You really do watch too much television!' He looked so chuffed, Jamie didn't want to piss on the lad's strawberries.

'What now?' asked a pleased-as-punch young Warren.

'Home James,' he grinned with.

'We've got a whole department these days dealing with identity theft, why d'we have to get our hands dirty scrambling about with this one?'

'Is it what Tigger Woods is doing these days?' Sandy checked.

'No. He's in intelligence gathering,' Jake Goodwin advised.

'Usually these days it's all about cyber theft, cloning people's Facebook pages, stealing their pin numbers and all that stuff. What's the betting he's just copied some poor kid's name from a grave stone or nicked a brown envelope from a letter box like they do, just to set himself up as this Nyman so he can carry on driving?'

'Heard about a worrying thing,' said Sandy. 'These home heating systems you can control from your phone. Latest wheeze is nick someone's phone and put their heating on full blast.'

'And?' Nicky asked without looking up.

'Do it when they're out at work, costs them a small fortune.'

'Why?' was her next question.

'To get your own back on someone you don't like. Do it every day for a month'll cost a few bob.'

'Excuse me,' said Jake loudly. 'Are we seriously suggesting this Nyman has gone to all this trouble just so he can drive for twenty months?' Jake queried. 'I'd like to bet there's more to this than just getting a driving licence, surely you can buy them on-line. Take the test under his false name, be easy so they tell me.'

'Could be he bought the licence in his name on line, and then added all the rest of it to match.'

'Always possible he just chops and changed his name to suit him. Changed from Tommy Muir to Dominic Muir when he started, then when he was getting into mischief he changed to Nyman, and when the ban ends he can go back to his original name. Remember there's nothing legal about names, you can call yourself anything you want.'

'He did two years for drug offences as Tommy Muir.' He hesitated. 'Why does Dom Muir sound a stupid name?' he asked and then went on. 'As Spencer Nyman on the other hand he is innocent.'

'Until we prove him guilty.'

'We've got his Land Rover, his address, both his names so we could easy have him stopped and have him charged with all the motoring offences for a banned driver. No insurance, driving while disqualified and such, but where will it all lead us?'

Inga Larsson having wandered slowly from her office answered Jake's query. 'If anything it would stop him getting up to whatever he's getting up to with that Diagne woman.' Jamie Hedley wanted to ask why she was looking at him so seriously. 'Cat amongst the pigeons,' she said and smiled aware the team were always in favour of her using British phrases. 'Chaos,' she added to show she understood and once again looked down at Jamie.

DC Jamie Hedley was sat in the far corner of the bar when Tamara Diagne walked in alone. Jamie took her order and walked to the end of the bar and as he waited for a slow barman to get his act in gear he saw DC Sandy MacLachlan enter and sidle up to the bar without any form of acknowledgement. Jamie guessed Tamara had once again been given a lift by somebody, and reckoned it was more than likely Nyman aka Tommy Muir or even Dom Muir.

Jamie didn't bother to wait to see whether Nyman entered the bar next door when his drinks were eventually served, and took them over to the corner seat.

'What's this all about?' she shot at him moodily.

'Boss wants to know what we'll find at Cluny if we go in.'

'How the hell should I know?' she threw back and sipped. 'Just raid the soddin' place! You've wasted enough bloody time already.'

'It's not as easy as that. We have to think of our public face,' he told her as Tamara sighed and shook her head. 'We go in there and find there's only a few old women and just bits and pieces, how do we explain to Joe Public we're still no further forward with the woman they found there? Imagine how we'd look on Twitter.'

'Why you so bothered what a load of old cronies are moaning about?'

'Because a woman has been attacked and left there to die and the public has an input. After all they come up with the cash.'

'So?'

'How would your mother feel if it was you?' he suggested. 'We go chasing next to bugger all and blow any chance of finding who attacked you. I'm sorry Mrs Diagne we buggered up the clues at the Priory but we did find two hundred fags and a big box of chocolates.'

'Very funny.' Time for her to sip again. 'And you've dragged me out to this dive for why exactly?'

'Like I said. What will we find? Is it in all honesty worth our while my boss wants to know, before she commits time and money.'

'Prat about like this all the time it's a wonder you catch any sod at all. All this politically correct stuff and nonsense.'

'She has to take costs into consideration,' he said firmly. 'Its public money we're dealing with, not a load of dosh we nicked from an ATM and let me tell you, times are still hard. Still budget constraints.'

'I've offered you the chance to close the bloody place down, great chance for your lot to pin something on those bitches in there.' She shrugged. 'Could be nicked DVDs, even a bit o'grass maybe,' she stopped to chuckle and shake her head.

'This just DVDs?'

'Nah. All sorts really could easy be anything. When folks are hard up best to nick what they're desperate for. DVDs just easy slip in yer pocket, got to be worth a quid or two. Food for homeless is a good racket too. Markets and car boots are best places, no staff, no security, be all knocked off stuff any roads.' She stopped to grin. 'Had this community order against me one time and all that business.'

'All behind you now?' he checked.

'Course,' Tamara chuckled. 'You just need to close the place down and get that old bitch out, so's my old man can't use it for anything. Has to be worth something.'

'Why can't he use it after?'

'How in God's name d'you think he's gonna find another bloody crook like Appleyard from where he's banged up?'

'Thought you said he'd got people out here sorting it for him.'

'They don't grow on trees, people like that. Folk who want to run a place like that, not something you can advertise in the Job Centre. All right all the time she's there and all those scabby awful women. What's he replace them all with?'

This was a different Tamara sat there opposite him in the Harvest Moon. Whatever happened to the delights Jamie had previously enjoyed, watching her savouring the best of those oatcakes, chutney and selection of cheese?

'Dom Muir not with you today then?' he asked and out of the corner of his eye could see Sandy casually dressed leant up just by the pumps, peering through into the other bar.

'This one of your lucky dip of crap questions?'

'Your driver I'm talking about. Dominic is it you call him?'

'Who are you on about?' she grimaced.

'The geezer with the Land Rover, Dom Muir.'

'No idea what you're bloody talking about,' and Jamie took her reaction as a clue when she gazed down at her glass rather than at him before she took a good drink, stood up abruptly and without saying a word headed towards the 'Toilets' sign and pushed open the door.

Jamie spotted her mobile sat there on the table in full view and gestured to Sandy to join him. Jamie quickly scouped it up and surreptitiously handed it to his colleague without a word and Sandy was gone. Then the only three others in the bar glanced up. Too late, all done.

When the door opened and Tamara rubbing her hands walked back in she appeared less agitated and resumed her position, took another sip and sat back.

'Where's my phone?' was the inevitable squeal you get from those who dare not be without their life crutch for a moment.

'Sorry.'

'Where's my fuckin' phone?' she shouted and Jamie sensed ears prick up.

'D'you take it to the loo?'

'Shit!' and she hurried back where she had just appeared from. In seconds the redhead was back. 'You got it?' she shouted, but Jamie had no chance to answer. 'Musta. Give it back pig!'

'I have not got your phone,' he said slowly.

'Turn out yer fuckin' pockets,' she demanded. 'C'mon.'

'Did you bring it with you?' Jamie asked as he got slowly to his feet and began to unload his trouser pockets. A black wallet, his Warrant Card, a pale blue handkerchief, a bit of loose change, a Samsung phone and small retractable pen. He then casually patted his thighs to show there was no more. He even patted the shirt pocket.

'Satisfied?'

'Must be somewhere,' and she truly looked desperate.

'On the kitchen table's a favourite of mine,' he suggested.

'Don't be stupid! Can't go out without your phone,' was a stupid remark as plenty of people do.

'Right,' said Jamie and gathered his belongings to feedback into his trouser pockets and then sat back down and crossed his legs. 'Where were we?'

'Not til I find my bloody phone.'

'They can wait.'

'What?' she exclaimed.

'The bored who've been texting you.'

'Nobody has.'

'In which case you've not missed anybody or anything life shatteringly important.' Jamie took a good drink of his lime and lemonade as Tamara continued to search for her phone, scanning the floor, moving chairs and even two of the half-a-dozen tables nobody was sat at.

'Gotta go,' she said suddenly and poured the remainder of her drink down.

'Need a lift?'

'You think I wanna be seen in a cop car?' she scoffed. 'No thank you,' was sharp.

'It's my own car, no blues and twos.'

'Same thing.'

'So Dominic is here.' Tamara just looked at him as if he had spoken in Serbo Croat.

'Just get it bloody sorted,' she said down to him and walked swiftly from the bar, but he watched her collect scruffy unshaven Spencer Nyman aka whoever, from the other bar.

This was a totally different Tamara than the one he'd become used to. This seriously was not the oatcakes demure young woman he'd been attracted to.

Jamie moved to where he could see vehicles exiting the car park and once Nyman had driven his Land Rover illegally off down the road he waited two minutes before leaving the premises to join Sandy at his car.

'Nice little job for our eTeam me thinks,' he said with Tamara's phone in his gloved hand.

35

A great deal had gone on during the ensuing two weeks in particular with regard to Cluny Priory, Tamara Diagne and her consort Nyman. Access to her Apple phone had proved vital in piecing everything together, and in addition provided the geeky eTeam with a whole host of other numbers they were able to obtain call print-outs of.

In the meantime the majority of the murder squad were still entrenched in their investigations into the death of Donald Mackenzie.

Jamie was however given knowledge of some of the information being gathered by the people crawling around inside people's phones and about the various raids being carried out as a result of the vital information they had gathered.

'Needed a word,' said DI Inga Larsson one morning as DC Jamie Hedley took a seat in her office once again having been dragged across to Lincoln early doors. At least it gave him an opportunity to nip to his small apartment to give it a once over and check the meagre amount of mail. 'What I am about to tell you will by necessity need to be released to the team later. I thought it only fair you be given the heads up in order for you to be aware of what people are likely to suggest.'

'Thanks,' but had no idea what he was thanking his boss for.

'Sorry to say you were set-up,' she said and then stopped. Jamie gathered in what she had said and immediately attempted to fathom what it meant. 'It is true your friend Tamara Diagne wanted her father's little business at the Cluny Priory destroyed, but what is not at all likely is she and her mother would then sail off into the sunset with all his ill-gotten gains and leave Terry Diagne with next to nothing when he gets out.'

'Only had her word,' he shrugged as if offering an excuse.

'I appreciate that, but. Spencer Nyman aka Tommy Muir is her boyfriend, lover, partner whatever.'

'She said she'd never heard of him,' got Jamie a look from Inga Larsson.

'Never heard of who?'

'Dom Muir.'

'Think you're not the only who has been had. My guess is she had no idea his real name is as you say Thomas Dominic Muir. Probably being honest, she didn't actually know of a Dom Muir because he was using her.' Inga smiled a knowing smile. 'Muir has a wife and two kids in Leeds and,' she allowed her head to shake slightly. 'Could have got the Nyman name he uses from anywhere.'

'This how she conned me?' the breath he blew out was full of frustration.

Inga sucked in. 'Sorry no. Diagne was trying to get you to get us to raid Cluny Priory by feeding you with info,' she tapped a wedge of paper in front of her. 'I'll let you read the full transcript. She told Spencer Nyman, the name of course she knew him by, she knew a copper and would see what she could find out.' Inga glanced away and then her look returned. 'Be honest with me now. Did she offer you sex?'

'No!'

'Fine, fine, but it is suggested in the texts between the two of them, if the worst comes to the worst she may have to use what she called the old sex bait.' Inga grimaced as she sifted through the papers. 'He's not that bright,' she read looked at Jamie momentarily before going on. 'He'll go where his cock tells him, quote unquote.'

Jamie coloured up and scoffed his reaction. 'Wishful thinking,' and sat shaking his head. 'So are you saying she wanted me to instigate raiding Cluny because of what she told me? Was that lies too?'

'The stuff going on there?' Inga posed and Jamie nodded. 'Looks like it, but remember they're both still out there, Once we worked out what their little game was from all her texts the lads downstairs are there as we speak. Plan to clear the place of all the knocked-off gear, and just been told customs are becoming involved or will be. Yes, a load of porn, fifty or more top of the range phones, fags and a room stacked floor to ceiling with ripped off contraband gear so far. This'll all get rid of those women and no doubt they'll find plenty to pin on Appleyard, but your Tamara and Nyman were planning to take it over, once we've got rid of the nuns with Appleyard out of it and guess the plan was to use it as a base. We understand Nyman's got a few heavies lined up in case her old man sends people down there.'

'Why we allowing her and Nyman to run free?'

'They have big plans, so we've done exactly what she asked,' Inga grinned. 'Guess she thinks she flattered her eyelids and you did as she asked, now it's all theirs.'

'And we just sit back and wait?'

'About the size of it, but reckoned you should know before the team. Be a bit of ribbing when they read this,' she tapped the papers. 'About you being conned by a pretty woman I'm guessing.' She shrugged her shoulders. 'Sorry.'

'No problem.' Jamie just shook his head and sighed. 'Not the first time though.'

'Don't want to go on but,' she hesitated. 'Paternity?'

His breath was released as a long sigh. 'Think you're right,' he admitted.

'Good man. For the best. All we have to do now while we wait for them to take over the Cluny business, is to work out what happened to poor old Mackenzie. He does seem to have become lost in all this and the other question is, what on earth did Carole-Anne Quentin have to do with anything?'

'She on Tamara's phone by any chance?'

'Unfortunately no not at all, so she's still a bit of a mystery. And before you ask, there's no mention of Mackenzie either.' Inga tapped the papers on her desk. 'I'll run a copy off for you.'

'Thanks ma'am.'

Toxicology results from the Post Mortem had taken longer than usual when Inga Larsson, iPad in hand stood out front of her team, bottom resting on a spare table.

'Wheesht!' was Sandy bringing the room to order for his boss.

'Thank you,' she acknowledged. 'Apparently, Mackenzie was injected with a neurotoxin. In particular,' she looked down. 'Tetrodotoxin which is found in Puffer Fish,' a few grimaced at. 'Worst bit about it is quite quickly your body becomes paralysed. You're in effect virtually frozen still yet your mind is fully functional. You realise you're about to die but there's nothing you can do about it. Something you'd not want to live through.'

'That's the problem, you don't live through it.'

'We'll get a full detailed report later but basically it blocks your sodium channels,' she read. 'That's what carries messages between brain and muscles and you lose all senses. CSI Leicester have added a quip about some people actually keep Puffer Fish as pets.'

DC Jamie Hedley was wondering what was coming next, still worrying about how he'd feel if the baby was not his and to a certain extent bemused when DI Inga Larsson beckoned him into her office again later in the day.

'Just a thought,' Inga said with Jamie stood in front of her desk like an impudent youngster, with him wondering how many more times he'd be called in like this. 'Give the names of all the people who do this odd-ball meal business to Jake, let's see what pops up on the systems.' She put an open hand up. 'This is not me prying into your private life, but we really do have to get to the bottom of this drug business. Could be quite innocent, always possible somebody assumed she was drugged up, as a lot are these days.'

'Yes ma'am.'

'Tell him all you can about them all.'

He was slightly bemused. He had somehow suddenly gone from being accused of leaking important information with a likely quick return to PHU, to a situation where if it was mentioned his name was no longer linked. He hoped his old pals down in PHU had been told who put them onto Cluny Loony and given them a fun day out.

The boss had been right, there had been a certain amount of banter about him being led up the garden path by Tamara his schoolboy crush. Lots of remarks about doing her homework and asking what went on behind the bike sheds.

DS Dennis Norton from Gainsborough sauntered into the Incident Room heading for Larsson's office.

'Boss asked me to keep you up to scratch on our cuckooing case ma'am. The one young Hedley got involved in.'

'Have a seat,' said Larsson as she got up to close the door.

'Forensics have finished on site pretty much. Not found a great deal to be honest apart from a couple of wraps of weed, probably because they were using it just as a distribution centre.'

'Do we know why? With this sort of set-up they took over some poor soul's place, caused utter chaos, turn it into twenty-four-seven rave and upset all the neighbours.'

'We've dealt with three others lately, around one a month just like this one,' Norton advised. 'These are a bit different. Take over some poor soul's home as somewhere all the dealers can congregate to get stocked up. Means if we raid their own places they're pretty much clean.'

'Any idea who's behind it?'

'Further up the scale we reckon has to be a Mr Big, but on a local basis we've clearly established a link with your Quinlan female...'

'Not mine,' Inga tossed back. 'She's just a silly bitch who got her head bashed in and we're still trying to lay that at some skurk's door.'

'Could be Mr Big laying down the law,' he suggested. 'Any rate she's linked phone wise to Chunky Knapp and we're putting her down as the organizer round these parts simply because she's the only one we've come across with a brain and the wherewithal. This fancy job she does means as part of her remit apparently, she coordinates care in the community linked to social services within the statutory medical requirements authorized by the NHS.'

'And what does she do exactly?'

'Always on the lookout for the next one's my guess. Picks out some old guy like Fish Pye,' Norton grinned. 'Old men each time it seems, who are not mobile and she removes their care provision to make them even more vulnerable.'

'Surely that's dangerous, what if something happens to them, she'd be right in the clag.'

Norton was shaking his head. 'Too clever by half this one. She only leaves them without a carer for a day or two, just long enough to get the dishing out all done and dusted. Spends her time coming up with all sorts of new modern schemes on the pretext of offering help. Plus before that from what neighbours are telling us, Quinlan gets a couple of the brighter lads to pop in and run errands for the old boy she's chosen, so he feels safe with them about. They go to the shop, mow the lawn, do the washing up and all that in exchange for a bit of weed probably or spice they can flog in town. She knows exactly when this new scheme will end so she fixes for a new carer to be there first thing next day. Easy.'

'All this organized through their phones.'

'Soon as old Pye was done with, these ragamuffins get a new pre-paid sim and off they go again, except…'

'Somebody gave her a bashing.'

'Exactly. Our guess is this is somebody getting their own back on what she's been up to. Somebody's old man or grandpa maybe got stitched up.'

'But it still went on without her,' Larsson reminded him. 'She couldn't have been involved, she was in hospital.'

Dennis Norton put his hands up. 'Clean as a whistle, what's the betting she's never come close to drugs and is nowhere near when the cuckooing is actually going on.'

'Smack on her head gave her a perfect alibi. Remember, we never found more than a personal use smidgen in her apartment. So, where's she getting it from?'

'If it is her it could be Quinlan is just the local Miss Fixit and plays a specific role.'

'Do us a favour,' Larsson requested. 'Have a look at these old boys who've had a scum visit and see if they've got a son, grandson or somebody useful who might have it in for her.'

'Never actually comes into contact with hash, coke or whatever.'

'Somebody took it upon themselves to give her a good bashing.'

'Remember she will probably get drug tested for work so she has to be completely clean.'

'Must mean she upset somebody, big time.'

'This a turf war?'

Jamie sauntered cautiously over to Jake Goodwin and explained what Inga Larsson had requested, and one by one Jake input details of his old pals. Jamie still felt conscious of Jake's eyes on him, guessed he still thought he was the one who was supposed to have made an error of judgment.

Knew the chances are his personal problems were probably going the rounds too, as he was obviously ribbing flavour of the month

Paul Miller he'd known since they were at Yarborough School, as it was then, together. Married with two children he now worked for the local Ford dealer. His younger brother Warren was as he had said an apprentice car mechanic attending college with hopes of joining the police Jamie was encouraging. Nathaniel 'Nutty' Charman, very much it appeared was controlled by his wife, worked for the local council in some office wallah role in Planning and had done so since leaving school.

Chris Tiernan was next for Jake to take note of, a landscape gardener and tree surgeon which probably meant he gave people's bushes and hedges a short back and sides once a year. Knowing Chris he guessed he'd take all the wood away and flog it to folk with wood burning stoves which are all the rage but environmentalists are set against.

Last but not least was Micky Aldridge who had worked for a removal firm for some time but Jamie was not absolutely sure what he did now for a living.

The comeback from Jake eventually was hardly awe inspiring. Charman had received three points for speeding nearly three years previous. Aldridge had paid a fine for not wearing his seat belt last year and Chris Tiernan had been done for having no car tax disc displayed on his old pickup way back when they were mandatory. Hardly candidates for Crook of the Year – certainly shoplifting, burglary or drunken misdemeanors. No fisticuffs, and Jamie guessed Jake Goodwin was to a degree disappointed he'd not found a great deal more.

'This it?' Inga asked at her office door, with the list in her hand Jake had produced. 'This the best you can do?' she threw at Jamie. 'These all the hard-nosed sleaze-bag crooks you go about with?' she chuckled. 'Anybody else?'

'Only the estate agent and the writer,' Jamie shrugged.

'What writer? What you on about?'

'Guy I met at the Blues, sorry at Gainsborough Trinity, I've got to know quite well. Been for a drink few times, meet up at the footie. Even came to the Romanian meal.'

'What's the writer bit all about?'

'Scott Casey, he's an author. Writes these murder mystery paperbacks. Sort of thing people take on holiday, bit like an up-to-

235

date Agatha Christie. Very good, well my old lady certainly thinks so, she's hooked.' Inga looked across at her DS. 'Another one for you Jake. See what you get with this...Scott Casey,' she glanced at Jamie just to make sure and he nodded.

'These books. Murders you say?' Jake enquired.

'Police Procedurals they classify them as I seem to think.'

'And where may I ask does he get his info?' Inga closed her eyes.

'Don't tell me,' scoffed Jake loudly. 'Please not you for God's sake! He picks your brains and you like a complete prat...' He chuckled. 'One minute it's a pretty girl, then...' he laughed. 'Let's start with PNC, see what pops up.'

'No, no, it's not like that,' Jamie insisted with a raised voice. 'I've told him when he's got things wrong, when sequences are all the wrong way round or it's all too fast. In one book he was suggesting toxicology results take just a few hours like they appear to on TV and other silliness.'

'Scott Casey, author?' said DS Nicky Scoley from the corner peering at her monitor.

'Yes,' said Jamie and it was soon Nicky's turn to be in the headlights.

'Scott Casey,' she said slowly. 'Author of three best sellers including "Thorns" and "Withered Rose" are part of his Rose Murder Mysteries. According to this, two of his books are based in Lancashire with a red rose theme and one in Yorkshire with the white rose.' She put a hand in the air to stop any comments. 'Wait a sec, something's just come to mind,' and they dutifully did as requested as she clicked from site to site. 'Come back to me,' she suggested to Inga 'I'll have a word with ASBO'.

'Nothing on PNC,' Jake advised. 'Found a scrote by that name but too young.'

Larsson turned back to Jamie in search of more information about his friends and became involved in a conversation about the odd-ball restaurants his friends were planning to visit.

'One in London apparently,' Jamie responded to her questions. 'With an African theme to the food, décor and drinks. Another is one in Prague where they have a model railway delivering food and drink to every table, and one place sells avocado with fries!'

'What about around here?' she wondered might suit her and Adam for something different. Maybe an anniversary.

'Not heard of any so far except The Deep in Hull. One in a tree house some place and an old train station decked out like a First Class carriage. Not a restaurant but there was a board game café in Lincoln until Covid shut it.'

'Board or bored?'

An hour later and DS Scoley had returned from her trip up to the techs and had been engrossed for ages in unravelling the Scott Casey entry in Wikipedia.

'How's it going?' the boss enquired without any sense of pressure other than what they were all under.

'All Scott Casey, but I've just come across a link in the references to it being the pen name of a Gordon Kenny.'

'It's a start,' Inga suggested. 'I'll leave it with you.'

'Hang on,' stopped the DI walking away. 'Wow! Get this,' Nicky suddenly enthused loudly to stop the room. 'On Wikipedia they only mention Scott Casey with stuff about his life after his first book success, and how he now writes full time, but I've just come across another press reference under this Gordon Kenny. Article in the literary press two years ago about him being a thorn amongst the roses and being brought up in a care home.'

Inga Larsson sidled up to her station. 'Show me.'

'Has to be him,' Nicky enthused. 'Must be. Real name…oh my word.' Nicky hand to mouth turned her head to look up at the boss peering down to read. 'Hang on their folks!' Nicky almost screamed. 'ASBO's used his specialist name search algorithm for me. Found a link between…you ready for this, a Darragh Gordon Kennedy and this Gordon Kenny who just happens to be on the Council Tax database and the last census.'

'Where?'

'West Lindsey,' she shot back enthusiastically. 'Born and brought up in Slaithwaite in West Yorkshire,' Nicky went on. 'Which of course is not…' She stopped and switched websites. 'It's him. This says born in Slaithwaite, West Yorkshire and Wikipedia says Scott Casey was born in West Yorkshire, although it doesn't specifically say Slaithwaite.'

'Bet that's been formulated by his agent.'

'Darragh Kennedy?' Inga looked aghast, closed her eyes tight then spoke as she allowed them to slowly reopen. 'You mean?'

'Bloody sure of it!'

'You saying?' Inga held her breath. 'Not *the* Darragh Kennedy.'

'Be serious! Please.' Jake Goodwin gasped from behind her.

'If this is one and the same, surely Kennedy was that teenager claiming to have killed his alcoholic father when the brute was beating the living daylights out of his mother?'

'But the mother confessed to it to protect her young son,' Jake added. 'Remember?' he almost shouted as he looked all round.

'The one who lazy Don Mackenzie believed, because she was the easy option and sent her down for a good few years.' Everything the Detective Inspector said was sharp and precise. 'The same Lynda Kennedy from whom Rita Appleyard then stole her identity to carry out her frauds, the same Lynda Kennedy who jumped in front of a bloody train. That Darragh Kennedy?' was abrupt and loud.

Ruth Buchan from the annexe next door was stood in the doorway clapping and came very close to cheering.

'Too much of a coincidence,' said Jake. 'If Gordon Kennedy is now Gordon Kenny.' He spun round in his seat to Jamie. 'You know this Gordon Kenny?' he demanded.

'I don't know any Darraghs, Gordons or Kennys. Only person I know is Scott Casey. First met him at a football do, that's how he introduced himself, that's the name on his books,' he insisted a mite too strongly.

'Hang on,' said Nicky back typing.

'Wait a sec,' said Jamie to stop her. 'He gave me a couple of books for my mum and once he slipped a business card inside. Had his name on it as Scott Casey I'm sure, otherwise I'd have wondered what was cracking off.'

'Darragh Kennedy sounds Irish to me,' said Ruth still in the doorway. 'But they say he's a Yorkshireman, from God's country,' got her a look from yellowbelly Jake.

'Listen to this,' said Nicky still peering at her monitor. 'He was born Darragh Gordon Kennedy and brought up in Yorkshire, but his father was Irish.'

'There you are,' Ruth butted in.

'Be where he gets his background from for the books.'

'Ireland?'

'No! Yorkshire.'

'Surely Don Mackenzie came from up that way too.'

'One slight snag ma'am,' said Nicky Scoley. 'Looks like him, but here's a question for you, what's the connection between this writer guy and our Carole-Anne Quinlan?'

'Back to square one with her,' said Jake with a wry grin.

'He write about nurses do we know?'

'Sex!' quipped Inga Larsson. 'Always sex somewhere I've seen somewhere and we've not had any up to now.'

'You speak for yourself!' made even Inga chuckle.

'Listen to this,' said Nicky still peering. 'His latest white rose book is all about conscience, with white being the symbol of cowardice. Normally associated with a white feather, but he uses the white rose.'

'If he killed Mackenzie in cold blood, that's cowardice if you like.'

'Book's called *Blood Red* and I'm sure I had bumph come through on an email from Amazon about new books a few weeks back. Rings a bell anyway.'

'My mum's read it,' Jamie reminded them all as he tried to fathom how he'd tell her if this was true. 'Read them all.'

'Somebody stabbed Don Mackenzie who in turn years ago convinced everybody including CPS, it was the small timid mother who stabbed her old man when he came home in another drunken rage. It wasn't. It was her son the one who claimed to have done it in the first place who Mackenzie refused to listen to.

' Inga spun to look at Jamie. 'This writer friend of yours. What sort of size is he? How big d'you reckon?'

Jamie grimaced. 'Six two or three and well built.'

'What's the betting he mentioned Quinlan being drugged up or you misunderstood his emphasis?' Jake suggested to Jamie. 'When in truth she's just fixing things amongst the scrotes maybe.'

Jamie blew out a breath as a sigh. 'Could be, I really can't remember to be honest. There was a discussion at the meal with the estate agent creep asking all sorts of stupid questions about what had happened to Quinlan, think he was just after all the juicy bits all the blood and guts he could put on Twitter. In amongst it all could be where somebody suggested she's into stuff.' He shrugged. 'Always possible.'

'He dropped a clanger did our killer. He's the one who knew she was somehow involved in drugs and all we need to know now is what connection he has with Quinlan.'

'Remind me,' said Inga who'd stood listening to her team. 'Why are we suggesting there's a connection between this Kenny, Kennedy and our Quinlan?'

'Ring,' said Jake as if the question was well known.

She nodded. 'Need more research into this guy and the estate agent too, but we've got to be sure of our facts. He on PNC this Kenny, by any chance? How do you imagine Quinlan knows this Gordon Kenny?' Inga nodded at Jake. 'Lovers tiff maybe.'

'Did she spin him a yarn about being a nurse and gave him the big sob story about working on the Cavid-19 front line and he found out?'

'Somebody close to him, wife, girlfriend perhaps died of the virus and she's treating it the way she did with us,' was Inga thinking out loud. 'Suggesting all sorts?'

'This seeking her fifteen minutes of fame, maybe? Opportunity missed by being pushed aside when the virus was at its peak. Suddenly she feels totally unimportant.'

'And she's not having that.'

'He finds out she's been lying and gives her a good bashing for her trouble.'

'Hold on, hold on!' Nicky Scoley almost shouted. 'Who's this?' she asked and turned her monitor to face her boss. 'According to the rap sheet, that's Appleyard.'

'Never our Appleyard,' said Inga.

'No way,' added Jake as he shuffled across for a gander.

'Thought I'd see if there's an Appleyard link to this Kenny. And suddenly she's popped up.'

'Who is it?'

'Maureen Appleyard.'

'Nice family if they're related' Inga Larsson suggested and caught Lizzie Webb's attention with a curl of her manicured finger. 'Have we put Don Mackenzie and this Rita Appleyard together to see what pops out?'

'Serious?' Lizzie asked. 'Don Mackenzie and a shoplifter lard arse like her?' she sniggered. 'She's a bit of lowlife and he was a DI.'

'And?'

'I just think…'

'She's female and he was male.' was smothered in a grin. 'If I find he's been a naughty policeman and there has been a link somewhere down the line, can you explain how either of them have any connection whatsoever with Carole-Anne Quinlan apart from her making use of one of Appleyard's pews? Because so far we've come up with a big fat zero.'

'She just doesn't compute.' Lizzie let out a puff of a sigh. 'Why is she still running free?' she asked.

'Who?'

'Appleyard.'

'Because I have the attack on Quinlan plus the little matter of the stabbing of Mackenzie to worry about without getting tangled up in the web of whatever it might be this Appleyard is up to. Understand they've charged her with a few bits and pieces and she's currently out on bail while they sort through the rest. Pretending to be a nun is a job for PHU. I think we've got enough on, don't you? Bring her in, rattle her cage, you never know what might drop out.' Inga was never happy when good friend Lizzie went off line in attempting to be a member of her squad rather than civilian backup. Easier said than done in their environment she realized.

'Try this for size,' Inga told Lizzie. Input a writer called Scott Casey with a real name of Darragh Gordon Kennedy and let's see who he links with. Mackenzie, Quinlan or Appleyard.'

'We've got Quinlan's call list remember up with ASBO.'

'But not got one for this Casey guy.'

'We might just get some form of link with one or other if we're lucky.' She hoped would send Lizzie back to her HOLMES 2 computer where she was the Queen Bee.

'If we're lucky it'll be Mackenzie, Quinlan *and* Appleyard.'

'Yeh right. But I won't hold my breath. And the question now is, which Appleyard?'

Suddenly it was a case of who wanted to speak first, with everyone fighting to read chapter and verse about this Maureen Dorothy Appleyard. Seniority won in the end.

'Maureen Appleyard,' said DS Goodwin seriously, but with a look of contentment lighting his strong face. 'Started off with time in a young offenders for ABH outside a nightclub when she was only seventeen. And there's more,' he chuckled.

'We get the picture,' Inga assured him.

'We've already come up with stuff on Rita Appleyard as you know.'

'Nice family.'

'Embezzlement apparently a few years ago now, she was done for running this charity on the pretext of helping old folk. Usual scenario one pound for the charity, one pound for Rita. Always been the problem with collecting boxes.'

'Actually worked at a charitable trust,' said Ruth to clarify the information from the angle she'd worked on. 'Where she apparently falsified documents so her bosses would authorize cheques. Instead of course she transferred the money into accounts in false names to hide her involvement.'

'Interesting,' said Inga. 'How crooks use other crooks to work for them. Never anybody decent and honest.'

'Being honest is no good to the likes of Appleyard.'

'Sorry, Jake,' Inga ushered her patient DS on.

'All came to light apparently when one of the charities was looking for publicity and suddenly somebody came up with this idea of a big cheque presentation with some celebrity.' Inga sniggered. 'When one of the marketing people went to the bank to ask them about getting a big cheque, they pointed out there was not enough in the account to cover it.'

'Whoops!'

'What in God's name has all this got to do with Quinlan, why was she dumped out there of all places?' Jake asked everybody, but knew there'd be no answer to make sense. 'Like I said, back to square one.'

'Remind me, did Mackenzie have anything to do with the Maureen Appleyard case at all?' The shake of Jake's head said it all without him uttering a word. 'Brilliant.' Inga just allowed her head to shake slowly, but then looked at Nicky Scoley. 'I know they're up to no good at Cluny, but the young girl still worries me. You don't think maybe muddled up with all this it might be like one of those illegals I've been reading about. More to do with slavery rather than hiding from some brute of a partner.'

'In this day and age in a society like ours it defies belief it really does, when the word slavery pokes its head up.'

'Could it be all this nun business is just an elaborate cover to hide women away like the Whyte girl?' Inga posed. 'Hide them from the gangs wanting to exploit and traffick them.'

'Not just the gangs you know,' said Jake. 'Kept as slaves in rich folks homes a lot of them. Poor women say they feel as if they're owned. Must be bloody horrendous.'

'Just imagine,' Nicky continued along the tangent. 'You get one life and you have to spend it like that. Compared with the sort of life we all lead. We don't know how lucky we are, we really don't.'

'We do know do we, this...' Inga had to glance down at her notes. 'Whyte Mulilima was not about to be sold, forced into prostitution or begging?'

'Why what you thinking?'

'Just something Trigger mentioned few weeks back when I bumped into him. He's intelligence gathering these days as you know and he just mentioned when I saw him how if we come across any slavery or the like he has a really good contact.' She didn't need to ask the question, the looks told her. 'I'll give him a call about Whyte, just in case.'

'Hope to God it doesn't turn out she was a slave after all.'

36

Author son of killer charged with murder

Scott Casey the award winning novelist has been charged with the murder of former police Detective Inspector Donald Mackenzie who was brutally stabbed to death in his garden shed recently.

Scott Casey arrested in a Lincoln County Police 'sting' operation organized by Detective Inspector Inga Larsson, was charged under his real name of Darragh Gordon Kennedy also known as Gordon Kenny. He is the son of Lynda Kennedy who stabbed her husband Padraig Kennedy to death in their home in 2003. Detective Inspector Mackenzie was the officer in charge of the murder investigation which led to the arrest of Mrs Kennedy.

During her trial it was submitted by the defence that the stabbing of Padraig Kennedy had in fact been carried out by their son Darragh.

The jury accepted her change of plea to guilty three days into the trial in Leeds and she was sentenced to 15 years imprisonment.

Lynda Kennedy committee suicide in 2016. She was hit by a train near Retford travelling from London Kings Cross to Edinburgh Waverley.

Darragh Kennedy aka Gordon Kenny aka Scott Casey will appear before Lincoln Magistrates in the morning.

Scott Casey is well known in particular for his debut novel "Thorns" first of his Rose Murder

Mystery series which is expected now to be made into a television series.

As was often the case, DI Inga Larsson's form of celebration was not to join the lads and lasses to down pints in the local hostelry as they'd have done back in Mackenzie's time, but instead the team would discuss the outcome over her provision of Swedish baking, something husband Adam had certainly got used to.

Jamie Hedley had done what he always did, and as he had been taught. Start of the day coffee organized, then check the overnights on the system. All what a colleague down in PHU called the 'curly wurlies' – all the dross incidents reported and logged overnight.

Had he been trying too hard to make a good impression or was the chances of being a proper member of MIT little more than just wishful thinking?

The boss's early reference to him knowing Gainsborough had come back to annoy him during his lonely hours. Was it the sole reason he was there? Had he once lived in Grimsby or Grantham would he still be back down in PHU dealing with the riff-raff day and night?

Being in MIT of course meant Jamie could just scan the majority of burglaries, car crimes, domestics of which there were always far too many and boozed-up brawls which had got out of hand.

'D'you listen to Breakfast Cavalcade?' he asked his boss as she prepared to discuss the situation so far. She just shook her head. 'DCI Stevens got a mention,' he enthused and keyed in the playback system on his PC. 'Listen to this.'

"£40 million pounds of Cocaine has been discovered in a people carrier taxi. The massive haul of the drug, a great deal of which was in high-purity blocks was seized by police when they found large sports bags inside the vehicle close to Gainsborough.

The driver and two men arrested are being held in Lincoln on suspicion of the importation of drugs. The vehicle is now undergoing close scrutiny but is believed normally to be used to transport the public to and from local airports.

Senior Investigating Officer Detective Chief Inspector Luke Stevens admitted: 'We have seized a massive quantity of high grade Cocaine which would we believe have netted the gang close to £40m had it reached street level. The majority of these drugs were we believe destined eventually for the north east of England.'

At the same time Lincoln County Police have confirmed that a number of women are helping with their enquiries into drug offences and stolen goods believed to have been discovered at the Cluny Priory outside the town.

At the present time neither the Mother Superior nor spokesperson for the holy order were available for comment but we would expect further information in our next bulletin.

We also understand the police have raided a number of properties at the coast in a search for illegal highs that at one time were considered legal."

'Thank you Jamie,' said Inga when the traffic report started and he turned it off.

'My pleasure ma'am.'

'Now it all fits,' said a disgruntled Jake Goodwin as he bowled in. 'Fraud lads have been checking these companies registered in the Isle of Man for me and the raid news has just blown the wind out my sails,' he said as he slumped down in his chair. 'Only one they can find that's not a shell company is one involved in property flipping.'

'Property…flipping?' Inga asked slowly.

'You buy a property and sell it on quickly for a hefty profit. Sometimes they give it a coat of paint, but…'

'Here we go.'

'But,' Jake repeated. 'Directors are the Diagne's, Mr *and* Mrs which I guess means she's running it and planned to keep on with it going forward.'

'Sarge,' said Sandy. 'This flippin' you call it. Didnae somewhere it's illegal, not that it'd bother her?'

'Brought in after the financial crash but they tell me it's only for residential properties requiring a mortgage. Doesn't stop cash purchases.'

'Aye didnae know.'

'Drugs would give her a decent cash flow.'

'One would think.'

'So, why was Tamara so keen on us raiding the place?' Jamie asked. 'Told me she wanted it bringing down.'

'Unless of course the drugs Stevens found turn out not to be connected to Josie Diagne. We assume unless she's lost her marbles they're nothing to do with Tamara either.'

Inga Larsson grimaced and sat shaking her head. 'Thanks Jake. And there was me thinking all we've got left is this Quinlan woman to sort out.'

'Apparently Dennis Norton has that Chunky Knapp downstairs,' Jake advised. 'What's his real name?' he asked them all.

'Dougal.'

'That's a dog's name! Anyway Norton downstairs has got this Dougal Knapp going no comment,' he said slowly.

'And two more for all this cuckooing business and drug trafficking, but what we still don't know is who gave her a bashing if it wasn't this Kennedy. I assume rightly or wrongly it has something to do with the drugs. Jamie.' He frowned his look at the boss. 'Can I leave that one with you to liaise with Gainsborough? No great shakes if we don't suss it, she'll be off sick for quite a while anyway. Just thinking of the boss's clear up rates.'

'And keeping PR happy,' Jake offered.

'Yes, chances are she's as guilty as hell but the law's the law, somebody gave her a good smacking and despite everything we owe her due diligence. Under the circumstances it's not worth a full blown operation but if you cover all bases particularly now Cluny has shut up shop, you might come across something. Word on the streets, you know the sort of thing. Right. Can we get back to the job in hand?' she asked but was going to anyway.

Jamie's mind immediately reacted to thoughts of the possibility of there being another altercation with Kerrie, and how he might react if he had to keep popping over to Gainsborough.

'Darragh Kennedy as we now surmise is Gordon Kenny,' the boss went on amidst his thoughts. 'Who happens to be the son of Lynda Kennedy who was jailed for murdering her husband when Darragh was only fourteen? DI Don Mackenzie was in charge at the time,' was how she started, sat out front, coffee beside her with all her team at their work stations. 'Who was it said it's a fine line between insanity and genius?'

'Why'd he change his name, ma'am?' Raza Latif asked.

'I think it was because he considered the name Darragh Kennedy would attract publicity which could very well put off more people than it gained. You know how precious some of these dotty snowflake old biddies can be.'

'You're probably right Jamie,' said Nicky Scoley. 'Would you buy a book by the Yorkshire Ripper's daughter or Myra Hindley's kid?'

'Possibly the first one out of sheer curiosity, but after that they'd give them a wide berth I reckon.'

'Women who read cosies would, you can be sure.'

'Somebody remembered the boy had said in one interview he'd done it,' Inga continued. 'Although the mother vigorously poo pooed this as the lad at fourteen was below the age to be tried and convicted, particularly with little or no evidence. Mackenzie had chosen to believe the mother's story and was the end of the matter. Now the actual tape recording of the lad admitting to killing his father is nowhere to be found.' Inga stopped momentarily to look round the room, then sipped her coffee. 'I can just imagine it. There it was, easy peasy, mother to jail, son to foster carers, all done and dusted and let's head off to the pub.' She nodded in the direction of Nicky Scoley.

'It was more than one foster home as it turned out,' she advised. 'Went from pillar to post and eventually he finished up in a home from where he absconded, none of which came as a real surprise. Social Services wiped their hands of him, and the trail just went cold almost within days of him doing a runner.'

'Disinterest from the authorities and lack of funds,' said Sandy. 'Is my guess. Poor sod.'

'As most of you know already I pulled up the records the crime scene photographer at the time had produced. No Crime Scene Investigators like we have today because it was back in the days of SOCO, but they were still good all the same.'

There was no need to display the photos again of the knife and dozen vicious deep stabs wounds. Then there was a description of the mother they were all aware of along with the head and shoulders photo of her being small and slight with close cropped hair she looked like a young lad.

'How in God's name did anybody ever think a little woman like her could kill the big burly brute of a husband? Yes a lot of it was blubber from the boozing, but be serious!'

'He'd have just pushed her away with one hand she looks so malnourished.'

'So would you be if all the dole money went to the pub,' Raza offered.

'My guess is,' Inga went on. 'She was not the only one living one hell of a life with that drunk. I reckon the son Darragh had seen his mother take a beating once too often and decided no more.'

'And what's the guessing he got badly treated too.'

'Why couldn't Mackenzie see it?' Jake Goodwin asked.

'I don't think he wanted to,' was Inga's quick retort. 'He had a confession from this little meek woman. Case closed, move on, get back to the golf.'

'Did he play golf?'

'Not as far as I know,' Inga chuckled. 'But you know what I mean. Couldn't be doing with the hassle is my guess.'

Jamie Hedley was worried sick sat there listening to all this as thoughts of the chances of going with the lads to some odd-ball restaurant having gone for a ball of chalk, annoyed him. How could he face them all having innocently taken a murderer to the Romanian meal? That Thomas idiot'll have a field day. Back to being the laughing stock just as he'd been over Kerrie and that Foskett bastard. Something else he'd probably have to face again.

He'd decided it was about time he moved back to Newark Road, got that DNA test done and maybe this'd be a good time to make a few new friends, make a fresh start.

Always possible that change would be made for him, by the boss packing him off back down to PHU and all the daily shit they deal with. That of course was if the Darke boss didn't intervene and just end his career forthwith.

With unemployment heading up and up despite all these government schemes what'll he do for a job, how much could he claim? What chance would he stand getting even something like a security job at a supermarket, with all the local hoodlums turning up to take the piss out of him? Be worse than PHU with all the daily drag of pickpockets, shoplifting, domestic abuse and the mental health issues they were lumbered with.

All because he was stupid enough to allow teenage lusting memories and his cock to rule his brain and been a complete arse meeting up with bloody Diagne bitch, all of which he'd stupidly kept to himself. Then there was the drugs business he'd got from somewhere he was sure Goodwin hadn't forgotten, and now all this.

Could his career become short lived with the boss's knowledge of him being a fool to cosy up to a killer at football? Shared a few pints with somebody with blood on his hands and then even invited a murderer to join a night out with the lads.

Why had he not twigged a thing and why oh why had Casey got pally with him of all people? That is apart from obviously being on the look-out for police investigation techniques he'd spouted about to him a few times.

As if all that was not enough with his future seriously in the balance, his mother'd be damn angry with him not about his career but the free books.

'You saying this is what it's all been aboot?' DC Sandy MacLachlan asked. 'Is this all about his mother committing suicide which sparked all this in Darragh Kennedy?'

Inga nodded. 'He could very well be of the opinion lazy Mackenzie in effect killed his mother, because he knew she hadn't murdered anybody. Been building up all that resentment inside over the years for the time she spent in nick. Then when she topped herself, it was more than he could handle.'

'Not very often I feel for murderers' said a sombre Jake. 'But in this case I think I just might make an exception.'

'Women who've shared a bed with him will be shocked to discover the second person they've been with. Kennedy would have been able to give off totally different behaviour and idiosyncrasies from the person they thought they knew. What is very difficult for such people in their position is not to think everybody in future they have a relationship with is, what they call double existers.'

'And what's the betting getting a few damn good thrashings off his father made him into the person we've met,' Jake suggested turned to look at Jamie sat in the corner. 'Or rather you've met.'

Sat listening to her team, Inga Larsson recalled from somewhere in the depths of her mind notice of early life trauma impairing the usual development of a child's emotions. Empathy and compassion she'd once read somewhere are crucial in preventing the adult version acting out thoughts including murder.

Lacking in human compassion removed by repeated trauma meant his victim was nothing more to him than just a body.

'I know we've got a great deal of pre-trial work to get through and if the domestic Raza's already dealing with turns into a Code Red on top of all this, there'll be all hell to pay but that aside, there's still one thing we're still no further forward with,' said Jake Goodwin seriously. They were all aware PNC stated the culprit had previous.

'Quinlan,' Inga responded sharply to ruffle his feathers and consciously and annoyingly drank more coffee forcing what remained of her team with Michelle also at the Hospital where the victim had been taken, to wait. 'Need a volunteer to start with who and why. This case is not going away any time soon, and there's a maniac out there,' she looked at Jamie. 'You happy with that Jamie?' she asked him sat downcast on his own in a corner.

'Me?' he reacted.

'Why not? You seem to know plenty of people over there. Somebody must know something, especially as Mackenzie's all over the media, people will want to add bits and pieces there's no doubt.'

'Yeh...fine,' he gasped when this was the last thing he'd expected. *'My office, now Jamie,'* was what he was expecting any time soon.

He'd moved over to Lincoln to get away from all the hassle with Kerrie and now he was being told to stay even longer with his mum. One step forward and two back or was this really two steps forward and only a little one back?

'Another thing, there's a job for your mum,' was unexpected. 'You say she's read all of the Casey books.'

'All more than once I think.'

'Bit of a long shot, but can you get her to point out in Kennedy's books who his murderers kill their roles rather than names and more importantly how. Shooting, stabbing, poison whatever. Always the possibility he's a serial killer reenacting his own fiction. Whatever she comes up with we'll get Lizzie to put it all through the HOLMES system and see if there are any unsolved with the same criteria.'

'She be happy with that?' Jamie nodded.

'I'll give her a ring, get her started.'

'And I'm sure we can afford a box of chocolates,' she smiled.

'If what you think is true, maybe he's already written about using that toxin stuff,' Nicky suggested and gestured her pleasure at Jamie still being involved.

'Ask yourself this everyone, silly question I know, but,' Inga asked them all sat there peering up at her. 'What does Quinlan do for a living?'

'Sort of...'

'Think Tank,' was Nicky.

'Exactly. And what is she linked to?'

'Hang on, hang on,' said Jake waving his hand. 'What we on about now?'

'Just something's come to mind out of the blue. This is a little grey cells moment.

'NHS,' said Jamie cautiously.

'What did your author friend use on Mackenzie?'

'Some toxin stuff.'

'How did he administer it?'

'Syringe,' Jake joined in instantly.

Inga Larsson clapped. 'And where could he get a syringe from?' and they just looked at her. 'Quinlan!' and she chuckled. 'Next question. Why didn't Kennedy kill Quinlan if was him responsible? Can't imagine he was disturbed not least by our false nuns and to be fair he did prop her up on a pew.'

'Ma'am,' said Sandy.

'Just a sec,' and Inga's hand went up. 'One question we need answering is has Kennedy done this before? Is that why he's selling loads of his books because readers know they contain seriously authentic killings not just made-up ones? Here's the big question. The Swede hesitated. 'Is he carrying out his novel murders for real?' She looked across. 'Sandy?'

'Don't matter.'

'Jamie,' Inga's eyes picked out. 'Any reason why you can't go back to Gainsborough for a couple of weeks?' He shook his head but did she hear the sigh? 'Scott Casey's all over social media as you'd expect, and I'm damn sure people will now be willing to talk, want their likes and be fraid of missing out and all that stupidity. How did Quinlan know Mackenzie and how did Quinlan know Scott Casey, apart him being a bit of a celebrity in the town? Damn sure somebody over there will be willing to blab.'

'And check up on that cuckooing business at the same time while I'm there?'

Inga nodded. 'Exactly. These odd meals out you've been telling us all about,' she went on. 'Eating in strange places and all that business. Talking to my dad last night and he was telling me about a restaurant in Stockholm called the Hairy Pig Deli.' Made a few snigger. 'They serve Wild Boar Sausages and Pies, Moose Lasagne and Reindeer. Plus pig shaped crackers,' made them all laugh at Jamie's expense. 'Bit far to go maybe for you and your mates, but what about instead one quiet lunchtime we lock you and your pals in a cell and serve you the usual microwaved pap we serve to the skurks?'

ACKNOWLEDGEMENTS

This is the book disturbed by Covid-19. The first draft was pretty much complete with all the characters created and set in their ways.

March 2020 and the lockdown meant research was not an essential journey so I had to stay put. Social distancing came into play and with pubs and restaurants closed great swathes of the book were not possible.

In the end as the lockdown began to ease I moved the timings in the hope there was not another virus surge, a second coming which of course did arrive after the story ends.

From there it was a case of simply waiting for the world to return to something like normal

I sincerely have to thank a good friend Gavin Scott who provided me with all the up to date detail of the workings of modern gyms and fitness facilities during that phase of the pandemic.

In addition to my grateful thanks to Gavin for bringing me up to date with his field of expertise, there are of course so many other friends and acquaintances who have provide me with distinct items of knowledge I have been able to use.

John Warner for example was kindly able to provide an insight into the systems appertaining at Gainsborough Trinity at that time.

That is particularly poignant with good friends of the nursing profession who in the case of *Best Served Cold* have been able to provide me with interesting insights into their world at that time.

In addition in this case I have to sincerely thank Lincolnshire Police who have been very constructive in the past in response to my queries. This time Sergeant Clive Farmer very kindly provided me with a copy of the Interviewing Protocols introduced during the pandemic. Thank you, Clive.

Any errors under these trying times are of course down to me.

My thanks of course to everyone who supports me and takes the time to read my efforts. Time now for whatever I can conjure up next.

To discover exactly what it is Inga Larsson and her team become involved in next, read on...

PREVIEW

As tall Freddie Curran brought his Ford Tourneo slowly to a halt outside the gate to their new property, his partner Kirsten in the front passenger seat stretched her arms out in front of her and yawned.

'Been great having a break, but you know, there's no place like home.'

'You call this home?' Freddie sniggered as he applied the handbrake and uncoupled his seat belt. 'Back to the hard graft more like, I'm afraid missus,' he said as he opened his door and stepped out. 'Brilliant!' he gasped as his partner emerged from her side. 'Mitch said he'd empty the bloody skip. That's a great start to come back to.'

'You know what he's like,' she shrugged away.

'Don't remind me. That's why he's cheap.'

'Can't have it both ways.'

'Look at the bloody front door! Told him to cut that ivy back for God's sake.'

This was their new property, but not one for them to enjoy in exactly the same way the previous three had not been home either. This was a teacher and an IT manager who for the best part of three years had become used to living in virtually one room and sleeping in another in their struggle to progress up the property ladder.

Just one more after this and then Freddie says they'll look for somewhere bigger and better to settle down properly and permanently. A place to truly call home was what Kirsten dreamt of.

The great adventure had all started off with that old former council house terraced place in the city they'd completely re-modelled, revamped and refurbished. Then the first two bedroomed semi in a slightly better part of town. From there it had been onto the three-bedrooms with a garage and quite a decent garden. Now number four, appropriately four bedrooms in a quiet village close to

Lincoln. Nestled at the end of a country lane but not too close to the nosey villagers. Chosen on purpose as they were both well aware how some sad folk with the location mantra will one day pay well over the odds to gain bragging rights over so-called friends. All of which they planned one day to make financial gain out of.

Therein lay the problem. With the property market in the doldrums for ages both pre and post Brexit and Coronavirus, selling was always a frustrating and tediously lengthy process.

Kirsten opened the white gate in the low fence and headed off key in hand along the fairly straight flagstone short path bordered by rose bushes to the red front door.

Freddie opened the tailgate of their Tourneo and lugged out two big travel bags he plonked on the grass verge. He then repeated the action humping out three back packs. With the door slammed shut he opened a rear door and lifted out two white paper carrier bags containing the set meal for three they'd just purchased on the way in.

The process had become a pre and post-holiday ritual over time. In this particular case on the Friday before they headed south once all the packing had been done to Kirsten's satisfaction, and they were ready to go, off they'd gone to find somewhere for a meal.

On this occasion they'd been to Windmill Farm and enjoyed the carvery. Freddie had chosen the beef and Kirsten turkey. Now on their return the process was repeated in that on the way back they'd stopped just as they had done previously at the end of holidays and short breaks, to pick up a take-away. This time it was her choice and she'd gone for Chinese.

In a home with as yet only a basic microwave and no dining table they could not go to any great lengths over cooking a meal even if they wanted to.

As he headed away from the car Freddie knew they were both looking forward to enjoying Kirsten's choice of meal comprising Shrimp Chop Suey, Tomato Beef, Roast Pork Chinese Style, Sweet and Sour Chicken, Barbecued Spare Ribs being Freddie's favourite and Special Fried Rice.

Freddie trundled up the path with the meal bags in one hand and two others in his left he placed carefully in the hall and strode back to the metallic car once more, and the first of their heavy bags. Tall Freddie had just gripped hold of his navy blue holdall containing their dirty washing his mother would deal with for them, when he heard a scream.

'Freddie!' told him it was Kirsten. 'Help Freddie! Please, oh my God!' he heard her shriek as she clattered noisily down the wooden stairs in front of him and ran sobbing straight into his arms now free of the load he'd just dumped down. 'Think he's dead!' she gasped her shout.

'What?' he exclaimed. 'Who?' he pushed her away at arms-length but retained hold of her shoulders. 'What you on about?'

'Up in bed…in our bed…a man, Freddie there's…a dead man up there!'

'You bloody what?'

'Blood everywhere, it's awful!' she shouted. 'Shit!'

'Stay there,' he snapped, released his hold and was indoors and scampering up the stairs two at a time as she bent over to wretch onto the path..

'For fucks sake!' she heard him shout. 'Get the cops,' he said on the stairs as he scampered down. 'Stay there, get back in the car, lock the doors,' with Kirsten still stood there white with fear and shaking. 'Now!' he hollered as he pulled out his phone and tapped nine three times too hard. 'Police,' he waited as Kirsten scampered for the car. 'I want to report a dead body,' he said. 'In our bedroom...my name?' he shouted. 'For God's sake. Freddie Curran.'

BODY OF EVIDENCE

Available late 2021

Printed in Great Britain
by Amazon